FRECKLES

FRECKLES

Gene Stratton Porter

GRAMERCY BOOKS
New York • Avenel

Foreword copyright © 1994 by Outlet Book Company, Inc.

This edition is published by Gramercy Books,
distributed by Outlet Book Company, Inc.,
a Random House Company,
40 Engelhard Avenue
Avenel, New Jersey 07001

Printed and bound in the United States of America

Designed by Melissa Ring

Library of Congress Cataloging-in-Publication Data
Stratton-Porter, Gene, 1863-1924.
Freckles / Gene Stratton Porter.
p. cm.
Summary: Orphaned and maimed, Freckles' bitterness about his fate is
lessened when he is hired to guard a stretch of lumber in the wild
Limberlost and, after meeting the beautiful "Swamp Angel," he
determines to find out about his past.
ISBN 0-517-10126-2
[1. Orphans--Fiction. 2. Swamps--Fiction. 3. Physically handicapped--
Fiction. 4. Indiana--Fiction.] I. Title.
PZ7.S9122Fr 1993   93-42393
[Fic]--dc 20   CIP
                                                 AC

8 7 6 5 4 3 2 1

Foreword

Imagine a vast, impenetrable area of dense swamps and bogs, deep woods and overgrown meadows, a mysterious thicket of mystery and danger. Along its edge runs the corduroy—a road built of small logs, laid about two feet apart, to keep wheels from sinking in the mire. You are in the Limberlost Swamp, a world loved by the fearless turn-of-the-century naturalist Gene Stratton Porter. It is a world she explored and studied, photographed, and wrote about in many books. Perhaps the Limberlost was named for the Limberlost Creek, which crosses a corner of the swampland, but some say the swamp got its name when a fellow nicknamed Limber wandered too far into the great Loblolly Swamp and got lost. The woods echoed with shouts of "Limber's lost!" He was never seen again, and legend gave the swamp a new name.

Gene Stratton Porter didn't let stories like that scare her off. Dressed in men's khakis, she would load herself down with photography equipment, pack a revolver for

protection, and stalk the birds, watching, waiting, ignoring the swarms of mosquitoes, the threat of snakes, the sweltering heat. With her camera and photographic glass plates, she would record the birds of the wild.

One spring day as she walked through the Limberlost, a huge iridescent black feather floated down across her path. She recognized it as the twenty-inch feather of the black vulture. Was there a nest nearby? Her careful search led her to a fallen hollow tree trunk; deep within was the nest with two eggs. She photographed the eggs and returned every two days for a series of pictures of the one baby bird that hatched, capturing his growth and development until he took flight and left the nest.

Finding that feather and discovering the vulture's nest was Gene Stratton Porter's inspiration for the book *Freckles*. In this enchanting story, you will confront the swamp with a young man named Freckles, whose life will be changed forever the day a huge black feather drifts down from the sky across *his* path. But let's start at the beginning.

When we first meet Freckles, he is alone, walking down the corduroy along the Limberlost in search of a job and a home. Nineteen years earlier he had been abandoned on the steps of a charity home. He was never adopted and has never known love. On his own now, friendless and homeless and with no name other than the nickname Freckles, he is "intensely eager to belong somewhere." Impulsively he follows the cheery sounds of camaraderie coming from the Grand Rapids Lumber Company and talks his way into employment. The job is a demanding one—guarding the rare and valuable trees of the Limberlost against timber thieves. Young Freckles will have to walk the seven miles of Limberlost trail at least twice a day to check for signs of trespassers.

"Every hour was torture to the boy. The restricted life of a great city orphanage was the other extreme of the world from the Limberlost. He was afraid for his life every minute.

But McLean, the boss of the lumber camp, and Duncan, the head teamster, have shown Freckles the first true kindness and acceptance of his life, and he's not about to let them down. As time passes, familiarity tames Freckles' fears of the swamp. Still, the days are long and the Limberlost is a solitary, lonely place. A person needs friends, and so Freckles turns for companionship to the creatures of the swamp—the birds, the insects, the wild animals. In the bleak winter months he brings nuts for the squirrels and makes friends with the birds. He transplants vines, ferns, and flowers, adds a carpeting of moss, and with "the heart of a painter" and "the soul of a poet" creates for himself a forest "room" of breathtaking beauty.

And then, one spring day, a huge, iridescent black feather drifts across his path; he is intrigued, then frustrated, for he cannot identify the feather. The Limberlost, which cast its spell upon him, drew him into its enchantment, and teased him with whispered secrets in the wind, is still beyond his reach. Freckles, the boy without a name, wants to call the insects, trees, flowers, butterflies, and birds he loves by *their* real names—but he can't. Finding the mystery feather inspires his quest for knowledge. Freckles identifies the large black vultures in a book, and then, jubilant, goes on to discover their nest in a fallen tree.

It just so happens that there is a photographer, called the Bird Woman, who is notified of his finding and comes to do a series of studies of the egg and baby vulture. Here Gene Stratton Porter has written herself into this fictional tale, playing the part she knows best, the self-sufficient naturalist/photographer. Working with the Bird Woman is a beautiful young girl (a character based on the author's own daughter, Jeannette)—and Freckles loses his heart to this "Swamp Angel." All the women in this delightful novel are modern by any standards, and the angel is no ornamental, turn-of-the-century beauty. She is smart, honest, independent, fearless, and loving.

As the story progresses, the plot takes some twists and turns along the way to its surprise ending, following Freckles' adventures with sinister villains and heroic rescues, detouring to spend time with Freckles and his angel, meandering through the Limberlost to observe life and love among the creatures of the wild.

This is a book to read again and again, an absorbing tale of uncommon courage and uncommon love. In Freckles' Limberlost world, love is so strong and so pure that people do not hesitate to risk their lives for each other, honesty and loyalty are fierce and uncompromising, and the American dream is alive and well.

NINA ROSENSTEIN

Westfield, New Jersey
1994

Chapter I

WHEREIN GREAT RISKS ARE TAKEN AND THE LIMBERLOST GUARD IS HIRED

Freckles came down the corduroy that crosses the lower end of the Limberlost. At a glance he might have been mistaken for a tramp, but he was truly seeking work. He was intensely eager to belong somewhere and to be attached to almost any sort of enterprise that would furnish him food and clothing.

Long before he came in sight of the camp of the Grand Rapids Lumber Company he could hear the cheery voices of the men and the neighing of the horses, and could smell the tempting odors of cooking food. A feeling of homeless friendlessness swept over him in a sickening wave. Without stopping to think, he turned into the newly made road and followed it to the camp, where the gang was making ready for supper and bed.

The scene was intensely attractive. The thickness of

the swamp made a dark, massive background below, and above towered gigantic trees. The men were calling jovially back and forth as they unharnessed tired horses that fell into attitudes of rest and crunched, in deep content, the grain given them. As he lovingly wiped the flanks of his big bays with handfuls of pawpaw leaves, Duncan, the brawny Scottish head teamster, softly whistled, "O wha will be my dearie, O!" and a cricket under the leaves at his feet accompanied him. The green-wood fire hissed and crackled merrily. Wreathing tongues of flame wrapped around the big black kettles, and, when the cook lifted the lids to plunge in his testing fork, gusts of savory odors escaped.

Freckles approached him. "I want to speak to the boss," he said.

The cook glanced at him and answered carelessly, "He can't use you."

The color flooded Freckles' face, but he said, simply, "If you will be having the goodness to point him out, we will give him a chance to do his own talking."

With a shrug of astonishment the cook led the way to a rough board table where a broad, square-shouldered man was bending over some account books.

"Mr. McLean, here's another man wanting to be taken on the gang, I suppose," he said.

"All right," came the cheery answer. "I never needed a good man more than I do just now."

The manager turned a page and carefully began on a new line.

"No use of your bothering with this fellow," volunteered the cook. "He hasn't but one hand."

The flush on Freckles' face burned deeper. His lips thinned to a mere line. He lifted his shoulders, took a step forward, and thrust out his right arm, from which the sleeve dangled empty at the wrist.

"That will do, Sears," came the voice of the boss sharply. "I will interview my man when I have finished this report." He turned to his work, while the cook hurried back to the fires.

Freckles stood one instant as he had braced himself to meet the eyes of the manager; then his arm dropped and a wave of whiteness swept over him. The boss had not even turned his head to see the deformity pointed out to him. He had used the possessive. When he said "my man" the hungry heart of Freckles went reaching toward him.

The boy drew a quivering breath. Then he whipped off his old hat and beat the dust from it carefully. With his left hand he caught the right sleeve, wiped his sweaty face, and tried to straighten his hair with his fingers. He broke a spray of iron-wort beside him and used the purple blossoms to beat the dust from his shoulders and limbs. The boss, busy over his report, was, nevertheless, vaguely aware of the effort being made behind him and scored one for the man.

McLean was a Scotsman. It was his habit to work slowly and methodically. The men of his camps never had known him to be in a hurry or to lose his temper. Discipline was inflexible, but the boss was always kind. His habits were simple. He shared camp life with his gangs. The only visible signs of his great wealth consisted of a big, shimmering diamond stone of ice and

fire that glittered and burned on one of his fingers and the dainty, beautiful thoroughbred mare he rode between camps and across the country on business.

No man of McLean's gangs could honestly say that he had ever been overdriven or underpaid. The boss never had exacted any deference from his men, yet so intense was his personality that no man of them ever had attempted a familiarity. They all knew him to be a thorough gentleman, and knew that up in the great timber city several millions stood to his credit.

He was the only son of that McLean who had sent out the finest ships ever built in Scotland. That his son should carry on this business after his death had been the father's ambition. He sent the boy through Edinburgh University and Oxford, and allowed him several years' travel before he should attempt his first commission for the firm.

Then he was ordered through southern Canada and Michigan to purchase a consignment of tall, straight timber for masts, and down into Indiana for oak beams. The young man entered these mighty forests, parts of which still lay untouched since the dawn of the morning of time. The clear, cool, pungent atmosphere was intoxicating. The intense silence, like that of a great empty cathedral, fascinated him. He gradually learned that to the shy wood creatures that darted across his path or peeped inquiringly from leafy ambush he was brother. He found himself approaching, with a feeling of reverence, those majestic trees that had stood through ages of sun, wind, and snow. Soon it became a difficult thing to fell them. When he had filled his order and returned home, he was amazed to find that in the swamps and forests he had lost his heart, and it was calling, forever calling him.

When he inherited his father's property, he promptly disposed of it, and, with his mother, made a home in a splendid residence in the outskirts of Grand Rapids. With three partners he organized a lumber company. His work was to purchase, fell, and ship the timber to the mills. Marshall managed the milling process and passed the lumber on to the factory. From the lumber, Barthol made beautiful and useful furniture, which Uptegrove scattered all over the world from a big wholesale house. Of the thousands who saw their faces reflected in the polished surfaces of that furniture and found comfort in its use, few there were to whom it suggested mighty forests and trackless swamps, and the man, big of soul and body, who cut his way through them, and with the eye of experience doomed the proud trees that were now entering the homes of civilization for service.

When McLean turned from his finished report he faced a young man, still under twenty, tall, spare, heavily framed, thickly freckled, and red-haired, with a homely Irish face, but in the steady gray eyes, straightly meeting his searching ones of blue, there was unswerving candor and a look of longing not to be ignored. He was dressed in the roughest of farm clothing and seemed tired to the point of falling.

"You are looking for work?" questioned McLean.

"Yes," answered Freckles.

"I am very sorry," said the boss, with genuine sympathy in his every tone, "but there is only one man I want at present—a good, big fellow with a stout heart and a strong body. I hoped that you would do, but I am afraid you are too young and hardly strong enough."

Freckles stood, hat in hand, his eyes fixed on McLean.

"And what was it you thought I might be doing?" he asked.

The boss scarcely could repress a start. Somewhere back of accident and poverty had been an ancestor who used cultivated English, even with an accent. The boy spoke in a mellow Irish voice, sweet and pure. It was scarcely definite enough to be called brogue, yet there was a trick in the turning of the sentence, the wrong sound of a letter here and there, that was almost irresistible to McLean and presaged a misuse of infinitives and possessives with which he was very familiar and which touched him closely. He was of foreign birth, and, despite years of alienation, in times of strong feeling he fell into inherited sins of accent and construction.

"It's no child's job," answered McLean. "I am the field manager of a big lumber company. We have just leased two thousand acres of the Limberlost. Many of these trees are of great value. We can't leave our camp, six miles south, for almost a year yet; so we have blazed a trail and strung barbed wires securely about the extent of this lease. Before we return to our work, I must put this Limberlost lease in the hands of a reliable, brave, strong man who will guard it every hour of the day, and sleep with one eye open at night. I should require the entire length of the trail to be walked at least twice every day, to make sure that our lines were up and no one had been trespassing."

Freckles was leaning forward, taking in every word with such intense eagerness that he was beguiling McLean into explanations he had never intended to make.

"But why wouldn't that be the finest job in the world · for me?" he pleaded. "I am never sick. I could walk the trail twice, three times every day, and I'd be watching sharp all the while."

"It's because you are little more than a boy and this will be a trying job for a work-hardened man," answered McLean. "You see, in the first place, you would be afraid. In stretching our lines we killed six rattlesnakes almost as long as your body and as thick as your arm. It's the price of your life to start through the marsh grass surrounding the swamp unless you are covered with heavy leather above your knees.

"You should be able to swim in case high water undermines the temporary bridge we have built where Sleepy Snake Creek enters the swamp. The fall and winter changes of weather are abrupt and severe and I should want strict watch kept every day. You would always be alone and I don't guarantee what is in the Limberlost. It is lying here as it has lain since the beginning of time, and it is alive with sounds and voices. I don't pretend to say what all of them come from, but, from a few slinking forms I've seen and hair-raising yells I've heard, I'd rather not confront their owners myself; and I am neither weak nor fearful.

"Worst of all, any man who will enter the swamp to

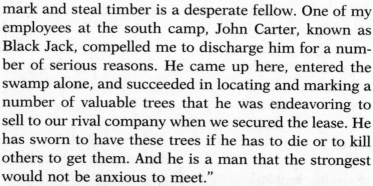

mark and steal timber is a desperate fellow. One of my employees at the south camp, John Carter, known as Black Jack, compelled me to discharge him for a number of serious reasons. He came up here, entered the swamp alone, and succeeded in locating and marking a number of valuable trees that he was endeavoring to sell to our rival company when we secured the lease. He has sworn to have these trees if he has to die or to kill others to get them. And he is a man that the strongest would not be anxious to meet."

"But if he came to steal trees wouldn't he bring teams and men enough that all any man could do would be to watch and be after you?" queried the boy.

"Yes," replied McLean.

"Then why couldn't I be watching just as closely, and coming as fast, as an older, stronger man?" asked Freckles.

"Why, by George, you could!" exclaimed McLean. "I don't know as the size of a man would be half so important as his grit and faithfulness, come to think of it. Sit down on that log there and we will talk it over. What is your name?"

Freckles shook his head at the offer of a seat and, folding his arms, stood straight as the trees about him. He grew a shade whiter, but his eyes never faltered.

"Freckles," he said.

"Good enough for every day," laughed McLean, "but I can scarcely put 'Freckles' on the company's books. Tell me your name."

"I haven't any name," replied the boy.

"I don't understand," said McLean.

"I was thinking from the voice and the face of you that you wouldn't," said Freckles slowly. "I've spent more time on it than I ever did on anything else in all me life and I don't understand. Does it seem to you that anyone would take a newborn baby and row over it until it was bruised black, cut off its hand, and leave it out on a bitter night on the steps of a charity home to the care of strangers? That's what somebody did to me."

McLean stared aghast. He found no reply ready, and presently in a low voice he suggested, "And after—?"

"The home people took me in and I was there the full legal age and several years over. For the most part we were a lot of little Irishmen together. They could always find homes for the rest of the children, but nobody would ever be wanting me on account of me arm."

"Were they kind to you?" McLean could have bitten his tongue for the question the minute it was asked.

"I don't know," answered Freckles. The reply sounded so hopeless, even to his own ears, that he hastened to qualify it by adding, "You see, it's like this, sir. Kindnesses that people are paid to lay off in job lots, and that belong equally to several hundred others, ain't going to be soaking into any one fellow so much."

"Go on," said McLean, nodding comprehendingly.

"There's nothing worth the taking of your time to tell," replied Freckles. "The home was in Chicago, and I was there all me life up to three months ago. When I was too old for the training they gave to the little children, they sent me out to the nearest ward school as long as the law would let them. But I was never like any of the other children, and they all knew it. I'd go and

come like a prisoner, and be working about the home early and late for me board and clothes. I always wanted to learn mighty bad, but I was glad when that was over.

"Every few days all me life I'd be called up, looked over, and refused a home and love, on account of me hand and ugly face. But it was all the home I'd ever known, and I didn't seem to belong anyplace else.

"Then a new superintendent was put in. He wasn't for being like any of the others and he swore he'd weed me out the first thing he did. He made a plan to send me down in the state to a man he said he knew that needed a boy. He wasn't for remembering to tell that man that I was a hand short, and the man knocked me down the minute he found I was the boy that had been sent him. Between noon and that evening, he and his son about my age had me in pretty much the same shape in which I was found in the beginning, so I lay awake that night and ran away. I'd like to have squared me account with that boy before I left, but I didn't dare for fear of waking the old man, and I knew I couldn't handle the two of them. But I'm hoping to meet him alone some day before I die."

McLean tugged at his mustache to hide the smile on his lips, and he liked the boy all the better for this confession.

"I didn't even have to steal clothes to get rid of starting in me home ones," Freckles went on, "for they had already taken all me clean, neat things for the boy and put me into his rags, and that went almost as sore as the beatings, for where I was we were always kept tidy and sweet-smelling, anyway. I hustled clear into this state before I learned that the man couldn't have kept me if he'd wanted to. When I thought I was good and away from him, I began hunting work, but it is with everybody else just as it is with you, sir. Big, strong, whole men are the only ones for being wanted."

"I have been thinking over this matter," answered McLean. "I am not so sure but that a man no older than you and like you in every way could do this work very well, if he were not a coward and had it in him to be trustworthy and industrious."

Freckles came forward a step.

"If you will give me a job where I can earn me food, clothes, and a place to sleep," he said, "if I can have a boss to work for like other men, and a place I feel I've a right to, I will do precisely what you tell me or die trying."

He said it so quietly and convincingly that McLean believed, although in his heart he knew that to employ a stranger would be wretched business for a man with the interests he had involved.

"Very well," the boss found himself answering. "I will enter you on my payrolls. We'll have supper and then I will provide you with clean clothing, wading boots, the wire-mending apparatus, and a revolver. The first thing in the morning, I will take you over the trail myself and explain fully what I want done. All I ask of you is to come to me at once at the south camp and tell me like a man if you find this job too hard for you. It will not surprise me. It is work that few men would perform faithfully. What name shall I put down?"

Freckles' eyes never left McLean's face, and the boss saw the swift spasm of pain that swept his lonely, sensitive face.

"I haven't any name," he said stubbornly, "no more than one somebody clapped on to me when they put me on the home books, with not the thought or care they'd named a house cat. I've seen how they enter those poor, little abandoned devils often enough to know. What they called me is no more my name than it is yours. I don't know what mine is and I never will, but I am going to be your man and do your work, and I'll be glad to answer to any name you choose to call me. Won't you please be giving me a name, Mr. McLean?"

The boss wheeled abruptly and began stacking his books. What he was thinking was probably what any other gentleman would have thought in the circumstances. With his eyes still downcast, and in a voice harsh with huskiness, he spoke.

"I will tell you what we will do, my lad," he said. "My father was my ideal man, and I loved him better than any other I have ever known. He died five years ago, but that he would have been proud to leave to you his name I firmly believe. If I give to you the name of my nearest kin and the man I loved best—will that do?"

Freckles' rigid attitude relaxed suddenly. His head dropped and big tears splashed down on the soiled calico shirt. McLean was not surprised at the silence, for he found that talking came none too easily just then.

"All right," he said. "I will write it on the roll—James Ross McLean."

"Thank you mightily," said Freckles. "That makes me feel almost as if I belonged, already."

"You do," said McLean. "Until someone armed with every right comes to claim you, you are mine. Now, come and take a bath, have some supper, and go to bed."

As Freckles followed into the lights and sounds of the camp, his heart and soul were singing for joy.

Chapter II

Next morning found Freckles in clean, whole clothing, fed, and rested. Then McLean outfitted him and gave him careful instruction in the use of his weapon. The boss showed him around the timberline and engaged him a place to board with the family of his head teamster, Duncan, whom he had brought from Scotland with him and who lived in a small clearing he was working out between the swamp and the corduroy. When the gang pulled out for the south camp, Freckles was left to guard a fortune in the Limberlost. That he was under guard himself those first weeks he never knew.

Every hour was torture to the boy. The restricted life of a great city orphanage was the other extreme of the world from the Limberlost. He was afraid for his life

14

every minute. The heat was intense. The heavy wading
boots rubbed his feet until they bled. He was already
sore and stiff from his long tramp and outdoor exposure. The seven miles of trail was agony at every step.
He practiced at night, under the direction of Duncan,
until he grew fairly sure in the use of his revolver. He
cut a stout hickory cudgel, with a knot on the end as big
as his fist, and it never left his hand. What he thought in
those first days he himself could not recall clearly afterward.

His heart stood still every time he saw the beautiful
marsh grass begin a sinuous waving *against* the play of
the wind, as McLean had told him it would. He bolted a
half mile with the first boom of the bittern, and his hat
lifted with every yelp of the sheitpoke. Once he saw a
lean, shadowy form following him and blazed away
with his revolver. Then he was frightened worse than
ever for fear it might have been Duncan's collie.

The first afternoon that he found his wires down, and
he was compelled to plunge knee deep into the black
swamp muck to restring them, he became so ill from
fear and nervousness that he scarcely could control his
shaking hand to do the work. With every step, he felt
that he would miss secure footing and be swallowed up
in that clinging sea of blackness. In dumb agony he
plunged forward, clinging to the post sand trees until he
had finished restringing and testing the wire. He had
consumed much time. Night closed in. The Limberlost
stirred gently, then shook herself, growled, and awoke
about him.

There seemed to be a great owl hooting from every

hollow tree and a little one screeching from every knot-
hole. The bellowing of monster bullfrogs was not sufficiently deafening to shut out the wailing of whippoor-
wills that seemed to come from every bush. Nighthawks
swept past him with their shivering cry and bats struck
his face. A prowling wildcat missed its catch and
screamed with rage. A lost fox bayed incessantly for its
mate.

The hair on the back of Freckles' neck rose like bris-
tles, and his knees wavered under him. He could not see
if the dreaded snakes were on the trail, nor, in the pandemonium, hear the rattle for which McLean had cautioned him to listen. He stood rooted to the ground in
an agony of fear. His breath whistled between his teeth.
The perspiration ran down his face and body in little
streams.

Something big, black, and heavy came crashing
through the swamp near him and with a yell of utter
panic Freckles broke and ran—how far he did not
know. But at last he gained some sort of mastery over
himself and retraced his steps. His jaws set like steel
and the sweat dried on his body. When he reached the
place from which he had started to run, he turned and
with measured steps made his way back down the line.
After a while he realized that he was only walking, so
for the second time he faced that sea of horrors. When
he again came toward the corduroy the cudgel fell to
test the wire at every step.

Sounds that curdled his blood seemed to close in
about him and shapes of terror to draw nearer and
nearer. Fear had so gained the mastery that he did not

dare look behind him. And, just when he felt that he should fall dead before he ever reached the clearing, he heard Duncan's rolling call, "Freckles! Freckles!" A great shuddering sob burst in the boy's dry throat. But he only told Duncan that finding the wire down had made him late.

The next morning he started out on time. Day after day, with his heart pounding like a trip-hammer, he ducked, dodged, ran when he could, and fought like a wildcat when he was brought to bay. If he ever had an idea of giving up, no one knew it; for he clung to his job without the shadow of wavering. All these things, insofar as he guessed them, Duncan, who had been set to watch the first weeks of Freckles' work, carried to the boss at the south camp. But the innermost, exquisite torture of the thing the big Scotsman never guessed, and McLean, with his finer perceptions, came only a little nearer.

After a few weeks, when Freckles found that he was still living, that he had a home, and the very first money he had ever possessed was safe in his pockets, he began to grow proud. He still sidestepped, dodged, and hurried to avoid being late again, but he was gradually developing the fearlessness that men acquire of dangers to which they are hourly accustomed.

His heart seemed to be in his mouth when his first rattler disputed the trail with him, but he mustered courage and drove at it with his club. After its head had been crushed, he sufficiently overcame an Irishman's inborn repugnance to snakes and cut off his rattles to show Duncan. With the mastery of his first snake, his greatest fear of them was gone.

Then he began to realize that with the abundance of food in the swamp, flesh hunters would not come out on the trail and attack him, and he had his revolver for defense if they did. He soon learned to laugh at the big, floppy birds that made horrible noises. One day, watching from behind a tree, he saw a crane solemnly performing a few measures of a belated nuptial song and dance with his mate. Realizing that it was intended in tenderness, no matter how it appeared, the lonely, starved heart of the boy went out to them in sympathy.

Before the first month was over he was fairly easy about his job, and by the next he rather liked it. Nature can be trusted to work her own miracle in the heart of any man whose daily task keeps him alone among her sights, sounds, and silences.

When, day after day, the only thing that relieved his utter loneliness was the companionship of the birds and beasts of the swamp, it was the most natural thing in the world that Freckles should turn to them for friendship. He began by instinctively protecting the weak and helpless. He was astonished at the quickness with which they became accustomed to him and the disregard they showed for his movements, once they learned that he was not a hunter and that the club he carried was used more frequently for their benefit than his own. He could scarcely believe what he saw.

From the effort to protect the birds and animals, it was only a short step to the possessive feeling, and with it sprang up the impulse to caress and provide. Through fall, when brooding was over and the upland birds sought the swamp in swarms to feast on its seeds and berries, Freckles was content with watching them and speculating about them. Outside of half a dozen of the very commonest, they were strangers to him. The likeness of their way to that of human folk was an hourly surprise.

When black frosts began stripping the Limberlost, cutting down the ferns, shearing the vines from the trees, mowing the succulent green things of the swale, and setting the leaves swirling down, he watched the departing troops of his friends with dismay. He began to realize that he was going to be left alone. He made special efforts toward friendliness with the hope that he could induce some of them to stay. It was then that he conceived the idea of carrying food to the birds; for he saw that they were leaving for lack of it. But he could not stop them. Day after day, flocks gathered and departed. By the time the first snow whitened his trail about the Limberlost, there were left only the little black-and-white juncos, the sapsuckers, yellowhammers, a few patriarchs among the flaming cardinals, the blue jays, the crows, and the quail.

Then Freckles began his magic work. He cleared a space of swale and twice a day he spread a birds' banquet. By the middle of December the strong winds of winter had beaten most of the seed from the grass and bushes. The snow fell, covering the swamp, and food was very scarce and hard to find. The birds scarcely waited until Freckles' back was turned to attack his provisions. In a few weeks they flew toward the clearing to

meet him. By the bitter weather of January they came halfway to the cabin every morning, and fluttered about him like doves all the way to the feeding ground. By February they were so accustomed to him, and so hunger-driven, that they would perch on his head and shoulders, and the saucy jays would try to pry into his pockets.

Then Freckles added to wheat and crumbs every scrap of refuse food he could find about the cabin. He carried down to his pets the parings of apples, turnips, potatoes, stray cabbage leaves, and carrots, and tied to the bushes meat bones to which scraps of fat and gristle still clung. One morning, coming to his feeding ground unusually early, he found a gorgeous cardinal and a rabbit sociably nibbling a cabbage leaf side by side. That instantly gave him the idea of cracking nuts, from the store he had gathered for Duncan's children, for the squirrels, in the effort to add them to his family. Soon he had them coming—red, gray, and black; and he became filled with a vast impatience that he did not know their names or habits.

So the winter passed. Every week McLean rode over to the Limberlost; never on the same day nor at the same hour. Always he found Freckles at his work, faithful and brave, no matter how severe the weather.

The boy's earnings constituted his first money, and when the boss explained to him that he could leave them safe at a bank and carry away a scrap of paper that represented the amount, he went, immediately on every payday, and made his deposit, keeping out barely what was necessary for his board and clothing. What he wanted to do with his money he did not know, but it gave him a sense of freedom and power to feel that it was there—it was his and he could have it when he chose. In imitation of McLean, he bought a small pocket account book, in which he carefully set down every dollar he earned and every penny he spent. As his expenses were small and the boss paid him well, it was astonishing how his little hoard grew.

That winter held the first hours of real happiness in Freckles' life. He was free. He was doing a man's work faithfully, through every rigor of rain, snow, and blizzard. He was gathering a wonderful strength of body, paying his way, and saving money. Every man of the gang and of that locality knew that he was under the protection of McLean, who was a power, and it had the effect of smoothing Freckles' path in many directions.

Mrs. Duncan showed him that individual kindness for which his hungry heart was longing. She had a hot drink ready for him when he came in from a freezing day on the trail. She knitted him a heavy mitten for his left hand and devised a way to sew up and pad the right sleeve which protected the maimed arm in bitter weather. She patched his clothing—frequently torn by the wire, and saved kitchen scraps for his birds, not because she either knew or cared a rap about them, but because she herself was near enough the swamp to be touched by its utter loneliness. When Duncan laughed at her for this, she retorted, "My God, mannie, if Freckles hadna the birds and the beasts he would be always alone. It was never meant for a human being to

be sa solitary. He'd get touched in the head if he hadna them to think for and to talk to."

"How much answer do ye think he gets to his talkin', lass?" laughed Duncan.

"He gets the answer that keeps the eye bricht, the heart happy, and the feet walking faithful the rough path he's set them in," answered Mrs. Duncan earnestly.

Duncan walked away looking very thoughtful. The next morning he gave an ear of the corn he was shelling for his chickens to Freckles, and told him to carry it to his wild chickens down there in the Limberlost. Freckles laughed delightedly.

"Me chickens!" he said. "Why didn't I ever think of that before? Of course they are! They are just little brightly colored cocks and hens! But 'wild' is no good. What would you say to me 'wild chickens' being a good deal tamer than yours here in your yard?"

"Hoot, lad!" cried Duncan.

"Make yours light on your head and eat out of your hands and pockets," challenged Freckles.

"Go tell your fairy tales to the wee people! They're juist brash on believin' things," said Duncan. "Ye canna invent any story too big to stop them from callin' for a bigger."

"I dare you to come see!" retorted Freckles.

"Take ye!" said Duncan. "If ye make juist one bird licht on your heid or eat frae your hand, ye are free to help yoursel' to my corncrib and wheat bin the rest of the winter."

Freckles sprang in air and howled in holy joy.

"Oh, Duncan! You're too aisy," he cried. "When will you come?"

"I'll come next Sabbath," said Duncan. "And I'll believe the birds of the Limberlost are tame as barnyard fowl when I see it, and no sooner!"

After that Freckles always spoke of the birds as his chickens and the Duncans followed his example.

The very next Sabbath, Duncan, with his wife and children, followed Freckles to the swamp. They saw a sight so wonderful it will keep them talking all the rest of their lives, and make them unfailing friends of all the birds save, perhaps, the hawks and the owls.

Freckles' chickens were awaiting him at the edge of the clearing. They cut the frosty air about his head into curves and circles of crimson, blue, and black. They chased each other from Freckles, and swept so closely themselves that they brushed him with their outspread wings.

At their feeding ground Freckles set down his old pail of scraps and swept the snow from a small level space with a broom improvised from twigs. As soon as his back was turned, the birds clustered over the food, snatching scraps to carry to the nearest bushes. Several of the boldest, a big crow and a couple of jays, settled on the rim and feasted at leisure, while a cardinal, which hesitated to venture, fumed and scolded from a twig overhead.

Then Freckles scattered his store. At once the ground resembled the spread mantle of Montezuma, except that this mass of gaily colored feathers was on the backs of living birds. While they feasted, Duncan gripped his wife's arm and stared in astonishment; for from the bushes and dry grass, with gentle cheeping and queer throaty chatter, as if to encourage each other, came flocks of quail. Before anyone saw it arrive, a big gray rabbit sat in the midst of the feast, contentedly gnawing a cabbage leaf.

"Weel, I be drawed on!" came Mrs. Duncan's tense whisper.

"Shu-shu," cautioned Duncan.

Then Freckles took off his cap. He began filling it with handfuls of wheat from his pockets. In a swarm the grain eaters rose about him like a flock of tame pigeons. They perched on his arms and the cap, and, in the stress of hunger, forgetting all caution, a brilliant cock cardinal and an equally gaudy jay fought for a perching place on his head.

"Weel, I'm beat," muttered Duncan, forgetting the silence imposed on his wife. "I'll hae to give in. 'Seein' is believin'.' A man wad hae to see that to believe it. We mauna let the boss miss that sight, for it's a chance will no likely come twice in a life. Everything is snowed under and thae craturs near starved, but trustin' Freckles that complete they are tamer than our chickens. Look hard, bairns!" he whispered. "Ye winna see the like o' yon again, while God lets ye live. Notice their color against the ice and snow, and the pretty skippin ways of them! And spunky! Weel, I'm beat fair!"

Freckles emptied his cap, turned his pockets, and scattered his last grain. Then he waved good-bye to his watching friends and struck off down the timberline.

A week later, Duncan and Freckles rose from break-

fast to face the bitterest morning of the winter. When
Freckles, warmly capped and gloved, stepped to the corner of the kitchen for his scrap pail, he found a big pan
of steaming boiled wheat on the top of it. He wheeled to
Mrs. Duncan with a shining face.

"Were you fixing this warm food for me chickens or
yours?" he asked.

"It's for yours, Freckles," she said. "I was afeared this
cold weather they wadna lay good without a warm bite
now and then."

Duncan laughed as he stepped to the other room for
his pipe; but Freckles faced Mrs. Duncan with a trace of
every pang of starved mother-hunger he ever had suffered written large on his homely, splotched, narrow
features.

"Oh, how I wish you were my mother!" he cried.

Mrs. Duncan attempted an echo of her husband's
laugh.

"Lord love the lad!" she exclaimed. "Why, Freckles,
are ye no bricht enough to learn without being taught
by a woman that I am your mither? If a great man like
yoursel' dinna ken that, learn it now and ne'er forget it.
Ance a woman is the wife of any man, she becomes wife
to all men, for having had the wifely experience she
kens! Ance a man-child has beaten his way to life under
the heart of a woman, she is mither to all men, for the
hearts of mithers are everywhere the same. Bless ye,
laddie, I am your mither!"

She tucked the coarse scarf she had knit for him
closer over his chest and pulled his cap lower about his
ears, but Freckles, whipping it off and holding it under

his arm, caught her rough, reddened hand and pressed it to his lips in a long kiss. Then he hurried away to hide the happy, embarrassing tears that were coming straight from his swelling heart.

Mrs. Duncan, sobbing unrestrainedly, swept into the next room and threw herself into Duncan's arms.

"Oh, the puir lad!" she wailed. "Oh, the puir mither-hungry lad! He breaks my heart!"

Duncan's arms closed convulsively about his wife. With a big, brown hand he lovingly stroked her rough, sorrel hair.

"Sarah, you're a guid woman!" he said. "You're a michty guid woman! Ye hae a way o' speakin' out at times that's like the inspired prophets of the Lord. If that had been put to me, now, I'd 'a' felt all I kent how to and been keen enough to say the richt thing. But dang it, I'd 'a' stuttered and stammered and got nae-thing out that would ha' done onybody a mite o' good. But ye, Sarah! Did ye see his face, woman? Ye sent him off lookin' leke a white light of holiness had passed over and settled on him. Ye sent the lad off too happy for mortal words, Sarah. And ye made me that proud o' ye! I wouldna trade ye an' my share o' the Limberlost with ony king ye could mention."

He relaxed his clasp, and setting a heavy hand on each shoulder, he looked straight into her eyes.

"Ye're prime, Sarah! Juist prime!" he said.

Sarah Duncan stood alone in the middle of her two-room log cabin and lifted a pair of bony, clawlike hands, reddened by frequent immersion in hot water, cracked and chafed by exposure to cold, black-lined by constant battle with swamp loam, and calloused by burns, and stared at them wonderingly.

"Pretty lookin' things ye are!" she whispered. "But ye hae juist been kissed. And by such a man! Fine as God ever made at His verra best. Duncan wouldna trade wi' a king! Na! Nor I wadna trade with a queen wi' a palace, an' velvet gowns, an' diamonds big as hazelnuts, an' a hundred visitors a day into the bargain. Ye've been that honored I'm blest if I can bear to souse ye in dishwater. Still, that kiss winna come off! Naething can take it from me, for it's mine till I dee. Lord, if I amna proud! Kisses on these old claws! Weel, I be drawed on!"

Chapter III

WHEREIN A FEATHER FALLS AND A SOUL IS
BORN

So Freckles fared through the bitter winter. He was very happy. He had hungered for freedom, love, and appreciation so long! He had been unspeakably lonely at the home; and the utter loneliness of a great desert or forest is not so hard to bear as the loneliness of being constantly surrounded by crowds of people who do not care in the least whether one is living or dead.

All through the winter Freckles' entire energy was given to keeping his lines up and his "chickens" from freezing or starving. When the first breath of spring touched the Limberlost, and the snow receded before it; when the catkins began to bloom, when there came a hint of green to the trees, bushes, and swale, when the rushes lifted their heads, and the pulse of the newly resurrected season beat strong in the heart of nature, something new stirred in the breast of the boy.

Nature always levies her tribute. Now she laid a powerful hand on the soul of Freckles, to which the boy's whole being responded, though he had not the least idea what was troubling him. Duncan accepted his wife's theory that it was a touch of spring fever, but Freckles knew better. He had never been so well. Clean, hot, and steady the blood pulsed in his veins. He was always hungry and his hardest day's work tired him not at all. For long months, without a single intermission, he had tramped those seven miles of trail twice every day, through every conceivable state of weather. With the heavy club he gave his wires a sure test, and between sections, first in play, afterward to keep his circulation going, he had acquired the skill of an expert drum major. In his work there was exercise for every muscle of his body each hour of the day, and at night a bath, wholesome food, and sound sleep in a room that never knew fire. He had taken on flesh and color, and developed a greater strength and endurance than anyone could ever have guessed.

And now the Limberlost did not contain last year's terrors. He had been with her in her hour of desolation, when, stripped bare and deserted, she had stood shivering, as if herself afraid. He had made excursions into the interior until he was familiar with every path and road that had ever been made. He had sounded the depths of her deepest pools, and had learned why the trees grew so magnificently. He had found that places of swamp and swale were few compared with miles of

solid timberland, concealed by summer's luxuriant
undergrowth.

The sounds that had at first struck cold fear into his
soul he now knew had left on wing and silent foot at the
approach of winter. As flock after flock of the birds returned and he recognized the old echoes reawakening,
he found to his surprise that he had been lonely for
them and was hailing their return with great joy. All his
fears were forgotten. Instead, he was possessed of an
overpowering desire to know what they were, to learn
where they had been, and whether they would make
friends with him as the winter birds had done; and if
they did, would they be as fickle? For, with the running
sap, creeping worm, and winging bug, most of Freckles'
chickens had deserted him, entered the swamp, and
feasted to such a state of plethora on its store that they
cared little for his supply, so that in the strenuous days
of mating and nest-building the boy was deserted.

He chafed at the birds' ingratitude, but he found
speedy consolation in watching and befriending the
newcomers. He surely would have been proud and
highly pleased if he had known that many of the former
inhabitants of the interior swamp now grouped their
nests about the timberline solely for the sake of his protection and company.

The yearly resurrection of the Limberlost is a mighty
revival. Freckles stood back and watched with awe and
envy the gradual reclothing and repopulating of the
swamp. Keen-eyed and alert through danger and loneliness, he noted every stage of development, from the first

piping frog and unsheathing bud, to full leafage and the return of the last emigrant.

The knowledge of his complete loneliness and utter insignificance was hourly thrust upon him. He brooded and fretted until he was in a fever, and yet he never guessed the cause. He was filled with a vast impatience and a longing that would not much further be denied.

It was June by the zodiac, June by the Limberlost, and by every delight of a newly resurrected season it should have been June in the hearts of all men. Yet Freckles scowled darkly as he came down the trail, and the running *tap, tap*, which tested the sagging wire and telegraphed word of his coming to his furred and feathered friends of the swamp, this morning carried the story of his discontent a mile ahead of him.

Freckles' special pet, a dainty, yellow-coated, black-sleeved, cock goldfinch, had for several days past remained on the wire, the bravest of all; and Freckles, absorbed with the cunning and beauty of the tiny fellow, never guessed that he was being duped. For the goldfinch was skipping, flirting, and swinging for the express purpose of so holding his attention that he would not look up and see a small cradle of thistledown and wool perilously near his head. In the beginning of brooding, the spunky little homesteader had heroically clung to the wire when he was almost paralyzed with fright. When day after day passed and brought only softly whistled repetitions of his call, a handful of crumbs on the top of a locust line post, and gently worded coaxings, he grew in confidence. Of late he had sung and swung during the passing of Freckles, who,

not dreaming of the nest and the solemn-eyed little hen so close above, thought himself unusually gifted in his power to attract the birds. This morning the goldfinch could scarcely believe his ears, and clung to the wire until an unusually vicious rap sent him spinning a foot in air and his *"Ptseet"* came with a squall of utter panic.

The wires were ringing with a story the birds could not translate and Freckles was quite as ignorant of the trouble as they.

A peculiar movement under a small walnut tree caught his eye. He stopped to investigate. It was an unusually large luna cocoon, and the moth was just bursting the upper end in its struggles to reach light and air. Freckles stood and stared.

"There's something in there trying to get out," he muttered. "Wonder if I could help it? Guess I best not be trying. If I hadn't happened along, there wouldn't have been anyone to help it, and maybe I'd only be hurting it. It's—it's—oh, skaggany! It's just being born!"

Freckles gasped with surprise. The moth cleared the opening and with great wobblings and contortions climbed up the tree. He stared speechless with amazement as the moth crept around a limb and clung to the underside. There was a great pursy body, almost as large as his thumb, and of the very snowiest white that Freckles had ever seen. There was a band of delicate lavender across its forehead, and its feet were of the same color. There were antlers, like tiny, straw-colored ferns, on its head, and on its shoulders little wet-looking flaps no bigger than his thumbnail. As Freckles gazed, tense with astonishment, he saw that those queer, little, wet-looking things were expanding, drooping, taking on color, and small, oval markings were beginning to show.

The minutes went by. Freckles' steady gaze never wavered. Without realizing it he was trembling with eagerness and anxiety. As he saw what was taking place, "It's going to have wings," he breathed in hushed wonder. The morning sun fell on the moth and dried its velvet down, and the soft air made it fluffy. The rapidly growing wings began to appear to be of the most delicate green, with lavender fore-ribs, transparent, eye-shaped markings edged with lines of red, tan, and black, and long, crisp trailers.

Freckles was whispering to himself for fear of disturbing the moth. It began a systematic exercise of raising and lowering its exquisite wings to dry them and to establish circulation. Freckles realized that it would soon be able to spread them and sail away. His long-coming soul sent up its first shivering cry.

"I don't know what it is! Oh, I wish I knew! How I wish I knew! It must be something grand! It can't be a butterfly! It's away too big. Oh, I wish there was someone to tell me what it is!"

He climbed on the locust post and, balancing himself by the wire, held a finger in the line of the moth's advance up the twig. It unhesitatingly climbed on and he stepped back to the path, holding it up to the light and examining it closely. Then he held it in the shade and turned it, gloating over its markings and beautiful coloring. When he held the moth back to the limb, it climbed on, still waving those magnificent wings.

"My, but I'd like to be staying with you!" he said. "But if I was to stay here all day you couldn't get any prettier than you are right now, and I wouldn't get smart enough to tell what you are. I suppose there's someone that knows. Of course there is! Mr. McLean said there were people that knew every leaf, bird, and flower in the Limberlost. Oh, Lord! How I wish You'd be telling me just this one thing!"

The goldfinch had ventured back to the wire, for there was his mate, only a few inches above the man creature's head; and, indeed, he simply must not be allowed to look up just then, so the brave little fellow rocked on the wire and piped up, just as he had done every day for a week, *"See me? See me?"*

"See you! Of course I see you," growled Freckles. "I see you day after day, and what good is it doing me? I might see you every morning for a year and then not be able to be telling anyone about it. 'Seen a bird—little, and yellow as any canary, with black silk wings.' That's as far as I'd get. What you doing here, anyway? Have you a mate? What's your name? 'See you?' I reckon I see you, but I might as well be blind, for any good it's doing me!"

Freckles impatiently struck the wire. With a screech of fear, the goldfinch fled precipitately. His mate tore from off the nest with a whirr—Freckles looked up and saw it.

"O-ho!" he cried. "So that's what you are doing here! You have a wife. And so close to my head I have been mighty near wearing a bird on my bonnet and never knew it!"

Freckles laughed at his own joke and in better humor
climbed up to examine the neat, tiny cradle and its contents. The hen darted at him in a frenzy. "Now, where
do you come in?" he demanded, when he saw that she
was not like the goldfinch.

"You be clearing out of here! This is none of your fry.
This is the nest of me little yellow friend of the wire,
and you shan't be touching it. Don't blame you for
wanting to see, though. My, but it's a fine nest and
beauties of eggs. Will you be keeping away or will I fire
this stick at you?"

Freckles dropped back to the trail. The hen darted to
the nest and settled on it with a tender, coddling movement. He of the yellow coat flew to the edge to make
sure that everything was right. It would have been plain
to even the veriest novice that they were partners in that
cradle.

"Well, I'll be switched!" muttered Freckles. "If that
ain't both their nest! And he's yellow and she's green, or
she's yellow and he's green. Of course, I don't know, and
I haven't any way to find out, but it's plain as the nose
on your face that they are both ready to be fighting for
that nest, so, of course, they belong. Don't that beat
you? Say, that's what's been sticking me for all of these
two weeks on that grass nest in the thorn tree down the
line. One day a blue bird is setting, and I think it is hers.
The next day a brown bird is on, and I chase it off because the nest is blue's. Next day the brown bird is on
again and I let her be because I think it must be hers.
Next day, be golly, blue's on again, and off I send her
because it's brown's; and now, I bet my hat, it's both

their nest, and I've only been bothering them and making a big fool of meself. Pretty specimen I am, pretending to be a friend to the birds, and so blamed ignorant I don't know which ones go in pairs, and blue and brown are a pair, of course, if yellow and green are—and there's the red birds! I never thought of them! He's red and she's gray—and now I want to be knowing, are they all different? Why, no! Of course, they ain't! There's the jays all blue, and the crows all black."

The tide of Freckles' discontent welled until he actually choked with anger and chagrin. He plodded on down the trail, scowling blackly and viciously spanging the wire. At the finches' nest he left the line and peered into the thorn tree. There was no bird brooding. He pressed closer to take a peep at the snowy, spotless little eggs he had found so beautiful, and at the slight noise up flared four tiny baby heads with wide-open mouths and hunger cries. Freckles stepped back. The brown bird lit on the edge and closed one cavity with a wiggling green worm, and not two minutes later the blue filled another with something white. That settled it. The blue and brown were mates. Once again Freckles repeated his "How I wish I knew!"

About the bridge spanning Sleepy Snake Creek the swale spread wide, the timber largely dropped away, and willows, rushes, marsh grass, and splendid wild flowers grew abundantly. Here lazy, big, black water snakes, for which the creek was named, sunned on the bushes, wild ducks and grebe chattered, cranes and herons fished, and muskrats plowed the bank in queer, rolling furrows. It was always a place full of interest and

Freckles loved to linger on the bridge, watching the marsh and water people. He also transacted affairs of importance with the wild flowers and sweet marsh grass. He enjoyed splashing through the shallow pools lying on either side of the bridge.

Then, too, where the creek entered the swamp was a place of unusual beauty. The water spread out in darksome, mossy, green pools. Water plants and lilies grew abundantly, throwing up great, rank, rich green leaves. Nowhere else in the Limberlost could be found a frog chorus to equal that of the mouth of the creek. The drumming and piping went on in never-ending orchestral effect, and the full chorus rang to its accompaniment throughout the season.

Freckles struck slowly into the path leading from the bridge to the line. It was the one spot at which he might relax his vigilance. The greatest timber thief the swamp had ever known would not have attempted to enter it by the mouth of the creek, on account of the water and because there was no protection from surrounding trees. He was swishing the rank grass with his cudgel, and thinking of the shade the denser swamp afforded, when he suddenly dodged sidewise. The cudgel whistled sharply through the air and Freckles sprang back.

Out of the clear sky above him, first level with his face, then skimming, dipping, tilting, whirling until it lit, quill down, in the path in front of him, came a glossy, iridescent, big black feather. As it struck the ground Freckles snatched it up and with an almost continuous movement faced the sky. There was not a tree of any size in a large open space. There was no wind to

carry it. From the clear sky it had fallen, and Freckles, gazing eagerly into the arch of June blue with a few lazy clouds floating far up in the sea of ether, had neither mind nor knowledge to dream of a bird hanging as if frozen there. He turned the big quill questioningly, and again his awed eyes swept the sky.

"A feather dropped from Heaven!" he breathed reverently. "Are the holy angels molting? But no; if they were, it would be white. Maybe all the angels are not for being white. What if the angels of God are white and those of the devil are black? But a black one has no business up there. Maybe some poor black angel is so tired of being punished it's slipping up to the gates, beating its wings trying to make the Master hear!"

Again and again Freckles searched the sky, but there was no answering gleam of golden gates, no form of sailing bird. Then he went slowly on his way, turning the feather over and wondering about it. It was a wing quill, eighteen inches in length, with a big heavy spine, gray at the base, shading to jet black at the tip, and it caught the play of the sun's rays in slanting gleams of green and bronze. Again Freckles' "old man of the sea" sat sullen and heavy on his shoulders and weighted him down until his step lagged and his heart ached.

"Where did it come from? What is it? Oh, how I wish I knew!" he kept repeating as he turned and studied the feather, with almost unseeing eyes, so intently was he thinking.

Before him spread a great, green pool filled with rotting logs and leaves, bordered with delicate ferns and grasses among which lifted the creamy spikes of the arrowhead, the blue of water hyacinth, and the delicate yellow of the jewel flower. As Freckles leaned, handling the feather and staring first at it and then into the depths of the pool, he once more gave voice to his old query, "I wonder what it is!"

Straight across from him, couched in the mosses of a soggy old log, a big green bullfrog, with palpitant throat and batting eyes, lifted his head and bellowed in answer, *"Fin' dout! Fin' dout!"*

"Wha—what's that?" stammered Freckles, almost too much taken aback to speak. "I—I know you are only a bullfrog, but, be jabbers, that sounded mightily like speech. Wouldn't you please to be saying it over?"

The bullfrog cuddled contentedly in the ooze. Then suddenly he lifted his voice and, like an imperative drumbeat, rolled it again: *"Fin' dout! Fin' dout! Fin' dout!"*

Freckles had the answer.

Like the lightning's flash, something seemed to snap in his brain. There was a wavering flame before his eyes. Then his mind cleared. His head lifted in a new poise, his shoulders squared, and his spine straightened. The agony was over. His soul floated free. Freckles came into his birthright.

"Before God, I will!" He uttered the oath so impressively that the recording angel never winced as he posted it up in the prayer column.

Freckles set his hat over the top of one of the locust posts used between trees to hold up the wire and fastened the feather securely in the band. Then he started

down the line, talking to himself as men who have worked long alone always fall into the habit of doing.

"What a fool I have been!" he muttered. "Of course that's what I have to do! There wouldn't likely anybody be doing it for me. Of course I can! What am I a man for? If I was a four-footed thing of the swamp, maybe I couldn't; but a man can do anything if he's the grit to work hard enough and stick at it, Mr. McLean is always saying, and here's the way I am to do it. He said, too, that there were people that knew everything in the swamp. Of course they have written books! The thing for me to be doing is to quit moping and be buying me some books. Never bought a book in me life, or anything else of much account, for that matter. Oh, ain't I glad I didn't waste me money! I'll surely be having enough to get a few. Let me see."

Freckles sat down on a log, took out his pencil and account book, and on a back page he figured it out. He had walked the timberline for ten months. His pay was thirty dollars a month and his board cost him eight. That left twenty-two dollars a month, and the two dollars were more than his clothing had cost him. At the very least he had two hundred dollars in the bank. He drew a deep breath of satisfaction and smiled up at the sky with heavenly sweetness.

"I'll be having a book about all the birds, trees, flowers, butterflies, and—yes, by gummy! I'll be having one about the frogs—if it takes every cent I have," he promised himself.

He put away the account book, which was his most cherished possession, caught up his stick, and started down the line. The even tap, tap, and the cheery, gladsome whistle carried far ahead of him the message that Freckles was himself again.

He fell into a rapid pace, for he had lost time that morning, and as he rounded the last curve he was almost running. There was just a chance that the boss might be there for his weekly report.

Then wavering, flickering, darting here and there over the sweet marsh grass came a great black shadow, which swept so closely before him that for the second time that morning Freckles dodged and sprang back. He had seen some owls and hawks of the swamp that he thought could be classed as large birds, but never anything like this, for six feet it spread its great, shining wings. Its big, strong feet could be seen drawn up among its feathers. The sun glinted on its sharp, hooked beak. Its eyes glowed, caught the light, and seemed able to pierce the ground at his feet. It cared no more for Freckles than if he had not been there; for it lit on a low tree, and a second later awkwardly hopped to the trunk of a lightning-riven elm, turned its back to him, and sent an eye searching the blue.

Freckles looked just in time to see a second shadow sweep the grass; and another bird, a trifle smaller and not quite so brilliant in the light, sailed slowly down and perched beside the first. They were evidently mates, for with a queer, rolling hop the firstcomer shivered his bronze wings, sidled up to the new arrival, and gave her a silly little peck on her wing. Then he coquettishly drew away and ogled her. He lifted his head and waddled from her a few steps, awkwardly ambled back, and

gave her such a simple sort of kiss on her beak that
Freckles burst into a laugh, but clapped his hand over
his mouth to stifle the sound.

The lover ducked and sidestepped a few feet. He
spread his wings and slowly and softly waved them precisely as if he were fanning his charmer, which was
indeed the result he accomplished. Then a wave of un-
controllable tenderness struck him and he hobbled up
to his bombardment once more. He faced her squarely
this time, and turned his head from side to side with
queer little jerks and indiscriminate peckings at her
wings and head, and smirkings that really should have
been irresistible. She yawned and shuffled away indif-
ferently. Freckles reached up, pulled the quill from his
hat, and, looking from it to the birds, nodded in settled
conviction.

"So you're me black angels, ye spalpeens! No wonder
you didn't get in! But I'll back you to come nearer it
than any other birds ever did. You fly higher than I can
see. Have you picked the Limberlost for a good thing
and come down to try it? Well, you can be me chickens
if you want to, but I'm blest if you ain't cool for new
ones. Why don't you take this stick for a gun and go
skinning a mile?"

Freckles broke into an unrestrained laugh, for the
bird-lover was keen about his courting and his mate
was evidently diffident. When he approached too bois-
terously she relieved him of a goodly tuft of feathers
and sent him backward in a series of squirmy little
jumps that gave the boy an idea of what had happened
up-sky to send the falling feather across his pathway.

"Score one for the lady! I'll be umpiring this," volunteered Freckles.

With a ravishing swagger, half-lifted wings, and deep, guttural hissing, the lover came on again. He suddenly lifted his body, but she coolly rocked forward on the limb, glided gracefully beneath him, and slowly sailed off into the Limberlost. He recovered himself and gazed after her in astonishment.

Freckles hurried down the trail shaking with laughter. When he neared the path to the clearing and saw the boss sitting motionless on the mare that was the pride of his heart, the boy broke into a run.

"Oh, Mr. McLean!" he cried. "I hope I haven't kept you waiting very long! And the sun is getting so hot! I have been so slow this morning! I could have gone faster, only there were that many things to keep me, and I didn't know you would be here. I'll hurry, after this. I've never had to be giving excuses before. The line wasn't down, and there wasn't a sign of trouble. It was other things that were making me late."

McLean, smiling down on the boy, immediately noticed the difference in him. This flushed, panting, talkative lad was not the same creature who had sought him in despair and bitterness. He watched in wonder as Freckles mopped the perspiration from his forehead and burst into a laugh. Then, forgetting all his customary reserve with the boss, the pent-up boyishness in Freckles broke loose. With an eloquence of which he never dreamed, he told his story. He talked with such enthusiasm that McLean never took his eyes from his face nor shifted in the saddle until he described the

strange bird-lover, and then the boss suddenly bent over the pommel and laughed with him.

Freckles decorated his story with keen appreciation and rare touches of Irish wit and drollery that made it most interesting as well as very funny. It was a first attempt at descriptive narration. With an inborn gift for striking the vital point, a naturalist's dawning enthusiasm for the wonders of the Limberlost, and the welling joy of his newly found happiness, he made McLean see the struggles of the moth and its newly painted wings, the dainty, brilliant bird-mates of different colors, the feather sliding through the clear air, the palpitant throat and batting eyes of the frog. And his version of the big bird's courtship won for the boss the best laugh he had enjoyed in years.

"They're back there in the middle of the swamp now," said Freckles. "Do you suppose there is any chance of them staying with me chickens? If they do, they'll be about the queerest I have; but I tell you, sir, I am getting some plum good ones. There's a new kind over at the mouth of the creek that uses its wings like feet and walks on all fours. It travels like a thrashing machine. There's another, tall as me waist, with a bill a foot long, a neck near two, not the thickness of me wrist and an elegant color. He's some blue and gray, touched up with black, white, and brown. The voice of him is such that if he'd be going up and standing by a tree and sawing at it a few times he could be cutting it square off. I don't know but it would be a good idea to try him on the gang, sir."

McLean laughed. "Those must be blue herons,

Freckles," he said. "And it doesn't seem possible, but your story of the big black birds sounds like genuine black vultures. They are common enough in the south. I've seen them thick about the lumber camps of Georgia, but I never heard of any this far north before. They must be strays. You have perfectly described our nearest equivalent to a branch of these birds that in Europe are called Pharaoh's Chickens, but if they are coming to the Limberlost they will have to drop Pharaoh and become Freckles' Chickens, like the rest of the birds; won't they? Or are they too odd and ugly to interest you?"

"Oh, not at all, at all!" cried Freckles, bursting into pure brogue in his haste. "I don't know as I'd be calling them exactly pretty, and they do move like a rocking-horse loping, but they are so big and fearless. They have a fine color for black birds, and their feet and beaks seem so strong. You never saw anything so keen as their eyes! And fly? Why, just think, sir, they must be flying miles straight up, for they were out of sight completely when the feather fell. I don't suppose I've a chicken in the swamp that can go as close to heaven as those big, black fellows, and then—" Freckles' voice trailed off and he hesitated.

"Then what?" interestedly urged McLean.

"He was loving her so," answered Freckles in a hushed voice. "I know it looked awful funny, and I laughed and told on him, but if I'd taken time to think I don't believe I'd have done it. You see, I've seen such a little bit of loving in me life. You can easily be understanding that at the home it was every day the old story of neglect and desertion. Always people that didn't care

enough for their children to raise them, even if they didn't try to kill them. So you see, sir, I had to like him for trying so hard to make her know how he loved her. Of course, they're only birds, but if they are caring for each other like that, why, it's just the same as people, ain't it?"

Freckles lifted his brave, steady eyes to the boss.

"If anybody loved me like that, Mr. McLean, I wouldn't be spending any time caring how they looked or moved. All I'd be thinking of was how they felt toward me. If they will stay, I'll be caring as much for them as any chickens I have. If I did laugh at him, I thought he was just fine!"

The face of McLean was a study. But the honest eyes of the boy were so compelling that he found himself answering, "You are right, Freckles. He's a gentleman, isn't he? And the only real chicken you have. Of course he'll stay! The Limberlost will be paradise for his family. And now, Freckles, what has been the trouble all spring? You have done your work as faithfully as anyone could ask, but I can't help seeing that there is something wrong. Are you tired of your job?"

"I love it," answered Freckles. "It will almost break me heart when the gang comes and begins tearing up the swamp and scaring away me chickens."

"Then what is the matter?" insisted McLean.

"I think, sir, it's been books," answered Freckles. "You see, I didn't realize it meself until the bullfrog told me this morning. I hadn't ever even heard about a place like this. Anyway, I wasn't understanding how it would be, if I had. Being among these beautiful things every

day, I got so anxious like to be knowing and naming
them, that it got to eating into me and went and made
me near sick, when I was well as I could be. Of course, I
learned to read, write, and figure some at school, but
there was nothing there, nor in any of the city that I
ever got to see, that would make a fellow even be
dreaming of such interesting things as there are here.
I've seen the parks—but good Lord, they ain't even beginning to be in it with the Limberlost! It's all new and
strange to me. I don't know a thing about any of it. The
bullfrog told me to *'find out,'* plain as day, and books
are the only way, ain't they?"

"Of course," said McLean, astonished at himself for
his heartfelt relief. He had not guessed until that minute what it would have meant to him to have Freckles
give up. "You know enough to study out what you want
yourself, if you have the books; don't you?"

"I am pretty sure I do," said Freckles. "I learned all I'd
the chance at in the home, and me schooling was good
as far as it went. Wouldn't let you go past fourteen, you
know. I always did me sums perfect, and I loved me
history books. I had them almost by heart. I never could
get the grammar to suit them. They said it was just born
in me to go wrong talking, and if it hadn't been I suppose I should have picked it up from the other children.
But I'd the best voice of any of them in the home or at
school. I could knock them all out singing. I was always
leader in the home, and once one of the superinten-
dents gave me carfare and let me go into the city and
sing in a boys' choir. The master said I'd the sweatest
voice of them all until it got rough like, and then he

made me quit for a while, but he said it would be coming back by now, and I'm railly thinking it is, sir, for I've
tried about the line a bit of late and it seems to go
smooth again and lots stronger. That and me chickens
has been all the company I've been having, and it will be
all I'll want if I can have some books and learn the real
names of things, where they come from, and why they
do such interesting things. It's been fretting me more
than I knew to be shut up here among all these wonders
and not knowing a thing. I wanted to ask you what
some books would cost me, and if you'd be having the
goodness to get me the right ones. I think I have enough
money."

Freckles handed up his account book and the boss
studied it gravely.

"You needn't touch your bank account, Freckles," he
said. "Ten dollars from this month's pay will get you
everything you need to start on. I will write a friend in
Grand Rapids today to select the very best and send
them at once."

Freckles' eyes were shining.

"Never owned a book in me life!" he said. "Even me
schoolbooks were never mine. Lord! How I used to wish
I could have just one of them for me very own! Won't it
be fun to see me saw-bird and me little yellow fellow
looking at me from the pages of a book, and their real
names and all about them printed alongside? How long
will it be taking, sir?"

"Ten days ought to do it nicely," said McLean. Then,
seeing Freckles' lengthening face, he added, "I'll have
Duncan get you a ten-bushel store box the next time he

goes to town. He can haul it down to the west entrance and set it up wherever you want it. You can put in your spare time filling it with the specimens you pick up until the books come, and then you can study what you have. I suspect you could find a lot of stuff that I could send to naturalists in the city and sell for you. Things like that winged creature, this morning. I don't know much in that line, but it must have been a moth and it might have been rare. I've seen them by the thousand in museums, and in all nature I don't remember rarer coloring than their wings. I'll order you a butterfly net and box and show you how scientists pin specimens. Possibly you can make a fine collection of these swamp beauties. It will be all right for you to take a pair of different moths and butterflies, but I don't want to hear of your killing any birds. They are protected by heavy fines."

McLean rode away and left Freckles staring aghast. Then he saw the point and grinned sheepishly. Standing on the trail, he twirled the feather and thought the morning over.

"Well, if life ain't getting to be worth living!" he said wonderingly. "Biggest streak of luck I ever had! 'Bout time something was coming my way, but I wouldn't ever thought anybody could strike such magnificent prospects through just a falling feather."

Chapter IV ——————————————————

WHEREIN FRECKLES BRAVELY FACES TROUBLE
AND OPENS THE WAY FOR NEW EXPERIENCES

On Duncan's return from his next trip to town there
was a big store box loaded on the back of his
wagon. He drove to the west entrance of the swamp, set
the box on a stump that Freckles had selected in a beautiful and sheltered place, and made it secure on its
foundation with a tree at its back.

"It seems most a pity to nail into that tree," said
Duncan. "I haena the time to examine into the grain of
it, but it looks as if it might be a rare ane. Anyhow, the
nailin' winna hurt it deep, and havin' the case by it will
make it safer if it is a guid ane."

"Isn't it an oak?" asked Freckles.

"Ay," said Duncan. "It looks like it might be ane of
thae fine-grained golden anes that mak' such grand
furniture."

50

When the body of the case was secure, Duncan made a door out of the lid, and fastened it on with hinges. He drove a staple, screwed on a latch, and gave Freckles a small padlock—so that he might safely fasten in his treasures. He made a shelf in the top for the books, and last of all covered the case with oilcloth.

It was the first time in Freckles' life that anyone had ever done that much for his pleasure, and it warmed his heart with pure joy. If the sides of the box had already been covered with the rarest treasures of the Limberlost, he could have been no happier.

When the big teamster stood back to look over his work, he laughingly quoted, " 'Neat, but no' gaudy,' as McLean says. All we're needing now is a coat of paint to make a cupboard that would turn Sarah green with envy. Ye'll find that safe an' dry, lad, an' that's all that's needed."

"Mr. Duncan," said Freckles, "I don't know why you are being so mighty good to me; but if you have any jobs up at the cabin that I could do for you or Mrs. Duncan, hours off the line, it would make me mighty happy."

Duncan laughed. "Ye needna feel ye are obliged to me, lad. Ye mauna think I could take a half day off in the best hauling season to go to town for boxes to rig up, and spend of my little for fixtures."

"I knew Mr. McLean sent you," said Freckles, his eyes wide and bright with happiness. "It's so good of him. How I wish I could do something that would please him as much!"

"Why, Freckles," said Duncan, as he knelt and began

gathering up his tools, "I canna see that it will hurt ye to be told that ye are doing every day a thing that pleases the boss as much as anything ye could do. Ye're being uncommon faithful, lad, and honest as old Father Time. McLean is trusting ye as he would his own flesh and blood."

"Oh, Duncan!" cried the happy boy. "Are you sure?"

"Why, I know," answered Duncan. "I wadna venture to say so else. In those first days he cautioned me na to tell ye that, but now he wadna care. D'ye ken, Freckles, that some of the single trees ye are guarding are worth a thousand dollars?"

Freckles caught his breath and stood speechless. He looked limp and his eyes popped.

"Ye see," said Duncan, "that's why they maun be watched so closely. They tak', say, for instance, a burl maple—bird's-eye they call it in the factory, because it's full o' wee knots and twists that look like the eye of a bird. They saw it out in sheets no muckle thicker than writin' paper. Then they make up the furniture out of cheaper wood and cover it with the maple—veneer, they call it. When it's all done and polished ye never saw onythin' grander. Gang into a retail shop the next time ye are in town and see some. By sawin' it thin that way they get finish for thousands of dollars' worth of furniture from a single tree. If ye dinna watch faithful, and Black Jack gets out a few he has marked, it means the loss of more money than ye ever dreamed of, lad. The other night, down at camp, some son of Baalam was suggestin' that ye might be sellin' the boss out to Jack and lettin' him tak' the trees secretly, and nobody wad ever ken till the gang gets here."

A wave of scarlet flooded Freckles' face and he blazed hotly at the insult.

"And the boss," continued Duncan, coolly ignoring Freckles' anger, "he lays back just as cool as cowcumbers an says, 'I'll give a thousand dollars to ony man that will show me a fresh stump when we reach the Limberlost,' says he. Some of the men just snapped him up that they'd find some. So you see how the boss is trustin' ye, lad."

"I am gladder than I can ever express," said Freckles. "And now will I be walking double time to keep some of them from cutting a tree to get all that money!"

"Mither o' Moses!" howled Duncan. "Ye can trust the Scots to bungle things a'thegither. McLean was only meanin' to show ye all confidence and honor. He's gone and set a high price for some dirty whelp to ruin ye. I was juist tryin' to show ye how he felt toward ye, and I've gone an' give ye that worry to bear. Damn the Scots! They're so slow an' so dumb!"

"Exciptin' prisint company?" sweetly inquired Freckles.

"No!" growled Duncan. "Headin' the list! He'd nae business to set a price on ye, lad, for that's about the amount of it, an' I'd nae business to tell ye. We've both done ye ill, an' both meanin' the verra best. Juist what I'm always tellin' Sarah."

"I am mighty proud of what you have been telling me, Duncan," said Freckles. "I need the warning, sure. For with the books coming I might be timpted to neglect me

work when double watching is needed. Thank you more than I can tell for putting me on to it. What you've told me may be the saving of me. I won't stop for dinner now. I'll be getting along the east line, and when I get around about three maybe Mother Duncan will let me have a glass of milk and a bite of something."

"Ye see now!" cried Duncan in disgust. "Ye'll start on that seven-mile tramp with na bite to stay your stomach. What was it I told ye?"

"You told me that the Scots had the hardest heads and the softest hearts of any people that's living," answered Freckles.

Duncan grunted in a sort of gratified disapproval.

Freckles picked up his club and started down the line, whistling cheerily, and he had an unusually long repertory upon which to draw.

Duncan went straight to the lower camp and, calling McLean aside, repeated the conversation verbatim, ending, "And nae matter what happens now or ever, dinna ye dare let onythin' make ye believe that Freckles hasna guarded faithful as ony man could."

"I don't think anything could shake my faith in the lad," answered McLean.

Freckles was whistling merrily. He kept one eye religiously on the line. The other he divided between the path, his friends of the wire, and a search of the sky for his latest arrivals. Every day since their coming he had seen them, either hanging like small, black clouds above the swamp or bobbing over logs and trees with their queer, tilting walk. Whenever he could spare time, he entered the swamp and tried to make friends with them, and they were the tamest of all his unnumbered subjects. They ducked, dodged, and ambled about him, over logs and bushes, and not even a near approach would drive them to flight.

For two weeks he had found them circling over the Limberlost regularly, but one morning the female was missing and only the big black chicken hung sentinel above the swamp. His mate did not reappear in the following days, and Freckles grew very anxious. He spoke of it to Mrs. Duncan and she quieted his fears by raising a delightful hope in their stead.

"Why, Freckles, if it's the hen bird ye are missing, it's ten to ane she's safe," she said. "She's laid, and is setting, ye silly! Watch him and mark whaur he lichts. Then follow and find the nest. Some Sabbath we'll all gang see it."

Accepting this theory, Freckles began searching for the nest. Because these chickens were large, like the hawks, he looked among the treetops until he almost sprained the back of his neck. He had half the crow and hawk nests in the swamp located. He searched for this nest instead of collecting subjects for his case. He found the pair the middle of one forenoon on the elm where he had watched their lovemaking. The big black chicken was feeding his mate; so it was proven that they were a pair, they were both alive, and undoubtedly she was brooding. After that Freckles' nest-hunting went on with renewed zeal, but as he had no idea where to look and Duncan could offer no helpful suggestion, the nest was no nearer being found.

Coming from a long day on the trail, Freckles saw

Duncan's children awaiting him much closer to the
swale than they usually ventured, and from their wild
gestures he knew that something had happened. He
broke into a run, but the cry that reached him was, "The
books have come!"

How they hurried! Freckles lifted the youngest to his
shoulder, the second took his club and dinner pail, and
when they came up they found Mrs. Duncan at work on
a big box. She had just loosened the lid and now she
laughingly sat down on it.

"Ye canna have a peep in here until ye have washed
and eaten supper," she said. "It's all ready on the table.
Ance ye begin on this, ye'll no be willin' to tak' your
nose o' it till bedtime, and I willna get my work done
the nicht. We've eaten long ago."

It was hard work, but Freckles smiled bravely. He
made himself neat, swallowed a few bites, and came so
eagerly that Mrs. Duncan yielded, although she said she
very well knew all the time that his supper would be
spoiled.

Lifting the lid, they removed the packing and found
in that box books on birds, trees, flowers, moths, and
butterflies. There was also one containing Freckles'
bullfrog, true to life. And besides these were a butterfly
net, a naturalist's tin specimen box, a bottle of gasoline,
a box of cotton, a paper of long, steel specimen pins,
and a letter telling what all these things were and how
to use them.

At the discovery of each new treasure, Freckles
shouted, "Will you be looking at this, now?"

Mrs. Duncan cried, "Weel, I be drawed on!"

The eldest boy turned a somersault for every extra, and the baby, trying to follow his example, bunched over in a little sidewise sprawl and cut his foot on the ax with which his mother had prized up the box lid. That sobered them and they carried the books indoors. Mrs. Duncan had a top shelf in her closet cleared for them, well out of the reach of meddling little fingers.

When Freckles started for the trail next morning, the shining new specimen box flashed on his back. The black chicken, a mere speck in the blue, caught the gleam of it and wondered what it was. The folded net hung by the boy's hatchet, and the bird book was in the box. He walked the line and tested each section scrupulously, watching every foot of the trail, for he was determined not to slight his work; but if ever a boy "made haste slowly" in a hurry, it was Freckles that morning. When at last he reached the space he had cleared out and fitted up around his case, his heart swelled with the pride of possessing even so much that he could call his own and his quick eyes feasted on the beauty of it.

He had made a large room with the door of the case set even with one side of it. On three sides, fine big bushes of wild rose climbed to the lower branches of the trees. Part of his walls were mallow, part alder, thorn, willow, and dogwood. Below there filled in a solid mass of pale pink sheep laurel, and yellow St. John's wort, while the amber threads of the dodder interlaced everywhere. At one side the swamp came close, and cattails grew in profusion. In front of them he had planted a row of water hyacinths without disturbing in the least the state of their azure bloom, and where the

ground rose higher for his floor, a row of foxfire, which
would soon be open.

To the left he had discovered a queer natural arrangement of the trees, which grew to giant size and were set
in a gradually narrowing space so that a long, open
vista stretched away until it was lost in the dim recesses
of the swamp. A little trimming back of underbush, rolling out of dead logs, leveling of floor, and carpeting of
moss made it easy to understand why Freckles had
named this the "cathedral," yet he had never been
taught that "the groves were God's first temples."

On either side of the trees that constituted the first
arch of this dim vista of the swamp he planted ferns
that grew waist high this early in the season, and so
skillfully had the work been done that not a frond
drooped because of the change. Opposite, he cleared a
space and made a flowerbed. He filled one end with
every delicate, lacy vine and fern he could successfully
transplant. The body of the bed was a riot of color. Here
he set growing dainty blue-eyed Marys and blue-eyed
grass side by side. He planted harebells; violets, blue,
white, and yellow; wild geranium, cardinal flower, col-
umbine, pink snake's mouth, buttercups, painted trilli-
ums, and orchis. Here were bloodroot, moccasin flower,
hepatica, pitcher plant, Jack-in-the-pulpit, and every
other flower of the Limberlost that was in bloom or
bore a bud presaging a flower. Every day saw the addi-
tion of new specimens. The place would have set a bota-
nist wild.

On the line side he left the bushes thick for conceal-
ment, and entered by a narrow path he and Duncan had

cleared in setting up the case. He called this the front door, though he used every precaution to hide it. He built rustic seats between several of the trees, leveled the floor, and thickly carpeted it with rank, heavy woolly dog moss. About the case he planted wild clematis, bittersweet, and wild grapevines, and trained them over it until it was almost covered. Every day he planted new flowers, cut back rough bushes, and coaxed out graceful ones. His pride in his room was very great, but he had no idea how surprisingly beautiful it would appear to anyone who had not witnessed its growth and construction.

This morning Freckles walked straight to his case, unlocked it, and set his apparatus and dinner inside. He planted a new specimen he had found near the trail, and, bringing his old scrap bucket from the corner in which it was hidden, from a nearby pool he dipped water and poured it over his carpet and flowers.

Then he took out the bird book, settled comfortably on a bench, and with a deep sigh of satisfaction turned to the section headed "V." Past "veery" and "vireo" he went, on down the line until his finger, trembling with eagerness, stopped at "vulture."

" 'Great black California Vulture,' " he read.

"Humph! This side of the Rockies will do for us."

" 'Common turkey buzzard.' "

"Well, we ain't hunting common turkeys. McLean said chickens, and what he says goes."

" 'Black vulture of the South.' "

"Here we are arrived at once."

Freckles' finger followed the line, and he read scraps aloud.

" 'Common in the South. Sometimes called Jim Crow. Nearest equivalent to C-a-t-h-a-r-t-e-s A-t-r-a-t-a.' "

"How the divil am I ever to learn them corkin' big words by meself?"

" '—the Pharaoh's Chickens of European species. Sometimes stray north as far as Virginia and Kentucky—' "

"And sometimes farther," interpolated Freckles, " 'cos I got them right here in Indiana so like these pictures I can just see me big chicken bobbing up to get his ears boxed. Hey?"

" 'Light-blue eggs—' "

"Golly! I got to be seeing them!"

" '—big as a common turkey's, but shaped like a hen's, heavily splotched with chocolate—' "

"Caramels, I suppose. And—"

" '—in hollow logs or stumps.' "

"Oh, hagginy! Wasn't I barking up the wrong tree, though? Ought to been looking near the ground all this time. Now it's all to do over, and I suspect the sooner I start the sooner I'll be likely to find them."

Freckles put away his book, dampened the smudge fire, without which the mosquitoes made the swamp almost unbearable, took his cudgel and lunch, and went out to the line. He sat down on a log, ate at dinnertime and drank his last drop of water. The heat of June was growing intense. Even on the west of the swamp, where one had full benefit of the breeze from the upland, it was beginning to be unpleasant in the middle of the day.

He brushed the crumbs from his knees and sat resting a little and watching the sky to see if his big chicken were hanging up there. But he came to the earth abruptly, for there were steps coming down the trail that were neither McLean's nor Duncan's—and there never had been others. Freckles' heart leaped hotly. He ran a quick hand over his belt to feel if his revolver and hatchet were there, caught up his cudgel and laid it across his knees—then sat quietly, waiting. Was it Black Jack, or someone even worse? Forced to do something to brace his nerves, he puckered his stiffening lips and began whistling a tune he had led in his clear tenor every year of his life at the home Christmas exercises.

> "Who comes this way, so blithe and gay
> Upon a merry Christmas day?"

His quick Irish wit roused to the ridiculousness of it and he burst into a laugh that steadied him amazingly.

Through the bushes he caught a glimpse of the oncoming figure. His heart flooded with joy, for it was a man from the gang. Wessner had been his bunkmate the night he came down the corduroy. He knew him as well as any of McLean's men. This was no timber thief. No doubt the boss had sent him with a message. Freckles sprang up and called cheerily, a warm welcome on his face.

"Well, it's good telling if you're glad to see me," said Wessner, with something very like a breath of relief.

"We been hearing down at the camp you were so mighty touchy you didn't allow a man within a rod of the line."

"No more do I," answered Freckles, "if he's a stranger, but you're from McLean, ain't you?"

"Oh, damn McLean!" said Wessner.

Freckles gripped the cudgel until his knuckles slowly turned purple.

"And are you really saying so?" he inquired with elaborate politeness.

"Yes, I am," said Wessner. "So would every other man of the gang if they wasn't too big cowards to say anything, unless maybe that other slobbering old Scotsman, Duncan. Grinding the lives out of us! Working us like dogs, and paying us starvation wages, while he rolls up his millions and lives like a prince!"

Green lights began to play through the gray of Freckles' eyes.

"Wessner," he said impressively, "you'd make a fine pattern for the father of liars! Every man on that gang is strong and hilthy, paid all he earns, and treated with the courtesy of a gentleman! As for the boss living like a prince, he shares fare with you every day of your lives!"

Wessner was not a born diplomat, but he saw he was on the wrong tack, and he tried another.

"How would you like to make a good big pile of money, without even lifting your hand?" he asked.

"Humph!" said Freckles. "Have you been up to Chicago and cornered wheat, and are you offering me a friendly tip on the invistmint of me fortune?"

Wessner came close.

"Freckles, old fellow," he said, "if you let me give you

a pointer, I can put you on to making a cool five hundred without stepping out of your tracks.

Freckles drew back.

"You needn't be afraid of speaking up," he said. "There isn't a soul in the Limberlost save the birds and the beasts, unless some of your sort's come along and's crowding the privileges of the legal tinints."

"None of *my* friends along," said Wessner. "Nobody knew I came but Black J—I mean a friend of mine. If you want to hear sense and act with reason, he can see you later, but it ain't necessary. We can make all the plans needed. The trick's so dead small and easy."

"Must be if you have the engineering of it," said Freckles. But he heard, with a sigh of relief, that they were alone.

Wessner was impervious. "You just bet it is! Why, only think, Freckles, slavin' away at a measly little thirty dollars a month, and here is a chance to clear five hundred in a day! You surely won't be the fool to miss it!"

"And how was you proposing for me to steal it?" inquired Freckles. "Or am I just to find it laying in me path about the line?"

"That's it, Freckles," blustered the Dutchman, "you're just to find it. You needn't do a thing. You needn't know a thing. You name a morning when you will walk up the west side of the swamp and then turn round and walk back down the same side again and the money is yours. Couldn't anything be easier than that, could it?"

"Depends entirely on the man," said Freckles. The lilt of a lark hanging above the swale beside them was not sweeter than the sweetness of his voice. "To some it

would seem to come aisy as breathing; and to some, wringin' the last drop of their hearts' blood couldn't force thim! I'm not the man that goes into a scheme like that with the blindfold over me eyes, for, you see, it means to break trust with the boss; and I've served him faithful as I know. You'll have to be making the thing very clear to me understanding."

"It's so dead easy," repeated Wessner, "it makes me tired of the simpleness of it. You see there's a few trees in the swamp that's real gold mines. There's three especial. Two are back in, but one's square on the line. Why, your pottering old Scots fool of a boss nailed the wire to it with his own hands! He never noticed where the bark had been peeled, nor saw what it was. If you will stay on this side of the trail just one day we can have it cut, loaded, and ready to drive out at night. Next morning you can find it, report, and be the busiest man in the search for us. We know where to fix it all safe and easy. Then McLean has a bet up with a couple of the gang that there can't be a raw stump found in the Limberlost. There's plenty of witnesses to swear to it, and I know three that will. There's a cool thousand, and this tree is worth all of that, raw. Say, it's a gold mine, I tell you, and just five hundred of it is yours. There's no danger on earth to you, for you've got McLean that bamboozled you could sell out the whole swamp and he'd never mistrust you. What do you say?"

Freckles' soul was satisfied. "Is that all?" he asked.

"No, it ain't," said Wessner. "If you really want to brace up and be a man and go into the thing for keeps, you can make five times that in a week. My friend knows a dozen others we could get out in a few days, and all you'd have to do would be to keep out of sight. Then you could take your money and skip some night, and begin life like a gentleman somewhere else. What do you think about it?"

Freckles purred like a kitten.

" 'Twould be a rare joke on the boss," he said, "to be stealin' from him the very thing he's trusted me to guard, and be getting me wages all winter throwed in free. And you're making the pay awful high. Me to be getting five hundred for such a simple little thing as that. You're treating me most royal indeed! It's away beyond all I'd be expecting. Seventeen cents would be a big price for that job. It must be looked into thorough. Just you wait here until I do a minute's turn in the swamp, and then I'll be eschorting you out to the clearing and giving you the answer."

Freckles lifted the overhanging bushes and hurried back to the case. He unslung the specimen box and laid it inside with his hatchet and revolver. He slipped the key in his pocket and went back to Wessner.

"Now for the answer," he said. "Stand up!"

There was iron in his voice, and he was commanding like an outraged general. "Anything you want to be taking off?" he questioned.

Wessner looked the astonishment he felt. "Why, no, Freckles," he said.

"Have the goodness to be calling me Mister McLean," snapped Freckles. "I'm after reservin' me pet name for the use of me friends! You may stand with your back to the light or be taking any advantage you want."

"Why, what do you mean?" spluttered Wessner.

"I'm meanin'," said Freckles tersely, "to lick a quarter-section of hell out of you, and may the Holy Virgin stay me before I leave you here carrion, for your carcass would turn the stummicks of me chickens!"

Down at the camp that morning, Wessner's conduct had been so palpable an excuse to force a discharge that Duncan moved near McLean and whispered, "Think of the boy, sir?"

McLean was so troubled that, an hour later, he mounted Nellie and followed Wessner to his home in Wildcat Hollow, only to find that he had left there a little before, heading for the Limberlost. McLean rode at top speed. When Mrs. Duncan told him that a man answering Wessner's description had gone down the west side of the swamp near noon, he left the mare in her charge and followed on foot. When he heard voices he entered the swamp and silently crept near just in time to hear Wessner whine, "But I can't fight you, Freckles. I hain't done nothing to you. I'm away bigger than you, and you've only one hand."

The boss slid off his coat and crouched among the bushes, like a tiger ready to spring. But as Freckles' voice reached him he held himself, with the effort of his life, to see what mettle was in the boy.

"Don't you be wasting of me good time in the numbering of me hands," howled Freckles. "The strength of me cause will make up for the weakness of me members, and the size of a cowardly thief don't count. You'll think all the wildcats of the Limberlost is turned loose on you when I come against you, and as for me cause—

I slept with you, Wessner, the night I come down the corduroy like a dirty friendless tramp, and the boss was for taking me up, washing, clothing, and feeding me, and giving me a home full of love and tenderness, and a master to look to, and good, well-earned money in the bank. He's trusting me his heartful, and here comes you, you spotted toad of the big road, and insults me, as is an honest Irish gentleman, by hinting that you conceive I'd be willing to shut me eyes and hold fast while you rob him of the thing I was set and paid to guard, and then act the sneak and liar to him, and ruin and eternally blacken the soul of me. You damned rascal," raved Freckles, "be fighting before I forget the laws of a gentleman's game and split your dirty head with me stick!"

Wessner backed away, mumbling, "But I don't want to hurt you, Freckles!"

"Oh, don't you!" raged the boy, now fairly frothing. "Well, you ain't resembling me none, for I'm itchin' like death to git me fingers in the face of you."

He danced up, and, as Wessner lunged out in self-defense, Freckles ducked under his arm like a bantam and punched him in the pit of the stomach so that Wessner doubled up with a groan. Before Wessner could straighten himself, Freckles was on him, fighting like the wildest fury that ever left the soil of the beautiful island. The Dutchman dealt thundering blows that sometimes landed and sent Freckles reeling, and sometimes missed, while he went plunging into the swale with the impetus of them. Freckles could not strike with half Wessner's force, but he could land three blows to

the Dutchman's one. It was here that Freckles' days of
alert watching on the line, the perpetual swinging of the
heavy cudgel, and the endurance of all weather stood
him in good stead; for he was as tough as a pine knot
and as agile as a panther. He danced, ducked, and
dodged. For the first five minutes he endured fearful
punishment. Then Wessner's breath commenced to
whistle between his teeth, when Freckles had only just
begun fighting. He sprang back with shrill laughter.

"Begolly! and will your honor be whistling the
hornpipe for me to be dancing of?" he cried.

Spang! went his fist into Wessner's face, and he was
past him into the swale.

"And would you be pleased to tune up a little live-
lier?" he gasped, and clipped his ear as he sprang back.
Wessner lunged at him in blind fury. Freckles, seeing an
opening, forgot the laws of a gentleman's game and
drove the toe of his heavy wading boot into Wessner's
middle until he doubled up and fell heavily. In a flash
Freckles was on him. For a time McLean could not see
what was happening. "Go! Go to him now!" he commanded himself, but so intense was his desire to see the
boy win alone that he could not stir.

At last Freckles sprang up and backed away. "Time!"
he yelled like a fury. "Be getting up, Mr. Wessner, and
don't be afraid of hurting me. I'll let you throw in an
extra hand and lick you to me complete satisfaction all
the same. Did you hear me call the limit? Will you get
up and be facing me?"

As Wessner struggled to his feet, he resembled a bat-
tlefield, for his clothing was in ribbons and his face and

hands streaming blood. "I—I guess I got enough," he mumbled.

"Oh, do you?" roared Freckles. "Well, this ain't your say. You come onto me ground, lying about me boss and intimatin' I'd steal from his very pockets. Now will you be standing up and taking your medicine like a man, or getting it poured down the throat of you like a baby? I ain't got enough! This is only just the beginning with me. Be looking out there!"

He sprang against Wessner and sent him rolling. He attacked the unresisting figure and fought him until he lay limp and still and Freckles had no strength left to lift an arm. Then he rose and stepped back, gasping for breath. With his first good lungful of air he shouted "Time!" But the figure of Wessner lay motionless.

Freckles watched him with a regardful eye and saw at last that he was completely exhausted. He bent over him, and, catching him by the back of the neck, jerked him to his knees. Wessner wore the face of a whipped cur, and, fearing further punishment, burst into great shivering sobs, while the tears washed tiny rivulets through the blood and muck. Freckles stepped back, glaring at Wessner, but suddenly the scowl of anger and the ugly, disfiguring red faded from the boy's face. He dabbed at a cut on his temple from which issued a tiny crimson stream, and jauntily shook back his hair. His face took on the innocent look of a cherub, and his voice rivaled that of a brooding dove, but into his eyes crept a look of diabolical mischief.

He glanced vaguely about him until he saw his club,

seized and twirled it like a drum major, stuck it upright
in the muck, and marched on tiptoe over to Wessner,
mechanically, as a puppet worked by a string. Bending
over, Freckles reached an arm about Wessner's waist
and helped him to his feet.

"Careful, now," he cautioned. "Be careful, Freddy;
there's danger of you hurting me."

Fishing a handkerchief from a back pocket, Freckles
tenderly wiped Wessner's eyes and nose.

"Come, Freddy, me child," he admonished Wessner,
"it's time little boys were getting home. I've me work to
do and can't be entertaining you any more today. Come
back tomorrow, if you ain't through yet, and we'll repeat the perfarmance. Don't be staring at me so wild
like. I would eat you, but I can't afford it. Me earnings,
being honest, come slow, and I've no money to be
squanderin' on the pailful of Dispeptic's Delight it
would be taking to work you out of my innards!"

Again an awful wrenching seized McLean. Freckles
stepped back as Wessner, tottering and reeling, like a
thoroughly drunken man, came toward the path, looking indeed as if wildcats had taken their fill of him.

The cudgel spun high in air, and catching it with an
expertness acquired by long practice on the line, the
boy twirled it a second, shook back his thick hair bonnily, and, stepping out into the trail, followed Wessner.
Because Freckles was Irish, it was impossible to do it
silently, and presently his clear tenor rang out though
there were bad catches where he was hard-pressed for
breath:

"It was the Dutch. It was the Dutch.
Do you think it was the Irish hollered help?
Not much.
It was the Dutch. It was the Dutch—"

Wessner turned and mumbled: "What you following me for? What are you going to do with me?"

Freckles called the Limberlost to witness. "How's that for the ingratitude of a beast? And me troubling meself to show him off me territory with the honors of war!"

Then he changed his tone completely and added, "Belike it's this, Freddy. You see, the boss might come riding down this trail any minute, and the little mare's so wheedlesome that if she'd come on to you in your present state all of a sudden, she'd stop that short she'd send Mr. McLean out over the ears of her. No disparagement intended to the sense of the mare!" he added hastily.

Wessner belched a fearful oath, and Freckles laughed merrily.

"That's a sample of the thanks a generous act's always for getting," he continued. "Here's me neglectin' me work to escort you out proper, and you saying such awful words. Freddy," he demanded sternly, "do you want me to soap out your mouth? You don't seem to be realizing it, but if you was to buck into Mr. McLean in your present state, without me there to explain matters, the chance is he'd cut the liver out of you; and I shouldn't think you'd be wanting such a fine gentleman as him to see that it's white!"

Wessner grew ghastly under his grime and broke into a staggering run.

"And now will you be looking at the manners of him?" questioned Freckles plaintively. "Going without even a 'thank you,' right in the face of all the pains I've taken to make it interesting for him!"

Freckles twirled the baton and stood like a soldier at attention until Wessner left the clearing, but it was the last scene of that performance. When the boy turned, there was a deathly illness in his face, and his legs wavered like reeds beneath his weight. He staggered back to the case and opening it he took out a piece of cloth. He dipped it into the water and, sitting on a bench, he wiped the blood and grime from his face, while his breath sucked between his clenched teeth. He was shivering with pain and excitement in spite of himself. He unbuttoned the band of his right sleeve, and, turning it back, exposed the blue-lined, calloused whiteness of his maimed arm, now vividly streaked with contusions, while in a series of circular dots the blood oozed slowly. Here Wessner had succeeded in setting his teeth. When Freckles saw what it was he forgave himself the kick in the pit of Wessner's stomach, and cursed fervently and deep.

"Freckles, Freckles," said McLean's voice.

Freckles snatched down his sleeve and rose to his feet.

"Excuse me, sir," he said. "You'll surely be believin' I thought meself alone."

McLean pushed him carefully to the seat, and, bending over him, opened a pocket case that he carried as regularly as his revolver and watch, for cuts and bruises were of daily occurrence among the gang.

Taking the hurt arm, he turned back the sleeve and bathed and bound up the wounds. He examined Freckles' head and body and convinced himself that there was no permanent injury, although the cruelty of the punishment the boy had borne set the boss shuddering. Then he closed the case, shoved it into his pocket, and sat down beside Freckles. All the indescribable beauty of the place was strong about him, but he saw only the bruised face of the suffering boy, who had hedged for the information he wanted like a diplomat, argued like a judge, fought like a sheik, and triumphed like a devil.

As the pain lessened and breath caught up with Freckles' pounding heart, he watched the boss from the corner of his eye. How had McLean gotten there and how long had he been there? Freckles did not dare ask. At last he arose and, going to the case, took out his revolver and the wire-mending apparatus and locked the door. Then he turned to McLean.

"Have you any orders, sir?" he asked.

"Yes," said McLean, "I have, and you are to follow them to the letter. Turn over that apparatus to me and go straight home. Soak yourself in the hottest bath your skin will bear and go to bed at once. Now hurry."

"Mr. McLean," said Freckles, "it's sorry I am to be telling you, but the afternoon's walking of the line ain't done. You see, I was just for getting to me feet to start, and I was on good time, when up came a gentleman, and we got into a little heated argument. It's either settled, or it's just begun, but between us, I'm that late I haven't started for the afternoon yet. I must be going at

once, for there's a tree I must find before the day's over."

"You plucky little idiot," growled McLean. "You can't walk the line! I doubt if you can get to Duncan's. Don't you know when you are done up? You go to bed. I'll finish your work."

"Never!" protested Freckles. "I was just a little done up for the present, a minute ago. I'm all right now. Riding boots are away too low. The day's hot and the walk a good seven miles, sir. Never!"

As he reached for the outfit he pitched forward and his eyes closed. McLean stretched him on the moss and applied restoratives. When Freckles returned to consciousness, McLean ran to the cabin to tell Mrs. Duncan to get a hot bath ready, and to bring Nellie. That worthy woman promptly filled the wash boiler and set a roaring fire under it. She pushed the horse trough off its base and rolled it up to the kitchen.

By the time McLean came again, leading Nellie and holding Freckles on her back, Mrs. Duncan was ready for business. She and the boss laid Freckles in the trough and poured on hot water until he squirmed. They soaked, rubbed, and scoured him. Then they let the hot water off and closed his pores with cold. Then they stretched him on the floor and chafed and rubbed and kneaded him until he cried out for mercy. As they rolled him into bed, his eyes dropped shut, but a little later they flared open.

"Mr. McLean," he cried, "the tree! Oh, do be looking after the tree!"

McLean bent over him. "Which tree, Freckles?"

"I don't know exact, sir; but it's on the east line and the wire is fastened to it. He bragged that you nailed it yourself, sir. You'll know it by the bark having been laid open to the grain somewhere low down, and it was five hundred dollars he offered me—to—be selling you out —sir!"

Freckles' head rolled over and his eyes dropped shut. McLean towered over him. Freckles' bright hair waved back on the pillow. His face was swollen, and purple with bruises. His left arm, with the hand battered almost out of shape, stretched beside him, and the right, with no hand at all, lay across a chest that was a mass of purple welts. McLean's mind traveled back to the night, nearly a year before, when he had engaged Freckles, a stranger.

McLean bent, covering the hurt arm with one hand and laying the other with a caress on the boy's forehead. Freckles stirred at his touch, and twittered as softly as the swallows under the eaves, "If you're coming this way—tomorrow—be pleased to step over—and we'll repeat the—chorus softly!"

"Bless the gritty devil," growled McLean.

Then he went out and told Mrs. Duncan to keep close watch on Freckles, and send Duncan to him at the swamp the minute he came home. Following the trail down to the line and back to the scene of the fight, the boss entered Freckles' study softly, as if his spirit, sleeping there, might be roused, and gazed about with astonished eyes.

How had the boy conceived it? What a picture he had wrought in living colors! He had the heart of a painter.

He had the soul of a poet. The boss stepped carefully over the velvet carpet and touched the walls of crisp verdure with gentle fingers. He stood long beside the flowerbed, and gazed at the banked wall of bright flowers as if he could never leave off.

Where had Freckles ever found, and how had he transplanted, such ferns? As McLean turned from them he stopped suddenly.

He had reached the door of the cathedral. That which Freckles had attempted would have been patent to anyone. What had been in the heart of the shy, silent boy when he had found that long, dim stretch of forest, decorated its entrance, cleared and smoothed its aisle, and carpeted its altar? What veriest work of God was in these mighty living pillars and the arched dome of green! How like stained cathedral windows were the long openings between the trees, filled with rifts of blue, rays of gold, and the shifting emerald of leaves! Where could be found mosaics to match this aisle paved with living color and glowing lights? Was Freckles a devout Christian, and did he worship here? Or was he an untaught heathen, and down this vista of entrancing loveliness did Pan come piping, and dryads, nymphs, and fairies dance for him?

Who can fathom the heart of a boy? McLean had been thinking of Freckles as a creature of unswerving honesty, courage, and faithfulness. Here was evidence of a heart aching for beauty, art, companionship, worship. It was writ large all over the floor, walls, and furnishing of that little Limberlost clearing.

When Duncan came, McLean told him the story of

the fight, and they laughed until they cried. Then they started around the line in search of the tree.

Said Duncan, "Now the boy is in for sore trouble!"

"I hope not," answered McLean. "You never in all your life saw a cur whipped so completely. He won't come back for the repetition of the chorus. We can surely find the tree. If we can't, Freckles can. I will bring enough of the gang to take it out at once. That will ensure peace for a time, at least, and I am hoping that in a month more the whole gang can be moved here. It will soon be fall, and then, if he will go, I intend to send Freckles to my mother to be educated. With his quickness of mind and body and a few years' good help he can do anything. Why, Duncan, I'd give a hundred-dollar bill if you could have been here and seen for yourself."

"Yes, and I'd 'a' done murder," muttered the big teamster. "I hope, sir, ye will make good your plans for Freckles, though I'd as soon see ony born child o' my ain taken from our home. We love the lad, me and Sarah."

Locating the tree was an easy task, because it was so well identified. When the rumble of the big lumber wagons passing the cabin on the way to the swamp wakened Freckles next morning, he sprang up and was soon following them. He was so sore and stiff that every movement was torture at first, but he grew easier, and shortly did not suffer so much. McLean scolded him for coming, yet in his heart triumphed over every new evidence of fineness in the boy.

The tree was a giant maple and so precious that they

almost dug it out by the roots. When it was down, cut in lengths, and loaded, there was still an empty wagon.

As they were gathering up their tools to go, Duncan said, "There's a big hollow tree somewhere mighty near here that I've been wanting for a watering trough for my stock; the one I have is so small. The Portland company cut this for elm butts last year, and it's six feet diameter and hollow for forty feet. It was a buster! While the men are here and there is an empty wagon, why mightn't I load it on and tak' it up to the barn as we pass?"

McLean said he was very willing, ordered the driver to pull out of line to go for the log, and detailed men with the loading apparatus to assist them.

He had told Freckles to ride on a section of the maple with him, but now the boy begged to go into the swamp with Duncan.

"I don't see why you want to go?" said McLean. "I have no business to let you out today at all."

"It's me chickens," whispered Freckles in distress. "You see, I was just after finding yesterday, from me new book, how they do be nesting in hollow trees, and there ain't any too many in the swamp. There's just a chance that they might be in that one."

"Go ahead," said McLean. "That's a different story. If they happen to be there, why, tell Duncan he must give up the tree until they have finished with it."

Then he climbed into a wagon and was driven away. Freckles hurried into the swamp. He was some little distance behind, but he could still see the men. Before he overtook them, they had turned from the west road and had entered the swamp toward the east.

They stopped at the trunk of a monstrous prostrate log. It had been cut about three feet from the ground, over three-fourths of the way through, and had fallen to the east, the body of the log still resting on the stump. The underbrush was almost impenetrable, but Duncan plunged in and with a crowbar began tapping along the trunk to decide how far it was hollow, so that they would know where to take it off. As they waited his decision, there came from the mouth of it—on wing—a great black bird that swept over their heads.

Freckles danced wildly. "It's me chickens! Oh, it's me chickens!" he shouted. "Oh, Duncan, come quick! You've found the nest of me precious chickens!"

Duncan hurried down to the mouth of the log, but Freckles raced before him. He crashed through poison vines and underbrush regardless of any danger, and climbed on the stump. When Duncan got there he was shouting like a wild thing.

"It's hatched!" he yelled. "Oh, me big chicken has hatched out me little chicken, and there's another egg. I can see it plain, and, oh, the funny little white baby! Oh, Duncan, can you see me little white chicken?"

Duncan could easily see it, and so could everyone else. Freckles crept back into the log and tenderly carried the hissing, blinking little thing out to the light in a leaf-lined hat. The men found it sufficiently wonderful to satisfy even Freckles, who had forgotten he was ever sore or stiff, and coddled over it with every blarneying term of endearment he knew.

Duncan gathered up his tools. "Deal's off, boys!" he said cheerfully. "This log mauna be touched until Freckles' chaukies have finished with it. We might as weel gang. Better put it back, Freckles. It's just out, and it may chill, Ye will probably hae twa the morn."

Freckles crept back into the log and carefully deposited the baby beside the egg. When he came back, he said, "I made a big mistake not to be bringing the egg out with the baby, but I was fearing to touch it. It's shaped like a hen's egg, and it's big as a turkey's and the beautifulest blue—just splattered with big brown splotches, like me book said, precise. But you never saw such a sight as it made on the yellow of the rotten wood beside that funny leathery-faced little white baby."

"Tell you what, Freckles," said one of the teamsters. "Have you ever heard of this Bird Woman that goes all over the country with a camera and makes pictures? She made some on my brother Jim's place last summer, and Jim's so wild about them he quits plowing and goes after her about every nest he finds. He helps her all he can to get them and then she gives him a picture. Jim's so proud of what he has he keeps them in the Bible. He shows them to everybody that comes, and brags about how he helped to take them. If you're smart, you'll send for her and she'll come and make a picture just like life. If you help her, she will give you one. It would be uncommon pretty to keep, after your birds are gone. I dunno what they are. I never see their like before. They must be something rare. Any you fellows ever see a bird like that hereabouts?"

No one ever had.

"Well," said the teamster, "failing to get this log lets me off till noon, and I'm going to town. I go right past her place. I've a big notion to stop and tell her. If she drives straight back in the swamp on the west road, and turns east at this big sycamore, she can't miss finding the tree, even if Freckles ain't about to show her. Jim says her work is a credit to the state she lives in, and any man is a measly creature that isn't willing to help her all he can. My old daddy used to say that all there was to religion was doing to the other fellow what you'd want him to do to you, and if I was making a living taking bird pictures, seems to me I'd be mighty glad for a chance to take one like that. So I'll just stop and tell her, and by gummy! maybe she will give me a picture of the little white sucker for my trouble."

Freckles touched his arm. "Will she be rough with it?" he asked.

"Government land! No!" said the teamster. "She's dead down on anybody that shoots a bird or tears up a nest. Why, she's half killing herself in all kinds of places and weather to teach people to love and protect the birds. She's that plum careful of them that Jim's wife says she has Jim a standin' like a big fool holding an ombrelly over them when they are young and tender until she gets a focus, whatever that is. Jim says there ain't a bird on his place that don't actually seem to like having her around after she has wheedled them a few days, and the pictures she gets nobody would ever believe that didn't stand by and see them taken."

"Will you be sure to tell her to come?" asked Freckles.

Duncan slept at home that night. He heard Freckles
slipping out early the next morning, but he was too
sleepy to wonder why, until he came to do his morning
chores. When he found that none of his stock was at all
thirsty, and saw the water trough brimming, he knew
that the boy was trying to make up to him for the loss of
the big trough that he had been so anxious to have.

"Bless his fool little hot heart!" said Duncan. "And
him so sore it is tearing him to move for anything. Nae
wonder he has us all loving him!"

But Freckles was moving briskly, and his heart was so
happy that he forgot all about the bruises. He hurried
about the trail, and on his way down the east side he
slipped in to see the chickens. The mother bird was on
the nest. He was afraid the other egg might just be
hatching, so he did not venture to disturb her. He made
the round and reached his study early. He had his lunch
along, and did not need to start on the second trip until
the middle of the afternoon. He would have long hours
to work on his flowerbed, improve his study, and learn
about his chickens. Lovingly he set his room to rights
and watered the flowers and carpet. He had carefully
chosen for his resting place the coolest spot on the west
side, where there was almost always a breeze; but today
the heat was so intense that it penetrated even there.

"I'm mighty glad there's nothing calling me inside!"
he said. "There's no bit of air stirring, and it will just be
steaming. Oh, but it's luck Duncan found the nest before it got so unbearing hot! I might have missed it altogether. Wouldn't it have been a shame to lose that sight?
The cunning little divil! When he gets to toddling down

that log to meet me, won't he be a circus? Wonder if he'll be as graceful a performer afoot as his father and mother?"

The heat became more insistent. Noon came, and Freckles ate his dinner and settled for an hour or two on a bench with a book.

Chapter V

WHEREIN AN ANGEL MATERIALIZES AND A MAN
WORSHIPS

Perhaps there was a breath of sound, Freckles could never afterward remember, but for some reason he lifted his head just as the bushes parted and the face of an angel looked through. Saints, nymphs, and fairies had floated down his cathedral aisle for him many times, with forms and voices of exquisite beauty.

Parting the wild roses by the entrance was beauty of which Freckles had never dreamed. Was it real or would it vanish as the other dreams had done? He dropped his book and, rising to his feet, took a step nearer, gazing intently. This was real flesh and blood. And it was in every way kin of the Limberlost, for no bird of its branches swung with easier grace than this dainty young thing rocked on the bit of morass on which she stood. A sapling beside her was not straighter nor rounder than her slender form. Her soft, waving hair clung about her face with the heat, and curled over her shoulders. It was all of one piece with the gold of the sun which filtered through the branches. Her eyes were just the deepest blue of the iris, her lips the reddest of the foxfire, and her cheeks exactly of the same satin as the wild rose petals caressing them. She was smiling at Freckles in perfect confidence, and she cried, "Oh, I'm so delighted that I've found you!"

The wildly leaping heart of Freckles burst from his body and fell in the black swamp muck at her feet with such a thud that he did not understand how she could avoid hearing it. He really felt that if she looked down she would see it.

"An'—an' was you looking for me?" he quavered, incredulous.

"I hoped I might find you," said the angel. "You see, I didn't do as I was told, and I'm lost. The Bird Woman said I should stay in the carriage until she came back. She's been gone hours. It's a perfect Turkish bath in there, and I'm all lumpy with mosquito bites. Just when I thought that I couldn't bear it another minute, along comes the biggest Papilio Ajax you ever saw. I knew how pleased she'd be, so I ran after it. It flew so slow and so low that I thought a dozen times I had it. Then all at once it went out of sight over the trees, and I couldn't find my way back to save me. I think I've walked over an hour. I have been mired to my knees. A thorn raked my arm until it is bleeding, and I'm so tired and warm."

She parted the bushes still further. Freckles saw that

her little blue cotton frock clung to her, limp with perspiration. It was torn across the breast. One sleeve hung
open from shoulder to elbow. A thorn had raked her
arm until it was covered with blood, and the gnats and
mosquitoes were clustering about it. Her feet were in
lace hose and low shoes.

Freckles gasped. In the Limberlost in low shoes! He
caught an armful of moss from his carpet and buried it
in the ooze in front of her for a footing.

"Get out here where I can see where you are stepping.
Quick, for the life of you!" he ordered.

She smiled on him indulgently.

"Why?" she inquired.

"Did anybody let you come here and not be telling
you of the snakes?" urged Freckles.

"We met Mr. McLean on the corduroy, and he did say
something about snakes, I believe. The Bird Woman put
on leather and a nice, parboiled time she must be having! Worst dose I ever had, and I'd nothing to do but
swelter."

"Will you be coming out of there?" groaned Freckles.

She laughed as if it were a fine joke.

"Maybe if I'd be telling you I killed a rattler, curled up
on that same place you're standing, as long as me body
and the thickness of me arm, you'd be moving where I
can see your footing," he urged insistently.

"What a perfectly delightful little brogue you speak,"
she said. "My father is Irish, and half ought to be
enough to entitle me to do that much. 'Maybe—if I'd—
be telling you,' " she imitated, rounding and accenting
each word carefully.

Freckles was beginning to feel a wildness in his head. He had derided Wessner to a finish at that same hour yesterday. Now his own eyes were filling with tears.

"If you was understanding the danger!" he continued, desperately.

"Oh, I don't think there is much!"

She tilted on the morass.

"If you killed one snake here, it's probably all there is near; and anyway, the Bird Woman says a rattlesnake is a gentleman and always gives warning before he strikes. I don't hear any rattling. Do you?"

"Would you be knowing it if you did?" asked Freckles, almost impatiently.

How the laugh of the young thing rippled!

"'Would I be knowing it,'" she mocked. "Well, you should see the swamps of Michigan where they dump rattlers out of the marl dredges three and four at a time!"

Freckles stood astounded. She did know. She was not in the least afraid. She was depending on a rattlesnake to live up to his share of the contract and rattle in time for her to move. The one characteristic an Irishman admires in a woman, above all others, is courage. Freckles worshiped anew. He changed his tactics.

"I'd be pleased to be receiving you at me front door," he said, "but as you have arrived at the back will you come in and be seated?"

He waved toward a bench.

The angel came instantly.

"Oh, how lovely and cool!" she cried.

As she moved across his room Freckles had hard

work to keep from falling on his knees; for they were very weak, and he was hard driven by an impulse to worship.

"Did you arrange this?" she asked.

"Yes," said Freckles, simply.

"Someone must come with a big canvas and copy each side of it," she said. "I never saw anything so beautiful! How I wish I might stay here with you! I will, some day, if you will let me; but now, if you can spare the time, will you help me look for the carriage? If the Bird Woman comes back and finds me gone she will be almost distracted."

"Did you come in on the west road?" asked Freckles.

"I think so," she said. "The man who told the Bird Woman said that was the only place the wires were down. We drove away in, and it was dreadful—over stumps and logs, and in to the hubs. I suppose you know, though. I should have stayed in the carriage, but I was so tired. I never dreamed of getting lost. I suspect I will get scolded finely. I go with the Bird Woman half the time during the summer vacations. My father says I learn a lot more than I do at school, and get it straight. I never came within a smell of getting lost before. I thought, at first, it was going to be horrid; but since I've found you, maybe it will be good fun after all."

Freckles was amazed to hear himself excusing. "It was so hot in there. You couldn't be expected to bear it for hours and not be moving. I can take you back around the trail almost to where you were. Then you can get up in the carriage and I will go find the Bird Woman."

"You'll get killed if you do! When she stays this long, it means that she has a focus on something. You see, when she gets a focus, and lies in the weeds and water for hours, and the sun bakes her, and things crawl over her, and then someone comes along and scares her bird away just as she has it coaxed up—why, she *kills* them. If I melt, you won't go after her. She's probably blistered and half eaten up, but she will never quit until she is satisfied."

"Then it will be safer to be taking care of you," suggested Freckles.

"Now you're talking sense!" said the angel.

"May I try to help your arm?" he asked.

"Have you any idea how it hurts?" she parried.

"A little," said Freckles.

"Well, Mr. McLean said we'd probably find his son here—"

"His son!" cried Freckles.

"That's what he said. And that you would do anything you could for us; and that we could trust you with our lives. But I would have trusted you anyway, if I hadn't known a thing about you. Say, your father is rampaging proud of you, isn't he?"

"I don't know," answered the dazed Freckles.

"Well, call on me if you want reliable information. He's so proud of you he is all swelled up like the toad in *Aesop's Fables*. If you have ever had an arm hurt like this, and can do anything, why, for pity sake, do it!"

She turned back her sleeve, holding out to Freckles an arm of palest cameo, shaped so exquisitely that no sculptor could have chiseled it.

Freckles unlocked his case and taking out some cotton cloth he tore it in strips. Then he brought a bucket of the cleanest water that he could find. She yielded herself to his touch like a baby, and he bathed away the blood and bandaged the ugly, ragged wound. He finished his surgery by lapping the torn sleeve over the cloth and binding it down with a piece of twine, with the angel's help about the knots.

Freckles worked with trembling fingers and a face tense with earnestness.

"Is it feeling any better?" he asked.

"Oh, it's well now!" cried the angel. "It doesn't hurt at all, any more."

"I'm mighty glad," said Freckles. "But you had best go and be having your doctor fix it right, the minute you get home."

"Oh, bother! A little scratch like that!" jeered the angel. "My blood is perfectly pure. It will heal in three days."

"It's cut cruel deep. It might be making a scar," faltered Freckles, his eyes on the ground. " 'Twould—'twould be an awful pity. A doctor might know something to be preventing it."

"Why, I never thought of that!" exclaimed the angel.

"I noticed you didn't," said Freckles softly. "I don't know much about it, but it seems like most girls would."

The angel thought intently, with Freckles still kneeling beside her. Suddenly she gave herself an impatient little shake, lifted her glorious eyes full to his, and the smile that broke over her sweet, young face was the loveliest thing that Freckles had ever seen.

"Don't let's bother about it," she proposed, with just the faintest hint of a confiding gesture toward him. "It won't make a scar. Why, it just couldn't, when you have dressed it so nicely."

The velvety touch of her warm arm was tingling in Freckles' fingertips. Dainty laces and fine white stuffs peeped through her torn dress. There were beautiful rings on her fingers. Every article about her was of the finest material and in excellent taste. There was the trembling Limberlost guard in his coarse clothing, with his cotton rags and his old pail of swamp water. Freckles was sufficiently accustomed to contrasts to notice them, and sufficiently fine to be hurt by them always.

He lifted his eyes to hers with a shadowy pain in them, and found them of serene, unconscious purity. What she had said was straight from a kind, untainted, young heart. She meant every word of it. Freckles' soul went sick. He scarcely knew whether he could muster strength to get to his feet.

"We must go and find the carriage," said the angel, rising.

In instant alarm for her, Freckles sprang up, grasped the cudgel, and led the way, sharply watching every step. He went as near the log as he felt that he dared, and with a little searching found the carriage. He cleared a path for the angel and, with a sigh of relief, saw her enter it safely. The heat was intense. She pushed the damp hair back from her face.

"This is a shame!" said Freckles. "You'll never be coming here again."

"Oh, yes, I shall!" said the angel. "The Bird Woman says that these birds stay over a month in the nest and she would like to make a picture every few days for seven or eight weeks, perhaps."

Freckles barely escaped crying out for joy.

"Then don't you ever be torturing yourself and your horse to be coming in here again," he said. "I'll show you a way to drive almost to the nest on the east trail, and then you can come around to my room and stay while the Bird Woman works. It's nearly always cool there, and there's comfortable seats and water."

"Oh! Did you have drinking water there?" she cried. "I was never so thirsty or so hungry in my life, but I thought I wouldn't mention it."

"And I had not the wit to be seeing!" wailed Freckles. "I can be getting you a good drink in no time."

He turned to the trail.

"Please wait a minute," called the angel. "What's your name? I want to think about you while you are gone."

Freckles lifted his face with the brown rift across it and smiled quizzically.

"Freckles?" she guessed, with a peal of laughter. "And mine is—"

"I'm knowing yours," interrupted Freckles.

"I don't believe you do. What is it?" asked the girl.

"You won't be getting angry?"

"Not until I've had the water, at least."

It was Freckles' turn to laugh. He whipped off his big, floppy straw hat, stood uncovered before her, and said,

in the sweetest of all the sweet tones of his voice,
"There's nothing you could be but the Swamp Angel."

The girl laughed happily.

Once out of her sight, Freckles ran every step of the
way to the cabin. Mrs. Duncan gave him a small bucket
of water, cool from the well. He carried it in the crook
of his right arm, and a basket filled with bread and but-
ter, cold meat, apple pie, and pickles, in his left hand.

"Pickles are kind o' cooling," said Mrs. Duncan.

Then Freckles ran again.

The angel was on her knees, reaching for the bucket,
as he came up.

"Be drinking slow," he cautioned her.

"Oh!" she cried, with a long breath of satisfaction.
"It's so good! You are so kind to bring it!"

Freckles stood blinking in the dazzling glory of her
smile until he could scarcely see to pass up the basket.

"Mercy!" she exclaimed. "I think I had best be naming
you 'the Angel.' My Guardian Angel."

"Yes," said Freckles. "I look the character every day—
but today most emphatic!"

"Angels don't go by looks," laughed the girl. "Your father told us you had been scrapping. But he told us
why. I'd gladly wear all your cuts and bruises if I could
do anything that would make my father look as
peacocky as yours did. He strutted about proper. I
never saw anyone look prouder."

"Did he say he was proud of me?" marveled Freckles.

"He didn't need to," answered the angel. "He was ra-
diating pride from every pore. Now, have you brought
me your dinner?"

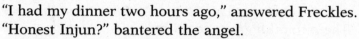

"I had my dinner two hours ago," answered Freckles.

"Honest Injun?" bantered the angel.

"Honest! I brought that on purpose for you."

"Well, if you knew how hungry I am, you would know how thankful I am, to the dot," said the angel.

"Then you be eating," cried the happy Freckles.

The angel sat down on a big camera, spread the lunch on the carriage seat, and divided it in halves. The daintiest parts she could select she carefully put back into the basket. The rest she ate. Again Freckles found her of the swamp, for though she was almost ravenous, she managed her food as gracefully as his little yellow fellow, and her every movement was easy and charming. As he watched her with famished eyes, Freckles told her of his birds, flowers, and books, and never realized what he was doing.

He led the horse out to a deep pool that he knew of, and the tortured creature drank greedily, and lovingly rubbed him with its nose as he wiped down its welted body with grass. Suddenly the angel cried, "There comes the Bird Woman!"

Freckles had intended leaving before she came, but now he was glad indeed to be there, for a warmer, more worn, and worse bitten creature he had never seen. She was staggering under a load of cameras and paraphernalia. Freckles ran to her aid. He took all he could carry of her load, stowed it in the back of the carriage and helped her in. The angel gave her water, knelt and unfastened the leggings, bathed her face, and offered the lunch.

Freckles brought up the horse. He was not sure of the

harness, but the angel knew, and soon they were out of the swamp. Then he showed them how to reach the chicken tree from the outside, indicated a cooler place for the horse, and told them how, the next time they came, the angel could find his room while she waited.

The Bird Woman finished her lunch and lay back, almost too tired to speak.

"Were you for getting Little Chicken's picture?" Freckles asked.

"Fine!" she answered. "He posed splendidly. But I couldn't do anything with his mother. She will take coaxing."

"The Lord be praised!" muttered Freckles under his breath.

The Bird Woman began to feel better.

"Why do you call the baby vulture 'Little Chicken'?" she asked, leaning toward Freckles in an interested fashion.

" 'Twas Duncan began it," said Freckles. "You see, through the fierce cold of winter the birds of the swamp were almost starving. It is mighty lonely here and they were all the company I was having. I got to carrying scraps and grain down to them. Duncan was that generous he was giving me of his wheat and corn from his chickens' feed, and he called the birds me swamp chickens. Then when these big black fellows came, Mr. McLean said they were our nearest kind to some in the old world that they called Pharaoh's Chickens, and he called mine 'Freckles' Chickens.' "

"Good enough!" cried the Bird Woman, her splotched purple face lighting with interest. "You must shoot

something for them occasionally, and I'll bring more food when I come. If you will help me keep them until I get my series, I'll give you a copy of each study I make, mounted in a book."

Freckles drew a deep breath and held hard.

"I'll be doing me very best," he promised, and from the deeps he meant it.

"I wonder if that other egg is going to hatch?" mused the Bird Woman. "I am afraid not. It should have been out today. Isn't it a beauty? I never saw either an egg or the young before. They are rare this far north."

"So Mr. McLean said," answered Freckles.

Before they drove away, the Bird Woman thanked him for his kindness to the angel and herself. She gave him her hand at parting, and Freckles joyfully realized that here was going to be another person for him to love. Freckles couldn't remember, after they had driven away, if they had even noticed his missing hand, and for the first time in his life he had forgotten it.

When the Bird Woman and the angel were well on the home road, the angel told of the little corner of paradise into which she had strayed and of her new name. The Bird Woman looked into the angel's face and guessed its appropriateness.

"Did you know Mr. McLean had a son?" asked the angel. "Isn't the little accent he has, and the way he twists a sentence, too dear? And isn't it too old-fashioned and funny to hear him call his father mister?"

"It sounds too good to be true," said the Bird Woman, answering the last question first. "I am so tired of these present-day young men who patronizingly call their fathers 'Dad,' 'Governor,' 'Old Man,' and 'Old Chap,' that the boy's attitude of respect and deference struck me as being as fine as silk. There must be something rare about that young man."

But she did not find it necessary to tell the angel that for several years she had known the man who so proudly proclaimed himself Freckles' father to be a bachelor and a Scotsman. The Bird Woman had a fine way of attending strictly to her own business.

Freckles turned back to the trail, but he stopped at every wild brier and looked at the pink satin of the petals. She was not of his world, and better than any other he knew it; but she might be his angel, and he was dreaming of naught but blind, silent worship. He finished the happiest day of his life, and that night he went back to the swamp as if drawn by a magnet. That Wessner would try for his revenge, he knew. That he would be abetted by Black Jack was almost certain, but fear had fled the happy heart of Freckles. He had kept his trust. He had won the respect of the boss. Nobody could ever wipe from his heart the flood of holy adoration that had welled up with the coming of his angel. He would do his best, and trust for strength to meet the dark day of reckoning that he knew would come sooner or later. He swung round the trail, briskly tapping the wire, and singing in a voice that could scarcely have been surpassed for sweetness.

At the edge of the clearing he came out into the bright

moonlight, and there sat McLean on his mare. Freckles hurried up to him.

"Is there trouble?" he asked anxiously.

"That's what I wanted to ask you," said the boss. "I stopped at the cabin to see you a minute, before I turned in, and they said you had come down here. You must not do it, Freckles. The swamp is none too healthy at any time, and at night it is rank poison."

Freckles stood combing his fingers through Nellie's mane, and the dainty creature was twisting her head around to his caresses. He pushed back his hat and looked up into McLean's face. "It's come to the 'sleep with one eye open,' sir. I'm not looking for anything to be happening for a week or two, but it's bound to come, and soon. If I'm to keep me trust as I've promised you and meself, I've to live here mostly until the gang comes. You must be knowing that, sir."

"I'm afraid, it's true, Freckles," said McLean. "And I've decided to double the guard until we get here. It will only be a few weeks, now; and I'm so anxious for you that you must not be left alone further. If anything should happen to you, Freckles, it would spoil one of the very dearest plans of my life."

Freckles heard with dismay the proposition to place a second guard.

"Oh! no, no, Mr. McLean," he cried. "Not for the world! I wouldn't be having a stranger around, scaring me birds and tramping up me study, and disturbing all me ways, for any money! I am all the guard you need! I will be faithful! I will turn over the lease with no tree missing—on me life, I will! Oh, don't be sending another man to set them saying I turned coward and asked for help. It will just kill the honor of me heart if you do it. The only thing I want is another gun. If it railly comes to trouble, six cartridges ain't many, and you know I am slow like about reloading."

McLean reached into his hip pocket and handed a shining big revolver down to Freckles, who slipped it beside the one already in his belt.

Then the boss sat brooding.

"Freckles," he said at last, "we never know the timber of a man's soul until something cuts into him deeply and brings the grain out strong. You've the making of a mighty fine piece of furniture, my boy, and you shall have your own way these few weeks yet. Then, if you will go, I am going to take you to the city and educate you, and you are to be my son, my lad—my own son!"

Freckles twisted his fingers in Nellie's mane to steady himself.

"But why should you be doing that, sir?" he faltered.

McLean slid his arm down about the boy's shoulders and gathered him close to him.

"Because I love you, Freckles," he said simply.

Freckles lifted a white face. "My God, sir!" he whispered. "Oh, my God!"

McLean tightened his clasp a second longer, then he rode away down the trail.

Freckles lifted his hat and faced the sky. The harvest moon looked down, sheeting the swamp in silver glory. The Limberlost sang her night song. The swale softly rustled in the wind. Winged things of night brushed his face; and still Freckles gazed upward, trying to fathom

these things that had come to him. There was no help from the sky. It seemed far away, cold, and blue. The earth, where flowers bloomed, angels walked, and love grew, was better. But to One, above the sky, he must make acknowledgment for these miracles. His lips moved and he began talking softly.

"Thank You for each separate good thing that has come to me," he said, "and above all for the falling of the feather. For if it didn't really fall from an angel, its falling brought an angel, and if it's in the great heart of You to exercise Yourself any further about me; oh, do please to be taking good care of her!"

Chapter VI ───────────────────

The next morning Freckles circled the Limberlost inexpressibly happy. He kept snatches of song ringing, as well as the wires. His heart was so full that tears of joy glistened in his eyes. He rigorously strove to divide his thoughts evenly between McLean and the angel. He realized to the fullest the debt he already owed the boss and the magnitude of last night's declaration and promises. He was hourly planning to deliver over his trust and then enter with equal zeal on whatever task his beloved boss saw fit to set him next. He wanted to be ready to meet every device that Wessner and Black Jack could think of to outwit him. He recognized their double leverage, for if they succeeded in felling even one tree McLean became liable for his wager.

Freckles' brow wrinkled in his effort to think deeply

and strongly, but from every swaying wild rose the angel beckoned to him. When he crossed Sleepy Snake
Creek and the goldfinch, waiting as ever, challenged,
"See me?" Freckles saw the dainty, swaying grace of the
angel instead. What is a man to do with an angel who
dismembers herself and scatters over a whole swamp,
thrusting a vivid reminder upon him at every turn?

Freckles counted the days. This first day he could do
little but test his wires, sing broken snatches, and
dream; but before the week would bring her again he
could do many things. He would carry all his books to
the swamp to show to her. He would complete his
flowerbed, arrange every detail he had planned for his
room, and make of it a bower fairies would envy. He
must devise a way to keep water cool. He would ask
Mrs. Duncan for a double lunch and a specially nice
one the day of her next coming, so that if the Bird
Woman should again be late, the angel might not suffer
from thirst and hunger. He would tell her to bring
heavy leather leggings, so that he might take her on a
trip around the trail. She should make friends with all
of his chickens and see their nests.

On the line he talked of her incessantly.

"You needn't be thinking," he said to the goldfinch,
"that because I'm coming down this line alone day after
day, it's always to be so. Some of these days you'll be
swinging on this wire, and you'll see me coming, and
you'll swing, skip and flirt yourself around, and chip up
right spunky, *'See me?'* I'll be saying 'See you? Oh, Lord!
See her!' You'll look, and there she'll stand. The sunshine won't look gold any more, nor the roses pink, nor

the sky blue, because she'll be the pinkest, bluest, goldest thing of all. You'll be yelling yourself hoarse with the jealousy of her. The saw-bird will stretch his neck out of joint, and she'll turn the heads of all the flowers. Wherever she goes, I can go back afterward and see the things she's seen, walk the path she's walked, hear the grasses whispering over all the things she's said; and if there's a place too swampy for her bits of feet; Holy Mother! maybe—maybe she'd be putting the beautiful arms of her about me neck and letting me carry her over!"

Freckles shivered as with a chill. He sent the cudgel whirling skyward, then dextrously caught it and set it spinning.

"You damned presumptuous fool!" he cried. "The thing for you to be thinking of would be to stretch out in the muck for the feet of her to be walking over, and then you could hold yourself holy to be even of that service to her.

"Maybe she'll be wanting the cup me blue-and-brown chickens raised their babies in. Perhaps she'd like to stop at the pool and see me bullfrog that had the goodness to take on human speech to show me the way out of me trouble. If there's any feathers falling that day, why, it's from the wings of me chickens—it's sure to be, for the only angel outside the gates will be walking this timberline, and every step of the way I'll be holding me breath and praying that she don't unfold wings and sail off before the hungry eyes of me."

So Freckles dreamed his dreams, made his plans, and watched his line. He counted not only the days, but the

hours of each day. As he told them off, each one bringing her nearer, he grew happier in the joy of her coming. He managed every day to leave some sort of offering at the great elm log for his black chickens. He
slipped under the line at every passing, and went over to
make sure that nothing was molesting them. Though it
was a long trip, he paid them several extra visits every
day for fear a snake, hawk, or fox might have found the
baby. For now his chickens not only represented all his
former interest in them, but they furnished the motive
that was bringing his angel.

Possibly he could find other subjects that the Bird
Woman wanted. The teamster had said that his brother
went after her every time that he found a nest. Well, he
had never counted the nests that he knew of, and it
might be that among all the birds of the swamp there
were some that would be rare to her.

The feathered folk of the Limberlost were practically
undisturbed save by their natural enemies. It was very
probable that among his chickens others as odd as the
big black ones could be found. If she wanted pictures of
half-grown birds, he could pick up fifty in one morning's trip around the line, for he had fed, handled, and
made friends with them ever since their eyes opened.

He had gathered bugs and worms all spring as he
noticed them on the grass and bushes, and dropped
them into the first little open mouth he had found. The
babies had gladly accepted this queer tri-parent addi-
tion to their natural providers.

When the week was up, Freckles had his room crisp
and glowing with fresh living things that rivaled every

tint of the rainbow. He carried bark and filled up all the muckiest places of the trail.

It was the middle of July. The heat of the last few days had dried up the water about and through the Limberlost, so that it was possible to cross it on foot in almost any direction—if one had any idea of direction and did not become completely lost in its rank tangle of vegetation and bushes. The brighter-hued flowers were opening. The trumpet creepers were flaunting their gorgeous horns of red-and-gold sweetness from the tops of lordly oak and elm, and down below whole pools were pink-sheeted in mallow bloom.

The heat was doing one other thing that was bound to make Freckles, as a good Irishman, shiver. As the swale dried, its inhabitants were seeking the cooler depths of the swamp. They liked neither the heat nor leaving the field mice, moles, and young rabbits of their chosen location. He saw them crossing the trail every day as the heat grew intense. The rattlers were sadly forgetting their manners, for they struck on no provocation whatever, and didn't even remember to rattle afterward. Daily Freckles was compelled to drive big black snakes and blue racers from the nests of his chickens. Often the terrified squalls of the parent birds would reach him far down the line, and he would run to the rescue of the babies.

He saw the angel when the carriage turned from the corduroy into the clearing. They stopped at the west entrance to the swamp, waiting for him to precede them down the trail, as he had told them it was safest for the horse that he should do so. They followed the east line to a point opposite the big chickens' tree, and Freckles carried in the cameras and showed the Bird Woman a path he had cleared to the log. He explained to her the effect the heat was having on the snakes, and, creeping back to Little Chicken, brought him out to the light. As she worked at setting up her camera, he told her of the birds of the line, and she stared at him, wide-eyed and incredulous.

They arranged that Freckles should drive the carriage into the east entrance in the shade and then take the horse around toward the north to a better place he knew. Then he was to entertain the angel at his study or on the line until the Bird Woman finished her work and came to them.

"This will take only a little time," she said. "I know where to set the camera now, and Little Chicken is big enough to be good and too little to run away or act very ugly, so I will soon be coming to see about those nests. I have ten plates along, and I surely won't use more than two on him; so perhaps I can get some nests or young birds this morning."

Freckles trod on air, for his dream had come true so soon. He was going down the timberline and the angel was following him. He asked to be excused for going first, because he wanted to be sure the trail was safe for her. She laughed at his fears, telling him that it was the polite thing for him to do, anyway.

"Oh!" said Freckles, "so you was after knowing that? Well, I didn't s'pose you did, and I was afraid you'd think me wanting in respect to be preceding you!"

The astonished angel looked at him, caught the irrepressible gleam of Irish fun in his eyes, and they stood and laughed together.

Freckles did not realize how he was talking that morning. He showed her many of the beautiful nests and eggs of the line. She could identify a number of them, but of some she was ignorant, so they made notes of the number and color of the eggs, material and construction of nest, color, size, and shape of the birds, and went on to look them up in the book.

At his room, when Freckles had lifted the overhanging bushes and stepped back for her to enter, his heart was all out of time and place. The study was vastly more beautiful than a week before. The angel drew a deep breath and stood staring, first at one side, then at another, then far off down the cathedral aisle. "It's just fairyland!" she cried, ecstatically. Then she turned and stared at Freckles exactly as she had at his handiwork.

"What are you planning to be?" she asked, slowly.

"Whatever Mr. McLean wants me to," he replied.

"What do you do most?" she asked.

"Watch me lines."

"I don't mean work!"

"Oh! In me spare time I keep me room and study in me books."

"Do you work on the room or the books most?"

"On the room just what it takes to keep it up, and the rest of the time on me books."

The angel eyed him sharply. "Well, maybe you are going to be a great scholar," she said, "but you don't look it. Your face isn't right for that, but it's got something big in it—something just great. I must find out

what it is and then you must go to work on it. Your
father is expecting you to do something. You can tell by
the way he talks. You ought to begin right away. You've
wasted too much time already."

Poor Freckles hung his head. He had never wasted an
hour in his life. There had never been one that was his
to waste.

The angel, studying him intently, read his thought in
his face. "Oh, I don't mean that!" she cried, with the
frank dismay of sixteen. "Of course, you're not lazy! Nobody would ever think that from your looks. It's this I
mean: there is something fine, strong, and full of power
in your face. There is something you are to do in this
world, and no matter how hard you work at all these
other things, nor how successfully you do them, it is all
wasted until you find the one thing that you can do best.
If you hadn't a thing in the world to do, and could go
anywhere you please and do anything you want, what
would you do?" persisted the angel.

"I'd go to Chicago and sing in the First Episcopal
choir," answered Freckles promptly.

The angel dropped back on a seat—the hat she had
taken off and held in her fingers rolled to her feet.
"There!" she exclaimed vehemently. "You can see what
I'm going to be. Nothing! Absolutely nothing! You can
sing? Of course you can sing! It is written all over you."

Anybody with half wit could have seen he could sing,
without having to be told, she thought. It's in the slen-
derness of his fingers and his quick nervous touch. It is
in the brightness of his hair, the fire of his eyes, the

breadth of his chest, the muscles of his throat and neck; and, above all, it's in every tone of his voice, for even as he speaks it's the sweetest sound I ever heard from the throat of a mortal.

"Will you do something for me?" she asked.

"I'll do anything in the world you want me to," said Freckles, largely; "and if I can't do what you want I'll go to work at once and I'll try till I can."

"Good! That's business!" said the angel. "You go over there and stand before that bank and sing something. Just anything you think of first."

Freckles faced the angel from his banked wall of brown, blue, and crimson, with its background of solid green, and lifting his face to the sky, he sang the first thing that came into his mind. It was a children's song that he had led for the little folks at the home many times, recalled to his mind by the angel's exclamation:

> "To fairyland we go,
>   With a song of joy, heigh-o;
>   In dreams we'll stand upon that shore
>   And all the realm behold;
>   We'll see the sights so grand
>   That belong to fairyland,
>   Its mysteries we will explore,
>   Its beauties will unfold.
>   Oh, tra, la, la, ho, ha, ha, ha!
>   We're happy now as we can be,
>   Our welcome song we will prolong,
>   And greet you with our melody.
>   Oh, fairyland, sweet fairyland, we love to sing—"

Nothing could have given the intense sweetness and rollicking quality of Freckles' voice better scope. He forgot everything but pride in his work with the sound of his voice. He was going full tilt on the chorus, and the Angel was shivering in ecstasy, when clip! clip! came the sharply beating feet of a swiftly ridden horse down the trail from the north. They both sprang toward the entrance.

"Freckles! Freckles!" called the voice of the Bird Woman.

They were at the trail on the instant.

"Both those revolvers loaded?" she asked.

"Yes," said Freckles.

"Is there a way you can cut across the swamp and get to the chicken tree in a few minutes, and with little noise?"

"Yes."

"Then go flying," said the Bird Woman. "Give the angel a lift up behind me, and we will ride the horse back to where you left him and wait for you. I finished Little Chicken in no time and put him back. His mother came so close, I felt sure she would enter the log. The light was fine, so I set and focused the camera and covered it with branches, attached the long hose, and went away off over a hundred feet and hid in some bushes to wait. A short, thick man and a tall, dark one passed me so closely I could almost have reached out and touched them. They carried a big saw on their shoulders. They said they could work until about noon, and then they must lay off until you passed and then try to load and get out at night. They went on—not entirely out of sight

—and began cutting a tree. Mr. McLean told me the other day what was likely to happen here, and if they get that tree down he loses his wager on you. Keep to the east and north and hustle. We'll meet you at the carriage. I am always armed. Give Babe one of your revolvers, and you keep the other. We will separate and creep up on them from different sides and give them a fusillade that will send them flying. You hurry, now!"

She gathered up the reins and started briskly down the trail. The angel, hatless and with sparkling eyes, was clinging about her waist.

Freckles wheeled and ran. He worked his way with great care, dodging limbs and bushes with noiseless tread, and cutting as close to where he thought the men were as he felt that he dared if he were to remain unseen. As he ran he tried to think. It was Wessner, burning for his revenge, aided by the bully of the locality, that he was going to meet. He was accustomed to that thought, but not to the complication of having two women on his hands who would undoubtedly have to be taken care of in spite of the Bird Woman's offer to help him. His heart was jarring as it never before had with running. He must follow the Bird Woman's plan and meet them at the carriage, but if they really did mean to try to help him, he must not allow it. Let the angel try to handle a revolver in his defense? Never! Not for all the trees in the Limberlost! She might shoot herself. She might forget to watch sharply and run across a snake that was not particularly well behaved that morning. Freckles permitted himself a grim smile as he went speeding on.

When he reached the carriage, the Bird Woman and the angel had the horse hitched to it, the outfit packed, and were calmly waiting. The Bird Woman held her revolver in her hand. She wore dark clothing. They had pinned a big focusing cloth over the front of the angel's light dress.

"Give Babe one of your revolvers, quick!" said the Bird Woman. "We will all creep up until we are in fair range. The underbrush is so thick and they are so hard at work that they will never notice us, if we don't make a noise. You fire first, then I will pop in from my direction, and then you, Baby, and shoot quite high, or else very low. We mustn't really hit them. We'll go close enough to the cowards to make it interesting, and keep it up until we have them going good."

Freckles protested.

The Bird Woman reached over, and, taking the small revolver from his belt, handed it to the angel. "Keep your nerve steady, dear. Watch where you step, and shoot high," she said. "Go straight at them from where you are. Wait until you hear Freckles' first shot, then follow me as closely as you can, to let them know that we outnumber them. If you want to save McLean's wager on you, now you go!" she commanded Freckles, who, with an agonized glance at the angel, ran toward the east.

The Bird Woman chose the middle distance, and for a last time cautioned the angel to lie down and shoot high, as she moved away.

Through the underbrush the Bird Woman crept, even more closely than she had intended, found a clear range, and waited for Freckles' shot. There was one long minute of sickening suspense. The men straightened for breath. Work was fearful with a handsaw in the heat of the swamp. As they rested, the big dark fellow took a bottle from his pocket and began oiling the saw.

"We got to keep mighty quiet," he said, "and wait to fell it until that damned guard has gone to his dinner."

Again they bent to their work. Freckles' revolver spat fire. Lead spanged on steel. The saw handle flew from Wessner's hand and he reeled with the jar of the shock. Black Jack straightened, uttering a fearful oath. The hat sailed off his head from the far northeast. The angel had not waited for the Bird Woman, and her shot could scarcely have been called high. At almost the same instant the third shot whistled in from the east. Black Jack sprang into the air with a yell of complete panic, for it ripped a heel from his boot. Freckles emptied his second chamber, and the dirt spattered over Wessner. Shots poured in thick and fast. Without even reaching for a weapon, both men broke for the east road in great, leaping bounds, while leaden slugs sang and hissed about them in deadly earnest.

Freckles was trimming his corners as closely as he dared, but if the angel did not really intend to hit, she was shaving the limit in a scandalous manner.

When the men reached the trail, Freckles yelled at the top of his voice, "Head them off on the south, boys! Fire from the south!"

As he had hoped, Jack and Wessner instantly plunged into the swale. A storm of lead spattered after them.

They crossed the swale, running low, with not even one backward glance and entered the woods beyond the corduroy.

Then the little party gathered at the tree.

"I'd better fix this saw so they can't be using it if they come back," said Freckles, taking out his hatchet and making sawteeth fly.

"Now we have to get out of here without being seen," said the Bird Woman to the angel. "It won't do for me to make enemies of these men, for I am liable to meet them about my work any day."

"You can do it by driving straight north on this road," said Freckles. "I will go ahead and cut the wires for you. The swale is almost dry. You will only be sinking a few inches at most. In a few rods you will strike a cornfield. I will take down the fence and let you into that. Follow the furrows and drive straight across it until you come to the other side. Be following the fence south until you come to a road through the woods east of it. Then take that road and follow east until you reach the pike. You will come out on your way back to town, and two miles north of anywhere they are likely to be. Don't for your lives ever let it out that you did this," he earnestly cautioned, "for it's black enemies you would be making."

Freckles snapped the wires and they drove through. The angel leaned from the carriage and held out his revolver. Freckles looked into her face and lost his breath. Her eyes were black, and her face a deeper rose than usual. He felt that his own was white as death.

"Did I shoot high enough?" she asked sweetly. "I really forgot about lying down."

Freckles winced. Did the child know how near she had gone? Surely she could not! Or was it possible that she had the nerve and skill to fire like that purposely?

"I will send the first reliable man I meet for McLean," said the Bird Woman, gathering up the lines. "If I don't meet one when we reach town, we will send a messenger. If it wasn't for having the gang see me, I would go myself; but I will promise you that you will have help in a little over two hours. You keep well hidden. They must think some of the gang is with you now. There isn't a chance that they will be back, but don't run any risks. Stay under cover. If they should come, it would probably be for their saw." She laughed as at a fine joke.

Chapter VII

WHEREIN FRECKLES WINS HONOR AND FINDS A
FOOTPRINT ON THE TRAIL

Round-eyed, Freckles watched the Bird Woman and
the angel drive away. After they were out of sight
and he was safely hidden among the branches of a
small tree, he remembered that he had neither thanked
them nor said good-bye. Considering what they had
been through, they would never come again. His heart
sank until he had palpitation in his wading boots.

Stretching along the limb, he thought deeply, though
he was not thinking of either Black Jack or Wessner.
Would the Bird Woman and the angel come again? No
other women that he had ever known would. But were
they like any other women he had ever known? He
thought of the Bird Woman's unruffled face and the angel's revolver practice, and presently he was not so sure
that they would not come back.

116

What were the people out in the big world like? His knowledge was so very limited. There had been people at the home who exchanged a stilted, perfunctory sort of kindness for their salaries. The visitors who called on receiving days he had divided into three classes: the psalm-singing kind, who came with a tear in the eye and hypocrisy in every feature of their faces; the kind who came in silks and jewels, and handed out to those poor, little mother-hungry souls worn toys that their children no longer cared for, in exactly the same spirit in which they pitched biscuits to the monkeys at the zoo, and for the same reason—to see how they would take them and be amused by what they would do; and the third class, whom he considered real people, who made him feel they cared that he was there and would have been glad to see him elsewhere.

Now, here was another class, who had all they needed of the world's best and were engaged in doing things that counted. They had things worthwhile to be proud of; and they had met him as a son and brother. With them he could, for the only time in his life, forget the lost hand that every day tortured him with a new pang. What sort of people were they and where did they belong among the classes he knew? He had to give it up, because he had never known others like them; but how he loved them!

Out in the world where he was soon going, were the majority like them, or were they of the hypocrite and bun-throwing classes? Freckles did not know, but he reached the ultimate conclusion that people like the

Bird Woman, the angel, McLean, and the Duncans were very rare, hence their exceeding preciousness.

He had forgotten the excitement of the morning and the passing of time when distant voices roused him, and he softly lifted his head. Nearer and nearer they came, and as the heavy wagons rumbled down the east trail he could hear them plainly. The gang were shouting themselves hoarse for the Limberlost guard. Freckles didn't feel that he deserved it. He would have given much to be able to go out to the men and explain how it was, but only to McLean could he tell his story.

At the sight of Freckles the men threw up their hats and cheered. McLean shook hands with him warmly, but big Duncan gathered him into his arms and hugged him like a bear and choked over a few words of praise. The gang drove in and finished felling the tree. McLean was angry beyond measure at this attempt on his property, for in their haste to fell the tree the thieves had cut too high and thus wasted a foot and a half of valuable timber.

When the last wagon rolled away, McLean sat down on the stump and Freckles told the story he was aching to tell. The boss could scarcely believe his senses. Also, he was greatly disappointed.

"I have been almost praying all the way over, Freckles," he said, "that you would have some evidence by which we could arrest those fellows and get them out of our way, but this will never do. We can't mix those women up in it. They have helped you save me the tree and my wager as well. Going about the country as she does, the Bird Woman could never be expected to testify against them."

"No, indeed; nor the angel, either, sir," said Freckles.

"The angel?" queried the astonished McLean.

The boss listened in silence while Freckles told of the coming and christening of the angel.

"I know her father well," said McLean at last, "and I have often seen her. You are right; she is a beautiful young girl, and she appears to be utterly free from the least particle of false pride or foolishness. I do not understand why her father risks such a jewel in this place."

"He's daring it because she is such a jewel, sir," said Freckles, eagerly. "Why, she's trusting a rattlesnake to rattle before it strikes her, and, of course, she thinks she can trust mankind as well. The man isn't made that wouldn't lay down the life of him for her. She don't need any care. Her face and the pretty ways of her are all the protection she would need in a band of howling savages."

"Did you say she handled one of the revolvers?" asked McLean.

"She scared all the breath out of me body," admitted Freckles. "Seems that her father has taught her to shoot. The Bird Woman told her distinctly to lie low and blaze away high, just to help scare them. The spunky little thing followed them right out into the west road, spitting lead like hail, and clipping all about the heads and heels of them; and I'm damned, sir, if I believe she'd cared a rap if she'd hit. I never saw much shooting, but if that wasn't the nearest to miss I ever

want to see! Scared the life near out of me body with the fear that she'd drop one of them. As long as I'd no one to help me but a couple of women that didn't dare be mixed up in it, all I could do was to let them get away."

"Now, will they come back?" asked McLean.

"Of course!" said Freckles. "They're not going to be taking that. You could stake your life on it, they'll be coming back. At least, Black Jack will. Wessner might not have the pluck, unless he were half drunk. Then he would be a terror. And the next time—" Freckles hesitated.

"What?"

"It will just be a question of who shoots first and straightest."

"Then the only thing for me to do is to double the guard and get the gang here the first minute possible. As soon as I feel that we have the rarest of the stuff out below, we will come. The fact is, in many cases, until it is felled it's hard to tell what a tree will prove to be. It won't do to leave you here longer alone. Jack has been shooting twenty years to your one, and it stands to reason that you are no match for him. Which of the gang would you like best to have with you?"

"No one, sir," said Freckles, emphatically. "Next time is where I run. I won't try to fight them alone. I'll just be getting wind of them, and then make tracks for you. I'll need to come like lightning, and Duncan has no extra horse, so I'm thinking you'd best get me one—or perhaps a wheel would be better. I used to do extra work for the home doctor, and he would let me take his bicycle to ride about the place. And at times the head nurse would lend me his for an hour. A wheel would cost less and be faster than a horse, and would take less care. I believe, if you are going to town soon, you had best pick up any kind of an old one at some secondhand store, for if I'm ever called to use it in a hurry there won't be the handlebars left after crossing the corduroy."

"Yes," said McLean, "and if you didn't have a first-class wheel, you could never cross the corduroy on it at all."

As they walked up to the cabin together, McLean insisted on another guard, but Freckles was stubbornly set on fighting his battle alone. He made one mental condition. If the Bird Woman was going to give up the Little Chicken series, he would yield to the second guard, solely for the sake of her work and the presence of the angel in the Limberlost. He did not propose to have a second man about unless it were absolutely necessary, for he had been so long alone that he loved the solitude, his chickens, and flowers. The thought of having a stranger to all his ways come in and meddle with his arrangements, frighten his pets, pull his flowers, and interrupt him when he wanted to study, so annoyed him that he was blinded to his real need of help.

With McLean it was a case of letting his sober, better judgment be overriden by the boy he was growing so to love that he could not bear to cross him, and to have Freckles keep his trust and win alone meant to him more than any money he might lose.

The next morning McLean brought the bicycle, and

Freckles took it down to the trail to test it. It was new, chainless, with as little as possible to catch in hurried riding, and in every way the best of its kind. Freckles went skimming around the trail on it on a preliminary trip before he locked it in his case and started his minute examination of his line on foot. He glanced around his room as he left it, and then stood staring.

On the moss in front of his prettiest seat lay the angel's hat. In the excitement of yesterday they had all forgotten it. He went and picked it up, oh! so carefully, gazing at it with hungry eyes, but touching it only to carry it over to his case, where he hung it on the shining handlebar of the new wheel and locked it in among his treasures. Then he went out to the trail with a new look on his face and a strange throbbing in his heart. He was not in the least afraid of anything that morning. He felt he was the veriest Daniel, and all his lions seemed weak and harmless.

What Black Jack's next move would be he could not guess, but that there would be a move of some kind was certain. The big bully was not a man to give up his purpose, or to have the hat swept from his head by a bullet and bear it meekly. Moreover, Wessner would cling to his revenge with a Dutchman's singleness of mind.

Freckles tried to think connectedly, but there were too many places about the trail where the angel's footprints were still plain. She had stepped in one mucky spot and left a sharp impression. The afternoon sun had baked it hard, and the horses' hoofs had not obliterated any part of it, as they had in so many places. Freckles stood fascinated, gazing at it. He measured it lovingly with his eye. He would not have ventured a caress on her hat any more than on her person, but surely this was different. Surely a footprint on a trail might belong to anyone who found and wanted it. He stooped under the wires and entered the swamp. With a little searching he found a big piece of thick bark loose on a log and, carefully peeling it, carried it out and covered the print with it so that the first rain would not wash it away.

When he got to his room, he tenderly laid the hat upon his bookshelf and, to wear off his awkwardness, mounted his bicycle and went spinning about the line again. It was like flying, for the path was worn smooth with his feet and baked hard with the sun almost all the way. When he came to the bark, he veered well to one side and smiled down at it in passing. Suddenly he was off the bicycle, kneeling beside it. He took off his hat, carefully lifted the bark, and gazed lovingly at the imprint.

"I wonder what she was going to say of me voice," he whispered. "She never got it said, but from the face of her, I believe she was liking it fairly well. Perhaps she was going to say that singing was the big thing I was to be doing. That's what they all said at the home. Well, if it is, I'll just shut me eyes, think of me little room, the face of her watching, and the heart of her beating, and I'll raise them. Damn them, if singing will do it, I'll raise them from the benches!"

   With this dire threat, Freckles knelt, as at a wayside
spring, and deliberately laid his lips on the footprint.
Then he rose up, looking as if he had been drinking at
the fountain of gladness.

Chapter VIII ─────────────────

WHEREIN FRECKLES MEETS A MAN OF AFFAIRS
AND LOSES NOTHING BY THE ENCOUNTER

"Weel, I be drawed on!" exclaimed Mrs. Duncan. Freckles stood before her, holding the angel's hat.

"I've been thinking this long time that ye or Duncan would see that sunbonnets werena braw enough for a woman of my standing, and ye're a guid laddie to bring me this beautiful hat."

She turned it about, examining the weave of the straw and the foliage trimmings, passing her rough fingers over the satin ties delightedly. As she held it up, admiring it, Freckles' astonished eyes saw a new side of Sarah Duncan. She was jesting, but under the jest the fact loomed strong that, though poor, overworked, and with none but God-given refinement, there was something in her soul crying out after that bit of feminine

finery, and it made his heart ache for her. He resolved that when he reached the city he would send her as fine a hat as the angel's, if it took fifty dollars to do it.

She lingeringly handed it back to him.

"It's unco guid of ye to think of me," she said lightly, "but I maun question your taste a wee. D'ye no think ye had best return this and get a woman with half her hair gray a little plainer headdress? Seems like that's far ower gay for me. I'm no' saying that it's no' exactly what I'd like to hae, but I mauna mak' mysel' ridiculous. Ye'd best give this to somebody young and pretty, say about sixteen. Where did ye come by it, Freckles? If there's anything been dropping lately, ye hae forgotten to mention it."

"Do you see anything heavenly about that hat?" queried Freckles, holding it up.

The morning breeze waved the ribbons gracefully, binding one about Freckles' sleeve and the other across his chest, where they caught and clung as if they were magnetized.

"Yes," said Sarah Duncan. "It's verra plain and simple, but it juist makes ye feel that it's all of the finest stuff. It's exactly what I'd call a heavenly hat."

"Sure," said Freckles, "for it's belonging to an angel!"

Then he told her about the hat and asked her what he should do with it.

"Take it to her, of course!" said Sarah Duncan. "Like it's the only ane she has and she may need it badly."

Freckles smiled. He had a pretty clear idea how nearly the hat came to being the only one the angel had.

However, there was a thing he felt he ought and wanted
to do, but he was not sure.

"You think I should be taking it home?" he said.

"Of course ye must," said Mrs. Duncan. "And without
another hour's delay. It's been here two days noo, and
she may want it and be too busy or afraid to come."

"But how can I take it?" asked Freckles.

"Gang spinning on your wheel. Ye can do it easy in an
hour."

"But in that hour, what if—?"

"Nonsense!" broke in Sarah Duncan. "Ye've watched
that timberline until ye're grown fast to it, lad. Give me
your boots and club and I'll gae walk the south end and
watch doon the east and west sides until ye get back."

"Mrs. Duncan! You never would be doing it," cried
Freckles.

"Why not?" inquired she.

"But you know you're mortal afraid of snakes and a
lot of other things in the swamp."

"I am afraid of snakes," said Mrs. Duncan, "but likely
they've gone into the swamp this hot weather. I'll juist
stay on the trail and watch, and ye might hurry the least
bit. The day's so bright it feels like storm. I can put the
bairns on the woodpile to play until I get back. Ye gang
awa and take the blessed little angel her beautiful hat."

"Are you sure it will be all right?" urged Freckles. "Do
you think if Mr. McLean came he would care?"

"Na," said Mrs. Duncan, "I dinna. If ye and me agree
that a thing ought to be done, and I watch in your place,
why, it's bound to be all right with McLean. Let me pin

the hat in a paper, and ye jump on your wheel and gang
flying. Ought ye put on your Sabbath-day clothes?"

Freckles shook his head. He knew what he had to do,
but there was no use in taking time to try to explain it to
Mrs. Duncan while he was so hurried. He exchanged his
wading boots for shoes, gave her his club, and went
spinning toward town. He knew very well where the
angel lived. He had passed her home many times, and
he passed it again without even taking his eyes from the
street, steering straight toward her father's place of
business.

Carrying the hat, Freckles passed a long line of clerks,
and, at the door of the private office, asked to see the
proprietor. When he had waited a moment, a tall, spare,
keen-eyed man faced him and in brisk, nervous tones
asked, "How can I serve you, sir?"

Freckles handed him the package and answered, "By
delivering to your daughter this hat, which she was after leaving at me place the other day when she went off
in a hurry. And by saying to her and the Bird Woman
that I'm more thankful than I'll be having words to express for the brave thing they was doing for me. I'm
McLean's Limberlost guard, sir."

"Why don't you take it yourself?" asked the man.

Freckles' clear gray eyes met those of the angel's father squarely, and he said, "If you were in my place,
would you take it to her yourself?"

"No, I would not," said that gentleman quickly.

"Then why ask why I did not?" came Freckles' lamb-
like query.

"Bless me!" said the angel's father. He stared at the

package, then at the lifted chin of the boy, and then at the package again, and muttered, "Excuse me!"

Freckles bowed.

"It would be favoring me greatly if you would deliver the hat and the message. Good morning, sir," and he turned away.

"One minute," said the angel's father. "Suppose I give you permission to return this hat in person and make your own acknowledgments."

Freckles stood one moment thinking intently, and then he lifted those eyes of unswerving truth and asked, "Why should you, sir? You are kind, indeed, to mention it, and it's thanking you I am for your good intentions, but my wanting to go or your being willing to have me ain't proving that your daughter would be wanting me or care to bother with me."

The angel's father looked keenly into the face of this extraordinary young man and he found it to his liking.

"There's one other thing I meant to say," said Freckles. "Every day I see something, and at times a lot of things, that I think the Bird Woman would be wanting pictures of badly, if she knew. You might be speaking of it to her, and if she'd want me to, I can send her word when I find things she wouldn't likely get elsewhere."

"If that's the case," said the angel's father, "and you feel under obligations for her assistance the other day, you can discharge them in that way. She is spending all her time in the fields and woods searching for subjects. If you run across things, perhaps rarer than she may find, about your work, it would save her the time she

spends searching for subjects and she could work in
security under your protection. By all means let her
know if you find subjects you think she could use and
we will do anything we can for you if you will give her
what help you can and see to it that she is as safe as
possible."

"It's hungry for human beings I get," said Freckles,
"and it's like heaven to me to have them come. Of
course, I'll be telling or sending her word every time me
work can spare me. Anything I can do it would make
me uncommon happy, but"—again truth had to be told,
because it was Freckles who was speaking—"when it
comes to protecting them, I'd risk me life, to be sure,
but even that mightn't do any good in some cases.
There's a good many dangers to be reckoned with in the
swamp, sir, that calls for every person to look sharp. If
there wasn't really thieving to guard against, why, Mr.
McLean wouldn't need be paying out good money for a
guard. I'd love them to be coming, and I'll do all I can,
but you must be told that there's danger of them running into timber thieves again any day, sir."

"Yes," said the angel's father, "and I suppose there's
danger of the earth opening up and swallowing the
town any day, but I'm damned if I quit business for fear
it will and the Bird Woman won't, either. Everybody
knows her and her work, and there is no danger in the
world of anyone in any way molesting her, even if he
were stealing a few of McLean's gold-plated trees. She's
as safe in the Limberlost as she is at home, so far as
timber thieves are concerned. All I am ever uneasy
about are the snakes, poison vines, and insects; and

those are risks she must run anywhere. You need not hesitate a minute about that. I shall be glad to tell them what you wish. Thank you very much, and good day, sir."

There was no way in which Freckles could know it, but by following his best instincts and being what he conceived a gentleman should be, he surprised the angel's father into thinking of him and seeing his face over his books many times that morning. Whereas, if he had gone to the angel as he had longed to do, her father would never have given him a second thought.

Out on the street he drew a deep breath. How had he acquitted himself? He only knew that he had lived up to his best impulse, and that is all anyone can do. He glanced over his bicycle to see that it was all right, and just as he stepped to the curb to mount he heard a voice that thrilled through and through him, calling, "Freckles! Oh, Freckles!"

The angel separated herself from a group of laughing, sweet-faced girls and came hurrying up to him. She was in snowy white—a quaint little frock, with a marvel of soft lace about her throat and wrists. Through the sheer sleeves of it her beautiful, rounded arms showed distinctly, and it was cut just to the base of her perfect neck. On her head was a pure white creation of fancy braid, with folds on folds of tulle, soft and silken as cobwebs, lining the brim. And a great mass of white roses clustered against the gold of her hair, crept about the crown, and fell in a riot to her shoulders at the back. There were gleams of gold with settings of blue on her fingers, and altogether she was the daintiest, sweetest

sight he had ever seen. Freckles, standing on the curb,
forgot himself in his cotton shirt, corduroys, and his
belt to which his wire cutter and pliers were still hanging, and gazed as a man gazes when first he sees the
woman he adores with all her charms enhanced by ap-
propriate and beautiful clothing.

"Oh, Freckles," she cried as she came up to him. "I
was wondering about you the other day. Do you know I
never saw you in town before. You watch that old line
so closely! Why did you come in? Is there any trouble?
Are you just starting back to the Limberlost?"

"I came to bring your hat," said Freckles. "You forgot
it in the rush the other day. I have just left it with your
father, and a message trying to express the gratitude of
me for how you and the Bird Woman were for helping
me out."

The angel nodded gravely and Freckles saw in a flash
that he had done the proper thing in going to her father.
Then his heart bounded until it jarred his body, for she
was saying that she could scarcely wait for the time to
come for the next picture of the Little Chicken's series.
"I want to hear the rest of that song and I hadn't even
begun seeing your room yet," she complained. "As for
singing, if you can sing like that every day, I can never
get enough of it. I wonder if I couldn't bring my banjo
and some of the songs I like best. I'll play and you'll
sing, and we'll put the birds out of commission."

Freckles stood on the curb with down-dropped eyes,
for he felt that if he lifted them the tumult of tender
adoration in them would show and frighten her.

"I was afraid your experience the other day would

scare you so that you'd never be coming again," he found himself saying.

The angel laughed gaily. "Did I look scared?" she asked.

"No," said Freckles, "you did not."

"Oh, I just enjoyed that," she cried. "Those hateful, stealing old things! I had a big notion to pink one of them, but I thought maybe some way it would be best for you that I shouldn't. They needed it. That didn't scare me. And as for the Bird Woman, she's accustomed to finding snakes, tramps, cross dogs, sheep, cattle, and goodness knows what! You can't frighten her when she's after a picture. Did they come back?"

"No," said Freckles. "The gang got there a little after noon and took out the tree, but I must tell you, and you must tell the Bird Woman, that there's no doubt but they will be coming back, and they will have to make it before long now, for it's soon the gang will be there to work on the swamp."

"Oh, what a shame!" cried the angel. "They'll clear out roads, cut down the beautiful trees, and tear up every-thing. They'll drive away the birds and spoil the cathe-dral. When they have done their worst, then all these mills about here will follow in and take out the cheap timber. Then the landowners will dig a few ditches, build some fires, and in two summers more the Limberlost will be in corn and potatoes."

They looked at each other, and groaned despairingly in unison.

"You like it, too," said Freckles.

"Yes," said the angel, "I love it. Your room is a little

piece right out of the heart of fairyland, and the cathedral is God's work, not yours. You only found it and opened the door after He had it completed. The birds, flowers, and vines are all so lovely. The Bird Woman says it is really a fact that the mallows, foxfire, iris, and lilies are larger and of richer coloring there than about the rest of the country. She says it's because of the rich loam and muck. I hate seeing the swamp torn up, and to you it will be like losing your best friend, won't it?"

"Something like," said Freckles. "Still, I've the Limberlost in me heart so that all of it will be real to me while I live, no matter what they do to it. I'm glad past telling if you will be coming a few more times, at least until the gang arrives. Past that time I don't allow meself to be thinking."

"Come, get a cool drink before you start back," said the angel.

"I couldn't possibly," said Freckles. "I left Mrs. Duncan on the trail, and she's terribly afraid of a lot of things. If she even sees a big snake, I don't know what she'll do."

"It won't take but a minute, and you can ride fast enough to make up for it. Please. I want to think of something fine for you, to make up a little for what you did for me that first day."

Freckles looked into the beautiful face of the angel in sheer wonderment. Did she truly mean it? Would she walk down that street with him, crippled, homely, in mean clothing, with the tools of his occupation about him, and share with him the treat she was offering? He could not believe it even of the angel. Still, in justice to the candor of her pure, sweet face, he would not believe that she would make the offer and not mean it. She really did think just what she said, but when it came to carrying out her offer and she saw the stares of her friends, the sneers of her enemies—if such as she could have enemies—and heard the whispered jeers of the curious, then she would see her mistake and be sorry. It was only a manly thing for him to think this out for her and save her from the results of her own blessed bigness of heart.

"I really must be off," said Freckles earnestly, "but I'm thanking you more than you'll ever know for your kindness. I'll just be drinking bowls of icy things all me way home in the thoughts of it."

Down came the angel's foot. Her eyes flashed indignantly. "There's no sense in that," she said. "How do you think you would have felt when you knew I was warm and thirsty and you went and brought me a drink, and I wouldn't take it because—because goodness knows why! You can ride faster to make up for the time. I've just thought out what I want to fix for you."

She stepped to his side and deliberately slipped her hand under his arm—that right arm that ended in an empty sleeve.

"You are coming," she said firmly. "I won't have it."

Freckles could not have told how he felt; neither could anyone else. His blood rioted and his head swam, but he kept his wits. He bent over her.

"Please don't, Angel," he said softly. "You don't understand." How Freckles came to understand was a problem.

"It's this," he persisted. "If your father came on me on the street, in my station and dress, with you on me arm, he'd have every right to be caning me before the people, and not a finger would I lift to stay him."

The angel's eyes snapped. "If you think my father cares about my doing anything that is right and kind, and that makes me happy to do—why, then you completely failed in reading my father, and I'll ask him and just show you."

She dropped Freckles' arm and turned toward the entrance to the building. "Why, look there!" she exclaimed.

Her father stood in a big window fronting the street, a bundle of papers in his hand, interestedly watching the little scene, with eyes that comprehended quite as thoroughly as if he had heard every word of it. The angel caught his glance and made a despairing little gesture toward Freckles. Her father answered her with a look of infinite tenderness. He nodded his head and waved the papers in the direction she had indicated, and the veriest dolt could have read the words his lips formed, "Take him along!"

A sudden trembling seized Freckles. At the sight of the angel's father he had stepped back as far from her as he could, leaned the bicycle against him, and snatched off his hat.

The angel turned on him with triumphing eyes. She was highly strung and not accustomed to being thwarted. "Did you see that?" she demanded. "Now are you satisfied? Will you come, or must I call a policeman to bring you?"

Freckles went. There was nothing else to do. Guiding his bicycle, he walked down the street beside her. On every hand she was kept busy giving and receiving the cheeriest greetings. She walked into the parlors exactly as if she owned them. A clerk came hurrying to meet her.

"There's a table vacant back here by a side window where it is cool. I'll save it for you," and he started back.

"Please not," said the angel. "I've taken this man unawares, when he's in a rush. I'm afraid if we sit down we'll take too much time and afterward he will blame me."

She walked up to the fountain, and a long row of people stared with all the varying degrees of insolence and curiosity that Freckles had felt they would. He glanced at the angel. *Now* would she see?

"On my soul!" he muttered under his breath. "They don't even touch her!"

She laid down her sunshade and gloves. She walked around to the end of the counter and turned the full battery of her eyes on the attendant.

"Please," she said.

The white-aproned individual stepped back and gave delighted assent. The angel walked up beside him, and selecting a tall, flaring glass, of almost paper thinness, she stooped and rolled it in a tray of cracked ice.

"I want to mix a drink for my friend," she said. "He has a long, hot ride before him, and I don't want him started off with one of those old palate-teasing sweetnesses that you mix just on purpose to drive a man back

in ten minutes." There was an appreciative laugh from
the line at the counter.

"I want a clear, cool, sparkling drink that has a tang
of acid in it. Where's the cherry phosphate? That, not at
all sweet, would be good, don't you think?"

The attendant did think. He pointed out the different
taps and the angel compounded the drink, while
Freckles, standing so erect he almost leaned backward,
fastened his eyes on her and paid no attention to anyone else. When she had the glass brimming, she tilted a
little of its contents into a second glass and tasted it.

"That's entirely too sweet for a thirsty man," she said.

She poured out half the mixture and, refilling the
glass, tasted it a second time. She submitted that result
to the attendant. "Isn't that about the thing?" she asked.

He replied enthusiastically, "I'd get my wages raised
ten a month if I could learn that trick."

The angel carried the brimming, frosty glass to
Freckles. He took off his hat, and lifting the icy liquid
even with her eyes and looking straight into them, he
said in the mellowest of all the mellow tones of his
voice, "I'll be drinking it to the swamp angel."

And as he had said to her that first day, the angel now
cautioned him, "Be drinking slowly."

As the screen door swung behind them, one of the
men at the counter asked of the attendant, "Now, what
did that mean?"

"Exactly what you saw," replied he, rather curtly.
"We're accustomed to it in here. Hardly a day passes,
this hot weather, but she's picking up some poor,
godforsaken mortal and bringing him in. Then she

comes behind the counter herself and fixes up a drink to suit the occasion. She's all sorts of fancies about what's what for all kinds of times and conditions, and you bet she can just hit the spot! Ain't a clerk here can put up a drink to touch her. She's a sort of knack at it. Every once in a while, when the boss sees her, he calls out to her to mix him a drink."

"And does she?" asked the man with an interested grin.

"Well, I guess! But first she goes back and sees how long it is since he's had a drink. What he drank last. How warm he is. When he ate last. Then she comes up here and mixes a glass of fizz with a little touch of acid, and a bit of cherry, lemon, grape, pineapple, or something sour and cooling. Then she passes it up over those blue eyes of her, and it hits the spot just as no spot was ever hit before. I honestly believe that the *interest* she takes in it is half the trick, for I watch her closely and I can't come within gunshot of her concoctions. She has a running bill here. Her father settles once a month. She gives nine-tenths of it away. Hardly ever touches it herself, but when she does she makes me mix it. Even the scrub boy of this establishment would fight for her. It lasts the year round, for in winter it's some poor, frozen cuss that she's warming up on hot coffee or chocolate."

"Mightly queer specimen she had this time," volunteered another. "Irish, hand off, straight as a ramrod, and something worthwhile in his face. Notice that hat peel off, and the eyes of him? There's a case of 'fight for her'! Wonder who he is?"

"I think," said a third, "that he's McLean's Limberlost guard, and I suspect she's gone to the swamp with the Bird Woman for pictures and knows him that way. I've heard that he is a master hand with the birds and that would just suit the Bird Woman to a T."

Out on the street the angel walked beside Freckles to the first crossing and there she stopped. "Now, will you promise to ride fast enough to make up for the five minutes that took?" she asked. "I am a little uneasy about Mrs. Duncan."

Freckles turned his bicycle into the street. It seemed to him he had poured that delicious, icy liquid into every vein in his body instead of his stomach. It even went to his brain.

"Did you insist on fixing that drink because you knew how intoxicating 'twould be?" he asked.

There was subtlety in the compliment and it delighted the angel. She laughed gleefully.

"Next time maybe you won't take so much coaxing," she teased.

"I wouldn't this, if I had known your father and been understanding you better. Do you really think the Bird Woman will be coming again?"

The angel jeered. "Wild horses couldn't drag her away," she cried. "She will have hard work to wait the week out. I shouldn't be in the least surprised to see her start any hour."

Freckles couldn't bear the suspense. It had to come. "And you?" he questioned, but he dared not lift his eyes.

"Wild horses me, too," she laughed. "Couldn't keep me away either! I dearly love to come, and the next time

I am going to bring my banjo, and I'll play, and you'll sing for me some of the songs I like best. Won't you?"

"Yes," said Freckles, because it was all he was capable of saying just then.

"It's beginning to act stormy," she said. "If you hurry you will just about make it. Now good-bye."

Chapter IX

WHEREIN THE LIMBERLOST FALLS UPON MRS.
DUNCAN AND FRECKLES COMES TO THE RESCUE

Freckles was halfway to the Limberlost when he dismounted. He could ride no farther, because he could not see the road. He sat down under a tree, and, leaning against it, burst into a storm of sobs that shook, twisted, and rent him. If they would remind him of his position, speak condescendingly, or notice his hand, he could bear it, but this—it would surely kill him! His hot, pulsing Irish blood could not bear it. What did they mean? Why did they do it? Were they like that to everyone? Was it pity?

It could not be, for he knew that the Bird Woman and the angel's father must know that he was not really McLean's son and it did not matter to them in the least. In spite of accident and poverty, they evidently expected him to do something worthwhile in the world. That

142

must be his remedy. He must go to work on his education. He must get away. He must find and do the great
thing of which the angel talked. For the first time his
thoughts turned anxiously toward the city and the beginning of his studies. McLean and the Duncans spoke
of him as "the boy," but he was a man. He must face life
bravely and act a man's part. The angel was a mere
child. He must not allow her to torture him past bearing
with her frank comradeship that meant to him high
heaven, earth's richness, and all that lay between, and
just *nothing* to her.

There was an ominous growl of thunder, and,
amazed at himself, Freckles snatched up his bicycle and
raced for the swamp. He was worried to find his boots
lying at the cabin door; the children playing on the
woodpile told him that mither said they were so heavy
she couldn't walk in them, and she had come back and
taken them off. Thoroughly frightened, he stopped only
long enough to slip them on himself, and then sped
with all his strength for the Limberlost. To the west, the
long, black, hardbeaten rail lay clear, but far up the east
side, straight across the path, he could see what was
certainly a limp, brown figure. Freckles pedaled with all
his might.

Face down, Sarah Duncan lay across the trail. When
Freckles turned her over, his blood chilled at the look of
horror frozen on her face. There was a low humming
and something spatted against him. Glancing about,
Freckles shivered in terror, for there was a swarm of
wild bees settled on a scrub thorn only a few yards
away. The air was thick with excited, unsettled bees

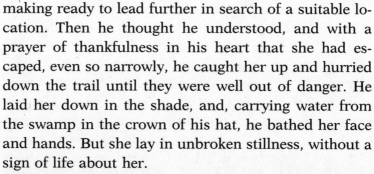

making ready to lead further in search of a suitable location. Then he thought he understood, and with a
prayer of thankfulness in his heart that she had escaped, even so narrowly, he caught her up and hurried
down the trail until they were well out of danger. He
laid her down in the shade, and, carrying water from
the swamp in the crown of his hat, he bathed her face
and hands. But she lay in unbroken stillness, without a
sign of life about her.

She had found Freckles' boots so large and heavy that
she had gone back and taken them off, although she
was mortally afraid to approach the swamp without
them. The thought of it made her nervous, and the fact
that she had never been there alone added to her fears.
She had not followed the trail many rods when her
trouble began. She was not Freckles, and not a bird of
the line was going to be fooled into thinking she was.

They kept whizzing from their nests and darting from
all sorts of unexpected places about her head and feet,
with quick whirrs that kept her starting and jumping.
Before Freckles was halfway to the town, poor Mrs.
Duncan was hysterical, and the Limberlost had neither
sung nor performed for her.

But there was trouble brewing. It was still and intensely hot, with that stifling stillness that precedes a
summer storm, and feathers and fur were tense and
nervous. The birds were singing only a few broken
snatches, and flying about, seeking places of shelter.
One moment everything seemed devoid of life, the next
there was an unexpected whirr, buzz, and sharp cry.

Inside, a pandemonium of growling, spatting, snarling, and grunting broke loose.

The swale bent flat before heavy gusts of wind, and the big black chicken swept lower and lower over the swamp. Patches of clouds gathered, shutting out the sun and making it very dark, and the next moment were swept away. The sun poured down with fierce, burning brightness, and everything was still. It was at the first growl of thunder that Freckles had really noticed the weather, and putting his own troubles aside resolutely, raced for the swamp.

Sarah Duncan paused on the line. "Weel, I wouldna stay in this place for a million a month," she said aloud, and the sound of her voice brought no comfort, for it was so little like she had thought it that she glanced hastily about to see if it had really been she that spoke. She tremblingly wiped the perspiration from her face with the skirt of her sunbonnet.

"Awfu' hot," she panted huskily. "B'lieve there's going to be a big storm. I do hope Freckles will hurry."

Her chin was quivering like a terrified child's. She lifted her bonnet to replace it and brushed it against a bush beside her. *Whirr*, almost into her face, went a big nighthawk stretched along a limb for its daytime nap. Mrs. Duncan cried out and sprang down the trail, light-ing on a frog that was just hopping across. The horrible croak it gave as she crushed it sickened her. She screamed wildly and jumped to one side. That carried her into the swale, where the grasses reached nearly to her waist, and, her horror of snakes returning, she made a flying leap for an old log lying along the line.

She lit on it squarely, but it was so damp and rotten that she sank straight through it to her knees. She caught at the wire as she went down, and, missing, raked her wrist over a barb until she laid it open in a bleeding gash. Her fingers closed convulsively around the second strand. She was too frightened to scream now. Her tongue stiffened. She clung frantically to the sagging wire, and finally managed to grasp it with the other hand. Then she could reach the top wire, and so she drew herself up and found solid footing. In order to extricate herself, she picked up the club that she had dropped. Leaning heavily on it, she managed to get back to the trail, but she was trembling so that she could scarcely walk. Going a few steps farther, she came to the stump of the first tree that had been taken out.

She sat bolt upright and very still, trying to collect her thoughts and reason off her terror. A squirrel above her dropped a nut, and as it came rattling down, bounding from branch to branch, every nerve in her tugged wildly. When the disgusted squirrel barked loudly, she sprang to the trail.

The wind rose higher, the changes from light to darkness were more abrupt, and the thunder came nearer and louder at every peal. In swarms the blackbirds rose from the swale and came flocking to the interior, with a clamoring cry, *"T'check, t'check."* Grackles marshaled to their tribal call, *"Trall-a-hee, trall-a-hee."* Red-winged blackbirds swept low, calling to belated mates, *"Fol-low-me, fol-low-me."* Huge, jetty crows gathered about her, crying, as if warning her to flee before it was everlastingly too late. A heron, fishing the nearby pool for Freckles' "find out" frog, fell into trouble with a muskrat and let out a rasping note that sent Mrs. Duncan a rod down the line without realizing that she had moved. She was too shaken to run far. She stopped and looked fearfully around her.

Several bees struck her and were angrily buzzing about before she noticed them. Then the humming swelled to a roar on all sides. A great, convulsive sob shook her, and she ran into the bushes, now into the swale, anywhere to avoid the swarming bees, ducking, dodging, fighting for her very life. Presently the humming seemed to grow a little fainter. She found the trail again, and ran with all her might from a few of her angry pursuers.

And as she ran, straining every muscle, she suddenly became aware that crossing the trail before her was a great, round black body, with brown markings on its back, like painted geometrical patterns. She tried to stop, but the louder buzzing behind warned her she dared not. Gathering her skirts still higher, with hair flying about her face and her eyes almost bursting from their sockets, she ran straight toward it. The sound of her feet and the humming of the bees alarmed the rattler, and it stopped squarely across the trail, lifting its head above the grasses of the swale and rattling inquiringly—rattled until the bees were outdone.

Straight at it went the panic-stricken woman, running wildly and uncontrollably. She took one great leap, clearing its body on the path, and then flew on with winged feet. The snake, coiling to strike, missed Mrs.

Duncan and landed among the bees instead. They settled over and about it, and realizing that it had found
trouble, it sank among the grasses and went threshing
toward the deep willow-fringed low ground where its
den was, until the swale looked as if a mighty reaper
were cutting a wide swath. The mass of enraged bees
darted angrily about, searching for it, and, colliding
with the scrub thorn, began a temporary settling there
to discover whether it was a suitable place. Completely
exhausted, Mrs. Duncan staggered on a few steps farther, fell face down on the path, where Freckles found
her, and lay still.

Freckles worked with her until she drew a long
quivering breath and opened her eyes.

When she saw him bending over her, she closed them
tightly, and gripping him, struggled to her feet. He
helped her up, and with his arm about and half carrying
her, they made their way to the clearing. She clung to
him and helped herself with all her remaining strength,
but open her eyes she would not until her children
came clustering about her. Then, brawny, big Scots-
woman though she was, she quietly keeled over again.
The children added their wailing to Freckles' panic.

This time he was so near the cabin that he could
carry her into the house and lay her on the bed. He sent
the oldest boy scudding down the corduroy for the
nearest neighbor, and between them they undressed her
and discovered that she was not bitten. They bathed
and bound up the bleeding wrist and coaxed her back to
consciousness. She lay sobbing and shuddering. The
first intelligent word she said was, "Freckles, look at

that jar on the kitchen table and see if my yeast is no running ower."

Several days went by before she could give Duncan and Freckles any detailed account of what had happened to her, and then she could not do it without crying like the youngest of her babies. Freckles was almost heartbroken and nursed her as well as any woman could have done, while big Duncan, with a heart full for them both, worked early and late to chink every crack about the cabin and examine every spot near it that could possibly harbor a snake. The effects of her morning on the trail kept her shivering half the time. She could not rest until she sent for McLean and begged him to save Freckles from further risk in that place of horrors. The boss went down to the swamp with his mind fully made up to do so.

Freckles stood and laughed at him. "Why, Mr. McLean, don't you let a woman's nervous system set you worrying over me," he said. "I'm not denying how she felt, because I've been through it meself, but that's all over and gone. It's the height of me glory to fight it out with the old swamp, and all that's in it, or will be coming to it, and then to turn it over to you as I promised you and meself I'd do, sir. You couldn't break the heart of me entire quicker than to be taking it from me now, when I'm just on the homestretch. It won't be over three or four weeks yet, and when I've gone it almost the year, why, what's that to me, sir? You mustn't let a woman get mixed up with business, for I've always heard about how it's bringing trouble."

McLean smiled. "What about that last tree?" he said.

Freckles blushed and grinned appreciatively.

"Angels and bird women don't count in the common run, sir," he affirmed, shamelessly.

McLean lay back in the saddle and laughed.

Chapter X

WHEREIN FRECKLES STRIVES MIGHTILY AND THE
SWAMP ANGEL REWARDS HIM

The Bird Woman and the angel did not seem to count in the common run, for they arrived on time for the third of the series and found McLean on the line talking to Freckles. The boss was filled with enthusiasm over a marsh article of the Bird Woman's that he had just read. He begged to be allowed to accompany her into the swamp and watch the method by which she secured an illustration in such a location.

The Bird Woman explained to him that it was an easy matter with the subject she then had in hand. And, since Little Chicken was too small to be frightened by him, and big enough to be getting troublesome, she was glad of his company. They went to the chicken log together, leaving to the happy Freckles the care of the angel, who had brought her banjo and a roll of songs

151

that she wanted to hear him sing. The Bird Woman told them that they might go to Freckles' room and practice until she finished with Little Chicken, and then she and McLean would come to the concert.

It was almost three hours before they finished and came down the west trail for their rest and lunch in Freckles' room. McLean walked ahead, keeping sharp watch on the trail and clearing it of fallen limbs from overhanging trees. He sent a big piece of bark flying into the swale, and then stopped short and stared down at the trail.

The Bird Woman bent forward. Together they studied that imprint of the angel's foot. At last their eyes met, the Bird Woman's filled with astonishment and McLean's wet with pity. Neither said a word, but they knew. McLean entered the swale and hunted up the bark. He tenderly replaced it and the Bird Woman carefully stepped over. As they reached the bushes at the entrance, the voice of the angel stopped them, for it was commanding and filled with impatience.

"Freckles James Ross McLean!" she was saying. "You fill me with dark-blue despair! You're singing as if your voice was glass and liable to break at any minute. Why don't you sing as you did a week ago? Answer me that, please."

Freckles smiled confusedly at the angel, who sat on one of his fancy seats, playing his accompaniment on her banjo.

"You are a fraud," she said. "Here you went last week and led me to think that there was the making of a great singer in you, and now you are singing—do you know how badly you are singing?"

"Yes," said Freckles meekly. "I'm thinking I'm too happy to be singing well today. The music don't come right only when I'm lonesome and sad. The world's for being all sunshine at prisint, for among you and Mr. McLean and the Bird Woman I'm after being *that* happy that I can't keep me thoughts on me notes. It's more than sorry I am to be disappointing you. Play it over, and I'll be beginning again, and this time I'll hold hard."

"Well," said the angel, disgustedly, "it seems to me that if I had all the things to be proud of that you have, I'd lift up my head and sing!"

"And what is it I've to be proud of, ma'am?" politely inquired Freckles.

"Why, a whole worldful of things," cried the angel, explosively. "For one thing, you can be good and proud over the way you've kept the timber thieves out of this lease, and the trust your father has in you. You can be proud that you've never even once disappointed him or failed in what he believed you could do. You can be proud over the way everyone speaks of you with trust and honor, and about how brave of heart and strong of body you are. I heard a big man say a few days ago that the Limberlost was full of disagreeable things—positive dangers, unhealthy as it could be, and that since the memory of the first settlers it has been a rendezvous for runaways, thieves, and murderers. This swamp is named for a man that got lost here and wandered around till he starved. That man I was talking with said he wouldn't take your job for a thousand dollars a

month—in fact, he said he wouldn't have it for any money, and you've never missed a day or lost a tree. Proud! Why, I should think you would just parade around about proper over that!

"And you can always be proud that you are born an Irishman. My father is Irish, and if you want to see him just get up and strut, give him a teeny opening to enlarge on his race. He says that if the Irish had decent territory they'd lead the world. He says they've always been handicapped by lack of space and of fertile soil. He says if Ireland had been as big and fertile as Indiana, why, England wouldn't ever have had the upper hand. She'd just be a little appendage. Fancy England an appendage! He says Ireland has the finest orators and the keenest statesmen in Europe today, and when England wants to fight, with whom does she fill her trenches? Irishmen, of course! Ireland has the greenest grass and trees, the finest stones and lakes, and they've jaunting cars. I don't know just exactly what they are, but Ireland has all there are, anyway. They've a lot of great actors, and a few singers, and there never was a sweeter poet than one of theirs. You should hear my father recite 'Dear Harp of My Country.' He does it this way."

The angel rose, made an elaborate old-time bow, and holding up the banjo, recited in clipping feet and meter, with rhythmic swing and a touch of brogue that was simply irresistible:

"Dear harp of my country" [*The angel ardently clasped the banjo*],

"In darkness I found thee" [*She held it up to the light*],

"The cold chain of silence had hung o'er thee long"
[*She muted the strings with her rosy palm*];

"Then proudly, my own Irish harp, I unbound thee"
[*She threw up her head and swept a ringing harmony*];

"And gave all thy chords to light, freedom, and song"
[*She crashed into the notes of the accompaniment she had been playing for Freckles*].

"That's what you want to be thinking of!" she cried. "Not darkness, and lonesomeness, and sadness, but 'light, freedom, and song.' I can't begin to think offhand of all the big, splendid things an Irishman has to be proud of, but whatever they are, they are all yours, and you are a part of them. I just despise that 'saddest-when-I-sing' business. You can sing! Now you go over there and do it! Ireland has had her statesmen, warriors, actors, and poets. Now you be her voice! You stand right out there before the cathedral door, and I'm going to come down the aisle playing that accompaniment, and when I stop in front of you—you sing!"

The angel's face wore an unusual flush. Her eyes were flashing and she was palpitating with earnestness.

She parted the bushes and disappeared. Freckles, straight as a young pine, and with the tenseness of a warhorse scenting battle, stood waiting. Presently, before he saw she was there, she was coming down the aisle toward him, playing compellingly, and rifts of light were touching her with golden glory. Freckles stood as if transfixed. The blood rioted in his veins.

The cathedral was majestically beautiful, from arched dome of frescoed gold, green, and blue in never-ending shades and harmonies, to the mosaic aisle she trod,

richly inlaid in choicest colors, and gigantic pillars that were God's handiwork fashioned and perfected down through ages of sunshine and rain. But the fair young face and divinely molded form of the angel were His most perfect work of all. Never had she looked so surpassingly beautiful. She was smiling encouragingly now, and as she came toward him, she struck the chords full and strong.

The heart of poor Freckles almost burst with dull pain and his great love for her. In his desire to fulfill her expectations he forgot everything else, and when she reached his initial chord he was ready. He literally burst forth:

> "Three little of Irish green,
>   United on one stem,
>   Love, truth, and valour do they mean
>   They form a magic gem."

The angel's eyes widened curiously and her lips fell apart. A heavier color swept into her cheeks. She had intended to arouse him. She had succeeded with a vengeance. She was too young to know that in the effort to rouse a man, women frequently kindle fires that they can neither quench nor control. Freckles was looking out over her head now and singing that song, as it had never been sung before, for her alone. And instead of her helping him, as she had intended, he was carrying her with him on the waves of his voice, away, away into a world she knew not of. When he struck into the chorus, wide-eyed and panting, she was swaying toward him and playing for dear life to keep up.

>"Oh, do you love? Oh, say you love,
>   You love the shamrock green!"

At the last note, Freckles' voice died away and his eyes fastened on the angel's. He had given his best and his all. He fell on his knees and folded his arms across his breast. The angel, as if magnetized, walked straight down the aisle to him, and running her fingers into the crisp masses of his red hair, tilted his head back and laid her lips on his forehead.

Then she stepped back and faced him. "Good boy!" she said, in a voice that wavered from the throbbing of her shaken heart. "Dear boy! I knew you could do it! I knew it was in you! Freckles, when you go out into the world, if you can face a great audience and sing like that, just once, you will be immortal, and anything you want will be yours."

"Anything!" gasped Freckles.

"Anything," said the angel.

Freckles found his feet, muttered something, and catching up his old bucket, plunged into the swamp blindly on a pretense of getting water. The angel walked slowly across the study and sat down on the rustic bench and, through narrowed lids, intently studied the tip of her shoe.

Out on the trail the Bird Woman wheeled on McLean with a dumbfounded look.

"God!" he muttered.

At last the Bird Woman spoke.

"Do you think the angel knew she did that?" she asked softly.

"No," said McLean, "I do not. But the poor boy knew it. Heaven help him!"

The Bird Woman stared across the gently waving swale. "I don't see how I am going to blame her," she said at last. "It is so exactly what I would have done myself."

"Say the rest," demanded McLean, hoarsely. "Do him justice."

"He is a born gentleman," conceded the Bird Woman. "He took no advantage. He never even offered to touch her. Whatever that kiss meant to him, he recognized that it was the loving impulse of a child under stress of strong emotion. He was fine and manly as any man ever could have been."

McLean lifted his hat. "Thank you," he said simply, and parted the bushes for her to enter Freckles' room.

It was her first visit and before she left she sent for her cameras and made studies of each side of it and of the cathedral. She was entranced with the delicate beauty of the place, and her eyes kept following Freckles as if she could not believe that it could be his conception and work.

That was a happy day. The Bird Woman had brought a lunch, and they spread it, with Freckles' dinner, on the study floor and sat about, resting and enjoying themselves. But the angel put her banjo into its case, silently gathered up her music, and no one mentioned the concert.

The Bird Woman left McLean and the angel to clear away the lunch and with Freckles examined the walls of his room and told him all she knew about his shrubs and flowers. She analyzed a cardinal flower and showed him what he had all summer wanted to know—why the bees buzzed ineffectually about it while the humming-birds found in it an ever ready feast. Some of his speci-mens were so rare that she was unfamiliar with them, and with the flower book between them they knelt, studying the different varieties. She wandered the length of the cathedral aisle with him and it was at her suggestion that he lighted his altar with a row of flam-ing foxfire.

As Freckles came up to the cabin from his long day at the swamp he saw Mrs. Chicken sweeping away to the south and wondered where she was going. He stepped into the bright, cozy little kitchen, and as he reached down the washbasin he asked Mrs. Duncan a question.

"Mother Duncan, do kisses wash off?"

So warm a wave swept her heart that a half-flush mantled her face. She straightened her shoulders and glanced down at her hands tenderly.

"Lord, na! Freckles," she cried. "At least, the anes ye get from people ye love dinna. They dinna stay on the outside. They strike in until they find the center of your heart and make their stopping place there, and nae-thing can take them from ye—I doubt if even death! Na, lad, ye can be reet sure kisses dinna wash off!"

Freckles set the basin down and muttered as he plunged his hot, tired face into the water, "I needn't be afraid to be washing, then, for that one struck in."

Chapter XI ──────────────────────────

"I wish," said Freckles at breakfast one morning, "that I had some way to be sending a message to the Bird Woman. I've something down at the swamp that I'm believing never happened before, and surely she'll be wanting it."

"What now, Freckles?" asked Mrs. Duncan.

"Why, the oddest thing you ever heard of," said Freckles. "The whole insect tribe gone on a spree. I'm supposing it's my fault, but it all happened by accident, like. You see, on the swale side of the line, right against me trail, there's one of these scrub wild crab trees. Where the grass grows thick about it, is the finest place you ever conceived of for snakes. Having women about has set me trying to clean out those fellows a bit, and yesterday I noticed that tree in passing. It struck me that it would be a good idea to be taking it out. First I thought I'd take me hatchet and cut it down, for it ain't thicker than me upper arm. Then I remembered how it was blooming in the spring and filling all the air with sweetness. The coloring of the blossoms is beautiful and I hated to be killing it. I just cut the grass short all about it. Then I started at the ground, trimmed up the trunk near the height of me shoulder, and left the top spreading. That made it look so truly ornamental that, idle like, I chips off the rough places neat, and this morning, on me soul, it's a sight! You see, cutting off the limbs and trimming up the trunk sets the sap running. In this hot sun it ferments in a few hours. There isn't much room for more things to crowd on that tree than there are, and to get drunker isn't noways possible."

"Weel, I be drawed on!" exclaimed Mrs. Duncan. "What kind of things do ye mean, Freckles?"

"Why, just an army of black ants. Some of them are sucking away like old topers. Some of them are setting up on their tails and hind legs, fiddling away with their forefeet and wiping their eyes. Some are rolling around on the ground, contented. There are quantities of big blue-bottle flies over the bark and hanging on the grasses about, too drunk to steer a course flying; so they just buzz away like flying, and all the time sitting still. The snake feeders are too full to feed anything—even more sap to themselves. There's a lot of hard-backed bugs—beetles, I guess—colored like the brown, blue, and black of a peacock's tail. They hang on until the legs of them are so weak they can't stick a minute longer, and then they break away and fall to the ground.

They just lay there on their backs, feebly clawing air.
When it wears off a bit, up they get and go crawling
back for more, and they so full they bump into each
other and roll over. Sometimes they can't climb the tree
until they wait to sober up a little. There's a lot of big
black-and-gold bumblebees, done for entire, stumbling
over the bark and rolling on the ground. They just lay
there on their backs, rocking from side to side, singing
to themselves like fat, happy babies. The wild bees keep
up a steady buzzing with the beating of their wings.

"The butterflies are the worst old topers of them all.
They're just a circus! You never saw the beat of the
beauties! They come every color you could be naming,
and every shape you could be thinking up. They drink
and drink until, if I'm driving them away, they stagger
as they fly and turn somersaults in the air. If I leave
them alone they cling to the grasses, shivering happy
like; and I'm blest, Mother Duncan, if the best of them
could be unlocking the front door with a lead pencil,
even."

"I never heard of anything sae surprising," said Mrs.
Duncan.

"It's a rare sight to watch them, and no one ever made
a picture of a thing like that before, I'm for thinking,"
said Freckles, earnestly.

"Na," said Mrs. Duncan. "Ye can be pretty sure there
didna. The Bird Woman must have word in some way,
if ye walk the line and I walk to town and tell her. If ye
think ye can wait until after supper, I am most sure ye
can gang yoursel', for Duncan is coming home and he'd
be glad to watch for ye. If he does na come, and na ane

passes that I can send word with today, I really will gang early in the morning and tell her mysel'."

Freckles took his lunch and went down to the swamp. He walked and watched eagerly. He could find no trace of anything, yet he felt a tense nervousness, as if trouble might be brooding. He examined every section of the wire, and kept watchful eyes on the grasses of the swale, in an effort to discover if anyone had passed through them. But he could discover no trace of anything to justify his fears.

He tilted his hat brim to shade his face and looked up for his chickens. They were both hanging almost out of sight in the sky.

"Gee!" he said. "If I only had your sharp eyes and convenient location now, I wouldn't need be troubling so."

He came around to his room and cautiously scanned the entrance before he stepped in. Then he pushed the bushes apart with his right arm and entered, his left hand on the butt of his favorite revolver. Instantly he knew that someone had been there. He stepped to the center of the room, closely scanning each wall and the floor. He could find no trace of a clue to confirm his belief, yet so intimate was he with the spirit of the place that he knew.

How he knew he could not have told, yet he did know that someone had entered his room, sat on his benches, and walked over his floor. He was most sure about the case. Nothing was disturbed, yet it seemed to Freckles that he could see where prying fingers had tried the lock. He stepped back of the case, carefully examining

the ground all about it, and close by the tree to which it was nailed he found a deep, fresh footprint in the spongy soil—a long, narrow print that was never made by the foot of Wessner. His heart tugged in his breast as he mentally measured the print, but he did not linger for now the feeling rose that he was being watched. It seemed to him he could feel the eyes of some intruder boring into his back. He knew he was examining things too closely. If anyone were watching he did not want him to know that he felt it.

He took the most open way, and carried water for his flowers and moss as usual, but he put himself into no position in which he was fully exposed, and his hand was near his revolver constantly. Growing restive at last under the strain, he plunged boldly into the swamp and searched minutely all about his room, but he could not discover the least thing to give him further cause for alarm. He unlocked his case, took out his bicycle and for the rest of the day he rode and watched as he never had before. Several times he locked up the wheel and crossed the swamp on foot, zigzagging to cover all the space possible. Every rod he traveled he used the caution that sprang from knowledge of danger and the direction from which it would probably come. Several times he thought of sending for McLean, but for his life he could not make up his mind to do it with nothing more tangible than one footprint to justify him.

He waited until he was sure Duncan would be at home, if he were coming for the night, before he went up to supper. The first thing he saw as he crossed the swale was the big bays in the yard.

There had been no one passing that day, and Duncan readily agreed to watch until Freckles rode to town. He told Duncan of the footprint, and urged him to watch closely. Duncan said he might rest easy, and, filling his pipe and taking a good revolver, the big man went down to the Limberlost.

Freckles made himself clean and neat and raced for town, but it was night and the stars were shining before he reached the home of the Bird Woman. From afar he could see that the house was ablaze with lights. When he reached the gate, the lawn and veranda were strung with fancy lanterns and alive with people. He thought his errand important, and to turn back never occurred to Freckles. This was all the time or opportunity he would have. He must see the Bird Woman, and see her now. He leaned his wheel inside the fence and walked up the broad front entrance. As he neared the steps he saw that the place was swarming with young people, and the angel, with an excuse to a group that surrounded her, came hurrying up to him.

"Oh, Freckles!" she cried delightedly. "So you could get off? We were so afraid you could not! I'm as glad as I can be!"

"I don't understand," said Freckles. "Were you expecting me?"

"Why, of course!" exclaimed the angel. "Haven't you come to my party? Didn't you get my invitation? I sent you one."

"By mail?" asked Freckles.

"Yes," said the angel. "I had to help with the preparations, and I couldn't find time to drive out. But I wrote you a letter and told you that the Bird Woman was giving a party for me, and we wanted you to come, sure. I told them at the office to put it with Mr. Duncan's mail."

"Then that's likely where it is at present," said Freckles. "Duncan only comes to town once a week, and at times not that. He's home tonight for the first in a week. He's watching an hour for me until I was coming to the Bird Woman with a bit of work I thought she'd be caring to hear about bad. Is she where I can see her?"

The angel's face clouded.

"What a disappointment!" she cried. "I did so want all my friends to know you. Can't you stay anyway?"

Freckles glanced from his wading boots to the patent leathers of some of the angel's friends nearby and smiled whimsically, but there was no danger of his ever misjudging her again.

"You know I cannot, Angel," he said.

"I am afraid I do," she said ruefully. "It's too bad! But there is a thing I want for you more than to come to my party, and that is to hang on and win with your work. I think of you every day, and I just pray that those thieves are not getting ahead of you. Oh, Freckles, do watch closely!"

She was so lovely a picture as she stood before him, ardent in his cause, that Freckles could not take his eyes from her to notice what her friends were thinking. If she did not mind, why should he? Anyway, if they really were the angel's friends, they were probably better accustomed to her ways than he.

Her face and bared neck and arms were like the wild-rose bloom. Her soft frock of white tulle lifted and stirred about her with the gentle evening air. The beautiful golden hair, which crept about her temples and ears as if it loved to cling there, was caught back and bound with a broad blue satin ribbon. There was a sash of blue wrapped about her waist, and knots of it catching up her draperies.

"Must I go for the Bird Woman?" she pleaded.

"Indeed, you must," answered Freckles, firmly.

The angel went away, but returned to say that the Bird Woman was telling a story to those inside and she could not come for a short time.

"You won't come in?" she pleaded.

"I must not," said Freckles. "I am not dressed to be among your friends, and I might be forgetting meself and stay too long."

"Then," said the angel, "we mustn't go through the house, because it would disturb the story; but I want you to come around the outside way to the conservatory and have some of my birthday lunch and get some cake to take to Mrs. Duncan and the babies. Won't that be fun?"

Freckles thought that it would be more than fun and followed delightedly.

The angel gave him a big glass, brimming with some icy, sparkling liquid that struck his palate as it had never been touched before, because a combination of frosty fruit juices had not been a frequent beverage with him. The night was warm and the angel most beautiful and kind. A sort of triple delirium of spirit, mind, and body seized upon him and developed a boldness all un-

natural. He slightly parted the heavy curtains that separated the conservatory from the company and looked in. He almost stopped breathing. He had read of things like that, but he had never seen them.

The open space seemed to stretch away through half a dozen rooms, all ablaze with lights, perfumed with flowers, and filled with elegantly dressed people. There were glimpses of polished floors, sparkling glass, and fine furnishings. From somewhere, the voice of his beloved Bird Woman rose and fell.

The angel crowded up beside him and was watching also.

"Doesn't it look pretty?" she whispered.

"Do you suppose Heaven is any finer than that?" asked Freckles.

The angel burst into a laugh.

"Do you want to be laughing harder than that?" queried Freckles.

"A laugh is always good," said the angel. "A little more won't hurt me. Go ahead."

"Well, then," said Freckles, "it's only that I feel all over as if I belonged in there. I could wear fine clothes, and move over those floors, and hold me own against the best of them."

"But where does my laugh come in?" demanded the angel, as if she had been defrauded.

"And you ask me where the laugh comes in, looking me in the face after that," marveled Freckles.

"I wouldn't be so foolish as to laugh at such a manifest truth as that," said the angel. "Anyone that knows you even half as well as I do knows that you are never guilty of a discourtesy, and you move with twice the grace of any man here. Why shouldn't you feel as if you belonged where people are graceful and courteous?"

"On me soul!" said Freckles. "You are kind to be thinking it. You are doubly kind to be saying it."

The curtains parted and a woman came toward them. Her silks and laces trailed along the polished floors. The lights gleamed on her neck and arms and flashed from rare jewels. She was smiling brightly and, until she spoke, Freckles had not fully realized that it was his loved Bird Woman.

Noticing his bewilderment, she cried, "Why, Freckles! Don't you know me in my war clothes?"

"I do in the uniform in which you fight the Limberlost," said Freckles.

The Bird Woman broke into a laugh. Then he told her why he had come and she could scarcely believe him. She could not say exactly when she would come, but she would make it as soon as possible, for she was most anxious for the study.

As they talked, the angel was busy packing a box of sandwiches, cake, fruit, and flowers. She gave him a last frosty glass, thanked him repeatedly for bringing news of new material, and then Freckles went out into the night. He rode for the Limberlost with his eyes on the stars. Presently he took off his hat, hung it to his belt, and ruffled his hair to the sweep of the night wind. He filled the air all the way with snatches of oratorios, gospel hymns, and dialect songs, in a startlingly varied pro-

gram. The one thing Freckles knew that he could do was to sing.

The Duncans heard him coming a mile up the corduroy and could not believe their senses. Freckles unfastened the box from his belt and gave Mrs. Duncan and the children all the eatables it contained, except one big piece of cake that he carried to the sweet-loving Duncan. He put the flowers back in the box and set it up among his books. He did not say anything, but they understood it was not to be touched.

"Thae's Freckles' flow'rs," said a tiny Scotsman, "but," he added cheerfully, "it's oor sweeties!"

Freckles slowly colored as he took Duncan's cake and started for the swamp. While Duncan ate, Freckles told him something about the evening, as well as he could find words to express himself, and the big man was so amazed he kept forgetting the treat in his hands.

Then Freckles mounted his bicycle and began a spin that terminated only when the biggest Plymouth Rock in Duncan's coop saluted a new day and long lines of light reddened the east. As he rode he sang, and as he sang he worshiped, but the god he tried to glorify was a dim and faraway mystery. The angel was warm flesh and blood.

Every time he passed the little bark-covered imprint on his trail he dismounted, removed his hat, solemnly knelt and laid his lips on the impression. Because he kept no account himself, only the laughing-faced old man of the moon knew how often it happened; and as from the beginning, to the follies of earth that gentleman ever has been kind.

With the near approach of dawn Freckles sang his last note. Wearied almost to falling, he turned from the trail into the path leading to the cabin for a few hours' rest.

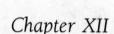

Chapter XII

WHEREIN BLACK JACK CAPTURES FRECKLES AND
THE ANGEL CAPTURES JACK

As Freckles left the trail from the swale near the
south entrance, four large, muscular men rose up
and swiftly and carefully entered the swamp by the
wagon road. Two of them carried a big saw, the third,
coils of rope and wire, and all of them were heavily
armed. They left one man on guard at the entrance. The
other three made their way through the darkness as
best they could and were soon at Freckles' room. He
had left the swamp on his bicycle from the west trail.
They counted on his returning on the bicycle and circling the east line before he came there.

A little below the west entrance to Freckles' room,
Black Jack stepped into the swale and binding a wire
tight about a scrub oak, carried it below the waving
grasses, stretched it taut across the trail, and fastened it

to a tree in the swamp. Then he obliterated all signs of his work, and arranged the grass over the wire until it was so completely covered that only minute examination would reveal it. They entered Freckles' room with coarse oaths and jests. In a few moments, his specimen case with its precious contents was rolled back into the swamp, and the saw was eating into one of the finest trees of the Limberlost.

The first report from the man on watch was that Duncan had driven away to the south camp. The second, that Freckles was coming. The man watching was sent back to see on which side the boy turned into the path. And, as they had expected, he took the east. He was a little tired and his head was rather stupid, for he had not been able to sleep as he had hoped, but he was very happy. Though he watched until his eyes ached, he could see no sign of anyone's having entered the swamp.

He called a cheery greeting to all his chickens. At Sleepy Snake Creek he almost fell from his bicycle with surprise: the saw-bird was surrounded by four lanky youngsters clamoring for breakfast. The father was strutting with all the importance of a drum major.

"No use to expect the Bird Woman today," said Freckles, "but now wouldn't she be jumping for a chance at that?"

As soon as Freckles was well down the east line, the watch was posted below the room on the west to report his coming. It was but a few moments before the signal came. Then the saw stopped, and the rope was brought out and uncoiled near a sapling. Wessner and Black

Jack crowded to the very edge of the swamp a little above the wire and crouched, waiting.

They heard Freckles before they saw him. He came clipping down the line at a good pace, and as he rode he was singing softly:

> "Oh, do you love,
> Oh, say you love—"

He got no further. The sharply driven wheel struck the tense wire and bounded back. Freckles shot over the handlebar and coasted down the trail on his chest. As he struck, Black Jack and Wessner were upon him. Wessner caught off an old felt hat and clapped it over Freckles' mouth, while Black Jack twisted his arms back of him and they rushed him into his room. Almost before he realized that anything had happened, he was trussed up to a tree and securely gagged.

Then three of the men resumed work on the tree. The other followed the path Freckles had worn to Little Chicken's tree, and presently he reported that the wires were down and two teams with the loading apparatus coming to take out the timber. All the time the saw was slowly eating, eating into the big tree.

Wessner went out to the trail and removed the wire. He picked up Freckles' bicycle, which did not seem to be injured, and leaned it against the bushes so that if anyone did pass on the trail he would not see it doubled up in the swamp grass.

Then he came and stood in front of Freckles and laughed in devilish hate. To his own amazement, Freckles found himself looking fear in the face, and marveled that he was not afraid. Four to one! The tree halfway eaten through, the wagons coming up the inside road—he, bound and gagged! The men with Black Jack and Wessner had belonged to McLean's gang when last he had heard of them, but who those coming with the wagons might be he could not guess.

If they secured that tree, McLean lost its value, lost his wager, and lost his faith in him. The words of the angel hammered in his ears. "Oh, Freckles, do watch closely!"

And the saw ate on.

When the tree was down and loaded, what would they do? Pull out and leave him there to report them? It was not to be hoped for. The place had always been lawless. It could mean but one thing.

A mist swept before his eyes and his head swam. Was it only last night that he had worshiped the angel in a delirium of happiness? And now, what? Wessner, released from a turn at the saw, walked over to the flowerbed and, tearing up a handful of rare ferns by the roots, started toward Freckles. His intention was obvious. Black Jack stopped him with an oath.

"You see here, Dutchy," he bawled, "mebby you think you'll wash his face with that, but you won't. A contract's a contract. We agreed to take out these trees and leave him for you to dispose of whatever way you please, provided you shut him up eternally on this deal. But I'll not see a tied man tormented by a fellow that he can lick up the ground with, loose, and that's flat. It raises my gorge to think what he'll get when we're gone, but you needn't think you're free to begin before. Don't you lay a hand on him while I'm here! What do you say, boys?"

"I say yes," growled one of McLean's latest deserters. "What's more, we're a pack of fools to risk the dirty work of silencing him. You had him face down and you on his back. Why the hell didn't you cover his head and roll him back into the bushes until we were gone? When I went into this, I didn't understand that he was to see all of us and that there was murder on the ticket. I'm not up to it. I don't mind lifting the trees we came for, but I'm cursed if I want blood on my hands."

"Well, you ain't going to get it," bellowed Jack. "You fellows only contracted to help me get out my marked trees. He belongs to Wessner and it ain't in our deal what happens to him."

"Yes, and if Wessner finishes him safely, we are practically in for murder as well as stealing the trees. And if he don't, all hell's to pay. I think you've made a damnable bungle of this thing; that's what I think!"

"Then keep your thoughts to yourself," roared Jack. "We're doing this, and it's all planned safe and sure. As for killing that buck—come to think of it, killing is what he needs. He's away too good for this world of woe, anyhow. I tell you, it's all safe enough. His dropping out won't be the only secret the old Limberlost has never told. It's too dead easy to make it look like he helped take the timber and then cut. Why, he's played right into our hands. He was here at the swamp all last night, and back again in an hour or so. When we get our plan worked out, even old fool Duncan won't lift a finger to

look for his carcass. We couldn't have him going in better shape."

"You just bet," said Wessner. "I owe him all he'll get,
and be damned to you, but I'll pay!" he snarled at
Freckles.

So it was killing, then. They were not only after this
one tree, but many, and with his body it was their plan
to kill his honor. To brand him a thief, like them, before
the angel, the Bird Woman, the dear boss, and the Duncans—Freckles' body sagged against the ropes in sick
despair.

Then he gathered his forces and thought swiftly.
There was no hope of McLean's coming. They had chosen a day when they knew he had a big contract at the
south camp. The boss could not possibly come before
tomorrow, and there would be no tomorrow for him.
Duncan was on his way to the south camp, and the Bird
Woman had said she would come as soon as she could.
After the fatigue of the party, it was useless to expect
her and the angel today, and God save them from coming! The angel's father had said they would be as safe in
the Limberlost as at home. What would he say to this?

The sweat broke out on Freckles' forehead. He tugged
at the ropes whenever he felt that he dared, but they
were passed about the tree and his body several times,
and knotted on his chest. He was helpless. There was no
hope, no help. And after they had conspired to make
him appear a runaway thief to his loved ones, what was
it that Wessner would do to him?

Whatever it was, Freckles lifted his head and resolved
that he would bear in mind what he had once heard the

Bird Woman say. He would go out bonnily. Never
would he let them see if he grew afraid. After all, what
did it matter what they did to his body if by some
scheme of the devil they could compass his disgrace?

Then hope suddenly rose high in Freckles' breast.
They could not do that! The angel would not believe.
Neither would McLean. He would keep up his courage.
Kill him they could; dishonor him they could not.

Yet, summon all the fortitude he might, that saw eating into the tree rasped his nerves worse and worse.
With whirling brain he gazed off into the Limberlost,
searching for something, he knew not what, and in
blank horror found his eyes fastened on the angel. She
was quite a distance away, but he could see her white
lips and wide, angry eyes.

Last week he had taken her and the Bird Woman
across the swamp over the path he followed in going in
from his room to the chicken tree. He had told them
last night that the butterfly tree was on the line close to
this path. In figuring on their not coming that day, he
failed to reckon with the enthusiasm of the Bird
Woman. They must be there for the study, and the angel
had risked crossing the swamp in search of him. Or was
there something in his room they needed? The blood
surged in his ears like the roar of the Limberlost in the
wrath of a storm.

He looked again, and it had been a dream. She was
not there. Had she been? For his life, Freckles could not
tell whether he had really seen the angel, or whether his
strained senses had played him the most cruel trick of

all. Or was it not the kindest? Now he could die with the vision of her lovely face fresh with him.

"Thank You for that, oh, God!" whispered Freckles. " 'Twas more than kind of You and I don't 'spose I ought to be wanting anything more. But if You can, oh, I wish I could know before this ends, if 'twas me mother"—Freckles could not even whisper the words, for he hesitated a second and ended—*"if 'twas me mother did it!"*

"Freckles! Freckles! Oh, Freckles!" the voice of the angel came calling. Freckles swayed forward and wrenched at the rope until it cut deeply into his body.

"Hell!" cried Black Jack. "Who is that? Do you know?" Freckles nodded.

Jack whipped out a revolver and snatched the gag from Freckles' mouth.

"Say quick, or it's up with you right now, and whoever that is with you!"

"It's the girl the Bird Woman takes about with her," whispered Freckles through dry, swollen lips.

"They ain't due here for five days yet," said Wessner. "We got on to that last week."

"Yes," said Freckles, "but I found a tree covered with butterflies and things along the east line yesterday that I thought the Bird Woman would want extra, and I went to town for her last night. She said she'd come soon, but she didn't say when. They must be here. I take care of the girl while the Bird Woman works. Untie me quick until she is gone. I'll try to send her back, and then you can go on with your dirty work."

"He ain't lying," volunteered Wessner. "I saw that tree

covered with butterflies and him watching around it
when we were spying on him yesterday."

"No, he leaves lying to your sort," snapped Black
Jack, as he undid the rope and pitched it across the
room. "Remember that you're covered every move you
make, my buck," he cautioned.

"Freckles! Freckles!" came the angel's impatient
voice, nearer and nearer.

"I must be answering," said Freckles, and Jack nodded. "Right here!" he called, and to the men: "You go on
with your work, and remember one thing yourselves.
The work of the Bird Woman is known all over the
world. This girl's father is a rich man, and she is all he
has. If you hurt either of them, this world has no place
far enough away nor dark enough for you to be hiding
in. Hell will be easy to what any man will get that
touches either of them!"

"Freckles, where are you?" demanded the angel.

Soul sick with fear for her, Freckles went toward her
and parted the bushes that she might enter. She came
through without apparently giving him a glance, and
the first words she said were, "Why have the gang come
so soon? I didn't know you expected them for three
weeks yet. Or is this some special tree that Mr. McLean
needs to fill an order right now?"

Freckles hesitated. Would a man dare lie to save himself? No. But to save the angel—surely that was different. He opened his lips, but the angel was capable of
saving herself. She walked in among them, exactly as if
she had been raised in a lumber camp, and never
waited for an answer.

"Why, your specimen case!" she cried. "Look! Haven't you noticed that it's tipped over? Set it straight, quickly!"

A couple of the men stepped out and carefully righted the case.

"There! That's better," she said. "Freckles, I'm surprised at your being so careless. It would be a shame to break those lovely butterflies for one old tree! Is that a valuable tree? Why didn't you tell us last night you were going to take a tree out this morning? Oh, say, did you put your case there to protect that tree from that stealing old Black Jack and his gang? I bet you did! Well, if that wasn't bright? What kind of a tree is it?"

"It's a golden oak," said Freckles.

"Like those they make dining tables and sideboards out of?"

"Yes."

"My! How interesting!" she cried. "I don't know a thing about timber, but my father wants me to learn about just everything I can. I am going to ask him to let me come here and watch you until I know enough to boss a gang myself. Do you like to cut trees, gentlemen?" she asked of the men, with angelic sweetness.

Some of them looked foolish and some grim, but one managed to say that they did.

Then the angel's eyes turned full on Black Jack, and she gave the most beautiful little start of astonishment.

"Oh! I almost thought that you were a ghost!" she cried. "But I see now that you are really and truly. Were you ever in Colorado?"

"No," said Jack.

"I see now you aren't the same man," said the angel. "You know, we were in Colorado last year, and there was a cowboy that was the handsomest man anywhere about. He'd come riding into town every night, and all we girls just adored him! Oh, but he was a beauty! I thought at first glance you were really he, but I see now he wasn't nearly so tall nor so broad as you, and only half as handsome."

The men burst into a roar of laughter and Jack flushed crimson. The angel joined in the laugh.

"Well, I'll leave it to you! Isn't he handsome?" she challenged. "As for that cowboy's face, it couldn't be compared with yours. The only trouble with you is that your clothes are spoiling you. It's the dress those cowboys wear that makes half their looks. If you were properly dressed, you could break the heart of the prettiest girl in the country."

With one accord the other men all focused on Black Jack, and for the first time realized that he was a superb specimen of manhood, for he stood six feet tall, was broad, well-rounded, and had dark, even skin, big black eyes, and full red lips.

"I'll tell you what!" exclaimed the angel. "I'd just love to see you on horseback. Nothing sets a handsome man off so splendidly. Do you ride?"

"Yes," said Jack, and his eyes were burning on the angel as if he would fathom the depths of her soul.

"Well," said the angel winsomely, "I know what I just wish you'd do. I wish you would let your hair grow a little longer. Then wear a blue flannel shirt a little open at the throat, a red tie, and a broad-brimmed felt hat, and ride past my house of evenings. I'm always at home then, and almost always on the veranda, and, oh! but I would like to see you! Will you do that for me?"

It is impossible to describe the art with which the angel put the question. She was looking straight into Jack's face, coarse and hardened with sin and careless living, which was now taking on a wholly different expression. The evil lines of it were softening and fading out under her clear gaze. A dull red flamed into his bronze cheeks, and his eyes were growing brightly tender.

"Yes," he said, and the glance he shot at the men was of such a nature that no one saw fit even to change countenance.

"Oh, goody!" she cried, tilting on her toes. "I'll ask all the girls to come to see, but they needn't stick in! We can get along without them, can't we?"

Jack leaned toward her. He was the charmed, fluttering bird, and the angel was the snake.

"Well, I rather guess!" he cried.

The angel drew a deep breath and looked him over rapturously.

"My! but you're tall!" she gurgled. "Do you suppose I will ever grow to reach your shoulders?"

She stood on tiptoe and measured the distance with her eyes. Then she fell into timid confusion, and her glance sought the ground.

"I wish I could do something," she half whispered.

Jack seemed to increase an inch in height.

"What?" he asked hoarsely.

"Lariat Bill used always to have a bunch of red flowers in his shirt pocket, and the red lit up his dark eyes and olive cheeks and made him splendid. May I put a bunch of red flowers on you?"

Freckles' eyes popped and he wheezed for breath. He wished that the earth would open and swallow him up. Was he dead or alive? Since his angel had set eyes on Black Jack she had never even glanced his way. Was she completely bewitched? Would she throw herself at the man's feet before them all? Couldn't she give him even one thought? Hadn't she seen that he was gagged and bound? Did she truly think that these were McLean's men? Why, she couldn't! It was only a few days ago that she had been near enough this man and angry enough with him to peel the hat from his head with a shot! Suddenly a thing she had jestingly said to him one day came back with startling force: "You must take angels on trust." Of course you must! She was his angel. She must have seen! His life, and what was far worse, her own, was in her hands. There was nothing he could do but trust her. Surely she was working out some plan.

The angel knelt beside his flowerbed and recklessly tore up by the roots a big bunch of foxfire.

"These stems are so tough and sticky," she said. "I can't break them. Loan me your knife," she ordered Freckles.

As she reached for the knife, her back was for one second toward the men. She looked into his eyes and deliberately winked.

She severed the stems, tossed the knife back to Freckles, and walking up to Jack, laid the flowers over his heart.

Freckles broke into a sweat of agony. He had said she would be safe in a herd of howling savages. Would she? If Black Jack even made a motion toward touching her, Freckles knew that from somewhere he would muster the strength to kill him. He mentally measured the distance to where his club lay and set his muscles for a spring. But no—by the splendor of God! The big fellow was baring his head with a hand that was unsteady. The angel pulled one of the long silver pins from her hat and fastened her flowers securely.

Freckles was quaking. What was to come next? What was she planning, and, oh! did she understand the danger of her presence among those men and the real necessity for action?

As the angel stepped back from Jack, she turned her head to one side and peered up at him, just as Freckles had seen the little yellow fellow do on the line a hundred times, and said, "Well, that does the trick! Isn't that fine? See how it sets him off, boys? Don't you forget the tie is to be red, and the first ride soon. I can't wait very long. Now I must go. The Bird Woman will be ready to start, and she will come here hunting me next, for she is busy today. What did I come here for anyway?"

She glanced inquiringly about, and several of the men laughed. Oh, the delight of it! She had forgotten her errand for him! Jack had a second increase in height. The angel glanced helplessly about as if seeking a clue. Then her eyes fell, as if by accident, on Freckles, and she cried, "Oh, I know now! It was those magazines the Bird Woman promised you. I came to tell you that we put them under the box where we hide things, at the

entrance to the swamp as we came in. I knew I should need my hands crossing the swamp, so I hid them there. You'll find them at the same old place."

Then Freckles spoke. "It's might risky for you to be crossing the swamp alone," he said. "I'm surprised that the Bird Woman would be letting you try it. I know it's a little farther, but it's begging you I am to be going back by the trail. That's bad enough, but it's far safer than by the swamp."

The angel laughed merrily. "Oh, stop your nonsense!" she cried. "I'm not afraid! Not in the least! The Bird Woman didn't want me to try following a path that I'd been over only once, but I was sure I could do it and I'm rather proud of the performance. Now, don't you go babying! You know I'm not afraid!"

"No," said Freckles gently, "I know you're not, but that has nothing to do with the fact that your friends are afraid for you. On the trail you can see your way a bit ahead, and you've all the world a better chance if you meet a snake."

Then Freckles had an inspiration. He turned to Jack imploringly.

"You tell her!" he pleaded. "Tell her to go by the trail. She will for you."

The implication of this statement was so gratifying to Black Jack that he seemed again to expand and take on magnitude before their very eyes.

"You bet!" exclaimed Jack. And to the angel: "You better take Freckles' word for it, Miss. He knows the old swamp better than any of us, except me, and if he says 'go by the trail,' you'd best do it."

The angel hesitated. She wanted to recross the swamp and try to get away on the horse. She knew Freckles would brave any danger to save her crossing the swamp alone, but she really was not afraid, and the trail added over a mile to the walk. She knew the path. She meant to run for dear life the instant she felt herself out of their sight, and tucked in the folds of her blouse was a fine little 32-caliber revolver that her father had presented her for her share in what he was pleased to call her millinery exploit. One last glance at Freckles showed her the agony in his eyes, and immediately she imagined he had some other reason. She would follow the trail.

"All right," she said, giving Jack a killing glance. "If you say so, I'll go back by the trail to please you. Goodbye, everybody."

She lifted the bushes and started for the entrance.

"You damned fool! Stop her!" growled Wessner. "Keep her till we're loaded, anyhow. You're playing hell! Can't you see that when this thing is found out, there she'll be to ruin all of us. If you let her go, every man of us has got to cut, and some of us will be caught sure."

Jack sprang forward. Freckles' heart muffled up in his throat. The angel seemed to divine Jack's coming. She was humming a little song. She deliberately stopped and began pulling the heads of the curious grasses that grew all about her. When she straightened, she took a step backward and called, "Ho! Freckles, the Bird Woman wants that natural history pamphlet returned. It belongs to a set she is going to have bound. That's one of the reasons we put it under the box. You be sure to

get them as you go home tonight, for fear it rains or gets damp with the heavy dews."

"All right," said Freckles, but it was in a voice that he had never heard before.

Then the angel turned and shot a parting glance at Jack, and she was overpoweringly human and bewitchingly lovely.

"You won't forget that ride and the red tie," she half asserted, half questioned.

Jack lost his head entirely. Freckles was his captive, but he was the angel's, soul and body. His face wore the holiest look it had ever known as he softly re-echoed Freckles' "all right." With her head held well up, the angel walked slowly away and Jack wheeled on the men.

"Drop your damned staring and saw wood," he shouted. "Don't you know anything at all about how to treat a lady?"

It might have been a question which of the crones that crouched over green-wood fires in the cabins of Wildcat Hollow, eternally sucking a corncob pipe and stirring the endless kettles of stewing coon and opossum, had taught him to do even as well as he had by the angel.

The men muttered and threatened among themselves, but they fell to working with a vengeance. Someone suggested that a man be sent to follow the angel and to watch her and the Bird Woman leave the swamp. Freckles' heart died within him, but Jack was in a delirium and past all caution.

"Yes," he sneered. "Mebby all of you had better give

over on the saw and run after the girl. I guess not!
Seems to me I got the favors. I don't see no bouquets on
the rest of you! If anybody follows her, I do, and I'm
needed here among such a pack of idiots. There's no
danger in that baby face. She wouldn't give me away!
You double and work like forty, and me and Wessner
will take the axes and begin to cut in on the other side."

"What about the noise?" asked Wessner.

"No difference about the noise," answered Jack. "She
took us to be from McLean's gang, slick as grease. Make
the chips fly!"

So all of them attacked the big tree.

Freckles sat down on one of his benches and waited.
In their haste to get the tree down and loaded, so that
the teamsters could start with it and leave them free to
attack another, they had forgotten to rebind him.

The angel was on the trail and safely started. The cold
perspiration made Freckles' temples clammy and ran in
little streams down his chest. It would take her a little
more time to go by the trail, but her safety was Freckles'
sole thought in urging her to go that way. He tried to
figure on how long it would take her to walk to the
carriage. He wondered if the Bird Woman had unhitched. He followed the angel every step of the way. He
figured on when she would cross the path of the clearing, pass the deep pool where his "find out" frog lived,
cross Sleepy Snake Creek, and reach the carriage.

He wondered what she would say to the Bird Woman,
and how long it would take them to pack and get
started. He knew now that they would understand, and
the angel would try to get the boss there in time to save

his wager. She could never do it, for the saw was more than half through, and Jack and Wessner cutting into the opposite side of the tree. It looked as if they could get at least that tree out before McLean could come, and if they did he lost his wager.

When it was down, would they rebind him and leave him for Wessner to wreak his insane vengeance on, or would they take him along to the next tree and dispose of him when they had stolen all the timber they could? Jack had said that he should not be touched until he left. Surely he would not run all that risk for one tree, when he had many others of far greater value marked. Freckles felt that he had some hope to cling to now, but he found himself praying that the angel would hurry.

Once Jack came over to Freckles and asked if he had any water. Freckles rose and showed him where he kept his drinking water. Jack drank in great gulps, and, as he passed the bucket back, he said, "When a man's got a chance of catching a fine girl like that, he ought not be mixed up in any dirty business. I wish to God I was out of this!"

Freckles answered heartily, "I wish I was, too!"

Jack stared at him a minute and then broke into a roar of rough laughter.

"Blest if I blame you," he said. "But you had your chance! We offered you a fair thing and you gave Wessner his answer. I ain't envying you when he gives you his."

"You're six to one," answered Freckles. "It will be easy enough for you to be killing the body of me, but, curse you all, you can't blacken me soul!"

"Well, I'd give anything you could name if I had your honesty," said Jack.

When the mighty tree fell, the Limberlost shivered and screamed with the echo. Freckles groaned in despair, but the gang took heart. That was so much accomplished. Now, if they could get it out quickly, they knew where to dispose of it safely, with no questions asked. Before the day was over, they could remove three others, all fit for veneer and worth far more than this. Then they would leave Freckles to Wessner and scatter for safety, with more money in their possession than they had ever dreamed of.

Chapter XIII ————————————————————

WHEREIN THE ANGEL RELEASES FRECKLES, AND
THE CURSE OF BLACK JACK FALLS UPON HER

On the line, the angel gave one backward glance at
Black Jack, to see that he had returned to his
work. Then she gathered her skirts above her knees and
leaped forward on the run. In the first three yards she
passed Freckles' bicycle. Instantly she imagined that
was why he had insisted on her coming by the trail. She
seized it and sprang on. The saddle was too high, but
she was an expert rider and could catch the pedals as
they came up. She stopped at Duncan's cabin long
enough to get out the wrench and lower the saddle, telling Mrs. Duncan the while what was happening and
that she must follow the east trail until she found the
Bird Woman, to tell her she had gone for McLean, and
to leave the swamp as quickly as possible.

Even with her fear for Freckles to spur her, Sarah

Duncan blanched and fell shivering at the idea of facing the Limberlost. The angel looked her in the eyes.

"No matter how afraid you are, you have to go," she said. "If you don't, the Bird Woman will go to Freckles' room, hunting me, and they will have trouble with her. If she isn't told to get out at once, they may follow me, and finding I'm gone, do some terrible thing to Freckles. I can't go—that's flat—for if they caught me, then there'd be no one to go for help. You don't suppose they are going to take out the trees they're after and then leave Freckles to run and tell? They are going to murder the boy; that's what they are going to do. You run, and run for life! For Freckles' life! You can ride back with the Bird Woman."

The angel saw Mrs. Duncan start off and then flew.

Those awful miles of corduroy! Would they never end? She did not dare use the bicycle too roughly, for if it broke she could never get there on time afoot. Where her way was impassable for the wheel, she jumped off, and, pushing it beside her or carrying it, she ran as fast as she could. The day was fearfully warm. The sun poured down with the fierce baking heat of August. The bushes claimed her hat, and she did not stop for it.

Where it was at all possible, the angel mounted and pounded over the corduroy again. She was panting for breath and almost worn out before she reached the level pike. She had no idea how long she had been—and only two miles covered. She leaned over the bars, almost standing on the pedals, racing with all the strength in her body. The blood surged in her ears and her head swam, but she kept a straight course, and rode

and rode. It seemed to her that she was standing still, and that the trees and houses were racing by her.

Once a farmer's big dog rushed angrily out into the road and she swerved until she almost fell, but she regained her balance and, setting her muscles, pedaled as hard as she could. At last she lifted her head. Surely it could not be over a mile more. She had covered two of corduroy and at least three of pike, and it was only six in all.

She was reeling in the saddle, but she gripped the bars with new energy and raced desperately. The sun blistered down on her bare head and hands. Just when she was choking with dust, and almost prostrate with heat and exhaustion—crash, she ran into a broken bottle. Snap! went the tire; the bicycle swerved and pitched over. The tired angel rolled into the thick yellow dust of the road and lay still.

From afar, Duncan began to notice a strange, dust-covered object in the road, as he headed for town with the first load of the day's felling.

He clucked to the bays and hurried them all he could. As he neared the angel, he saw it was a woman and a broken bicycle. He was beside her in an instant. He carried her to a shaded fence corner, stretched her on the grass, and wiped the dust from the lovely face all dirt-streaked, crimson, and bearing a startling whiteness about the mouth and nose.

Bicycles were common enough. Many of the farmers' daughters owned and rode them, but he knew these same farmers' daughters; this face was a stranger's. He glanced at the angel's tumbled clothing, the silkiness of her hair, with its pale satin ribbon, and noticed that she had lost her hat. His lips tightened in an ominous quiver. He left her and picked up the bicycle: as he had surmised, he knew it. This, then, was Freckles' swamp angel. There was trouble in the Limberlost, and she had broken down in racing for McLean. Duncan turned the bays into a fence corner, tied one of them, unharnessed the other, fastened up the trace chains, and hurried to the nearest farmhouse to send help to the angel. He found a woman, who took a bottle of camphor, a jug of water, and some towels, and started on the run.

Then Duncan put the bay to speed and raced for camp.

The angel, left alone, lay still for a second, then she shivered and opened her eyes. She saw that she was on the grass and the broken bicycle beside her. Instantly she realized that someone had carried her there and gone for help. She sat up and looked about. Her eyes fell on the load of logs and the one horse. Somebody was riding for help for her!

"Oh, poor Freckles!" she wailed. "They may be killing him by now. Oh, how much time have I wasted?"

She hurried to the other bay, and her fingers flew as she set him free. Snatching up a big blacksnake whip that lay on the ground, she caught the hames, stretched along the horse's neck, and, for the first time, the fine, big fellow felt on his back the quality of the lash that Duncan was accustomed to crack over him. He was frightened and ran at top speed.

The angel passed a wildly waving, screaming woman on the road, and a little later a man riding as if he, too,

were in great haste. The man called to her, but she only lay lower and slashed away harder with the whip. Soon the feet of the man's horse sounded farther and farther away.

At the south camp they were loading a second wagon when the angel thundered up on one of Duncan's bays, lathered and dripping, and cried, "Everybody go to Freckles! There are thieves stealing trees, and they have him bound. They're going to kill him!"

She wheeled the horse and headed back for the Limberlost. The alarm sounded over camp. The gang was not unprepared for it. McLean sprang to Nellie's back and raced after the angel. As they passed Duncan he wheeled and followed. Soon the pike was an irregular procession of barebacked riders, wildly driving flying horses toward the swamp.

The boss rode neck and neck with the angel. He repeatedly commanded her to stop and fall out of line, until he remembered that he would need her to lead him to Freckles. Then he gave up and rode beside her, for she was sending the bay at as sharp a pace as the other horses could keep and hold out. He could see that she was not hearing him. He glanced back and saw that Duncan was near. There was something terrifying in the look of the big man, and the way he sat his beast and rode. It would be a sad day for the man on whom Duncan's wrath broke. There were four others close behind him, and the pike filling up with the rest of the gang, so McLean took heart and raced beside the angel. Over and over he asked her where the trouble was, but he could get no reply. She only gripped the hames, leaned along the bay's neck, and slashed away with the blacksnake. The steaming horse, with crimson nostrils and heaving sides, stretched out and ran for home with all the speed there was in it.

When they passed the cabin, the Bird Woman's carriage was there and Mrs. Duncan in the door wringing her hands, but the Bird Woman was nowhere to be seen. The angel sent the bay along the path, and turned into the trail to the west, and the men bunched and followed her. When she reached the entrance to Freckles' room, there were four men with her, and two more very close behind. She slid from the horse, and, snatching the little revolver from her breast, darted for the bushes. McLean caught them back, and, with drawn weapon, pressed up beside her. There they stopped in astonishment.

The Bird Woman blocked the entrance. Over a small limb lay her revolver, and it was trained at short range on Black Jack and Wessner, who stood with their hands above their heads.

Freckles, with the blood streaming down his face, from an ugly cut in his temple, was gagged and bound to the tree again, and the rest of the men were gone. Black Jack was raving like a maniac, and when they looked closer it was only the left arm that he raised. His right, with the hand shattered, hung helpless at his side, and his revolver lay at Freckles' feet. Wessner's weapon was still in his belt, and beside him lay Freckles' club.

Freckles' face was of stony whiteness, with colorless lips, but in his eyes was the strength of undying cour-

age. McLean pushed past the Bird Woman, crying, "Hold steady on them for just one minute more!"

He snatched the revolver from Wessner's belt, and stooped for Jack's.

At that instant the angel rushed in. She tore the gag from Freckles, and, seizing the rope knotted on his chest, she tugged at it desperately. Under her fingers it gave way, and she hurled it to McLean. The men were crowding in, and Duncan seized Wessner. As the angel saw Freckles stand out, free, she reached her arms to him and pitched forward. A fearful oath burst from the lips of Black Jack. To have saved his life, Freckles could not have avoided the glance of triumph he gave Jack, as he folded his angel in his arms and stretched her on the mosses.

The Bird Woman cried out sharply for water as she ran to them. Somebody sprang for that, and another to break open the case for brandy. As McLean rose from binding Wessner, there was a cry that Black Jack was escaping.

He was already well into the swamp, working for its densest part and running in great leaping bounds. Every man that could be spared plunged after him.

Other members of the gang arrived and were sent to follow the tracks of the wagons. The teamsters had driven out of the west entrance and, crossing the swale, had taken the same route the Bird Woman and the angel had before them. There had been ample time for the drivers to reach the road, after which they could take any one of four directions. Traffic was heavy and lumber wagons were passing almost constantly, in all directions; so the men turned back and joined the more exciting hunt for a man. Other members of the gang were arriving, also farmers from along the pike and travelers attracted by the disturbance.

Watchers were set all about the trail at no great intervals, and they patrolled the line and roads through the swamp all that night, with lighted torches, and the next day McLean headed as thorough a search as he felt could be made of one side, while Duncan covered the other, but Black Jack could not be found. Spies were set about his home, in Wildcat Hollow, to ascertain if he reached there or aid was sent in any direction to him, but it was soon clear that his relatives were ignorant of his whereabouts and were themselves searching for him.

Great is the elasticity of youth. A hot bath and a sound night's sleep renewed Freckles' strength, and it needed but little more to work the same result with the angel. Freckles was on the trail early the next morning. Besides a crowd of people anxious to witness Jack's capture, he found four stalwart guards, one at each turn. In his heart he was compelled to admit that he was glad to have them there. Near noon, McLean turned his party over to join Duncan, and, taking Freckles, drove to town to see how it fared with the angel. McLean visited a greenhouse and bought an armload of its finest products, but Freckles would have none of them. He would carry his message in a glowing mass of the Limberlost's first goldenrod.

The Bird Woman received them and, in answer to their eager inquiries, said that the angel was in no way

seriously injured, only so bruised and shaken that their
doctor had ordered her to lie quietly for the day.
Though she was sore and stiff, they were having hard
work to keep her in bed. Her callers sent up their flowers with their grateful regards and the angel promptly
returned word that she wanted to see them.

She reached both hands to McLean. "What if one old
tree is gone? You don't care, sir? You feel that Freckles
has kept his trust as nobody ever did before, don't you?
You won't forget all those long first days of fright that
you told us of, the fearful cold of winter, the rain, heat,
and lonesomeness, and the brave days, and, lately,
nights, too, and let him feel that his trust is broken? Oh,
Mr. McLean," she begged, "say something to him! Do
something to make him feel that it isn't for nothing he
has watched and suffered it out with that old
Limberlost. Make him see how great and fine it is, and
how far, far better he has done than you or any of us
expected! What's one old tree, anyway?" she burst out
passionately.

"I was thinking before you came. Those two other
men were rank big cowards. They were scared for their
lives. If they were the drivers, I wager you gloves against
gloves they never took those logs out to the pike. My
coming upset them. Before you feel bad any more, you
go look and see if they didn't run out of courage the
minute they left Wessner and Black Jack, and dump
that timber and go on the run. I don't believe they ever
had the grit to drive out with it in daylight. Go see if
they didn't figure on going out the way we did the other
morning, and you'll find the logs before you strike the

road. They never risked taking them into the open,
when they got away and had time to think. Of course
they didn't!

"And, then, another thing. You haven't lost your wager! It will never be claimed, because you made it with a
stout, dark, red-faced man that drives a bay and a gray.
He was right back of you, Mr. McLean, when I came up
to you yesterday. He went deathly white and shook on
his feet when he saw those men would likely be caught.
Some one of them was something to him, and you can
just spot him for one of the men at the bottom of your
troubles, and urging those other younger fellows on to
steal from you. I suppose he'd promised to divide. You
settle with him and that business will stop."

She turned to Freckles. "And you be the happiest man
alive because you have kept your trust. Go look where I
tell you and you'll find the logs. I can just see about
where they are. When they go up that steep little hill,
into the next woods after the cornfield, why, they could
unloose the chains and the logs would roll off the wagons themselves. Now, you go see. And, Mr. McLean, you
do feel that Freckles has been brave and faithful? You
won't love him any the less even if you don't find the
logs—"

The angel's nerve gave way and she burst into a flood
of tears. Freckles couldn't bear it. He fairly ran from the
room, with the tears streaming from his own eyes, but
McLean took the angel out of the Bird Woman's arms,
and kissed her brave little face and stroked her hair and
petted her into quietness before he left.

As they drove back to the swamp, McLean so ear-

nestly seconded all that the angel had said that he soon
had the boy feeling much better.

"Freckles, your angel has a spice of the devil in her,
but she's superb! You needn't spend any time questioning or bewailing anything she does. Just worship
blindly, my boy. By heaven! She's sense, courage, and
beauty for half a dozen girls," said McLean.

"It's altogether right you are, sir," affirmed Freckles,
heartily. After a little he added, "There's no question but
the series is over now."

"Don't think it!" answered McLean. "The Bird Woman
is working for success, and success along any line is not
won by being scared out. She will be back on the usual
day, and, ten to one, the angel will be with her. They are
made of pretty stern stuff and they don't scare worth a
cent. Just before I left, I told the Bird Woman it would
be safe; and it will. You may do your usual walking, but
those four guards are there to stay. They are under your
orders absolutely. They are prohibited from firing on
any bird or molesting anything that you want to protect, but there they stay and this time it is useless for
you to say one word. I have listened to your pride too
long. You are too precious to me and that voice of yours
is too precious to the world to run any more risks."

"I am sorry to have anything spoil the series," said
Freckles, "and I'd love them to be coming, the angel
especial, but it can't be. You'll have to tell them so. You
see, Jack would have been ready to stake his life she
meant what she said and did to him. When the teams
pulled out, Wessner seized me, and he and Jack went to
quarreling over whether they should finish me then or

take me on to the next tree they were for felling. Between them they were pulling me about and hurting me bad. Wessner wanted to get at me right then, and Jack said he shouldn't be touching me till the last tree was out and all the rest of them gone. I'm believing Jack really hated to see me done for in the beginning. And I think, too, he was afraid if Wessner finished me then he'd lose his nerve and cut and they couldn't be managing the felling without him. Anyway, they were hauling me round like I was already past all feeling and they tied me up again. To keep me courage up, I twits Wessner about having to tie me and needing another man to help handle me. I told him what I'd do to him if I was free and he grabs up me own club and lays open me head with it. When the blood came streaming it set Jack raving, and he cursed and damned Wessner for a coward and a softy. Then Wessner turned on Jack and gives it to him for letting the angel make a fool of him. Tells him she was just playing with him, and beyond all manner of doubt she'd gone for you, and there was nothing to do on account of his cursed foolishness but finish me, get out, and let the rest of the timber go, for likely you was on the way right then. And it drove Jack plum crazy.

"I don't think he was for having a doubt of the angel before, but then he just raved. He grabbed out his gun and turned on Wessner. Sprang! It went out of his fist, and the order comes, 'Hands up!' Wessner reached for kingdom come like he was expecting to grab hold and pull himself up. Jack puts up what he has left. Then he leans over to me and tells me what he'll do to me if he

ever gets out of there alive. Then, just like a snake hissing, he spits out what he'll do to her for playing him. He
did get away, and, with his strength, that wound in his
hand won't be bothering him long. He'll do to me just
what he said, and when he hears it really was she that
went for you, why, he'll keep his oath about her.

"He's lived in the swamp all his life, sir, and everybody says it's always been the home of cutthroats, out-
laws, and runaways. He knows its most secret places as
none of the others. He's alive. He's in there now, sir.
Some way he'll keep alive. If you'd seen his face, all
scarlet with passion, twisted with pain, and black with
hate, and heard him swearing that oath, you'd know it
was a sure thing. I ain't done with him yet and I've
brought this awful thing on her."

"And I haven't begun with him yet," said McLean, setting his teeth. "I've been away too slow and too easy,
believing there'd be no greater harm than the loss of a
tree. I've sent for a couple of first-class detectives. We
will put them on his track and rout him out and rid the
country of him. I don't propose for him to stop either
our work or our pleasure. As for his being in the swamp
now, I don't believe it. He'd find a way out last night, in
spite of us. Don't you worry! I am at the helm now and
I'll see to that gentleman in my own way."

"I wish to my soul you had seen and heard him!" said
Freckles, unconvinced.

They entered the swamp, taking the route followed by
the Bird Woman and the angel. They really did find the
logs, almost where the angel had predicted they would
be. McLean went on to the south camp and had an in-

terview with Crowen that completely convinced him that the angel was correct there also. But he had no proof, so all he could do was to discharge the man, though his guilt was so apparent that he himself offered to withdraw the wager.

Then McLean sent for a pack of bloodhounds and put them on the trail of Black Jack. They clung to it, on and on, into the depths of the swamp, leading their followers through what had been considered impassable and impenetrable ways, and, finally, around near to the west entrance and out into the swale. Here the dogs bellowed, raved, and fell over each other in their excitement. They raced back and forth from swamp to swale, but follow the scent farther they would not, even though cruelly driven. At last their owner attributed their actions to snakes, and, as they were very valuable dogs, gave over the effort to urge them on. So that all they really established was the fact that Black Jack had eluded their vigilance and crossed the trail some time in the night. He had escaped to the swale, from which he probably crossed the corduroy, and, reaching the lower end of the swamp, had found friends. At any rate, it was a great relief to feel that he was not in the swamp, and it raised the spirits of every man on the line, though many of them expressed regrets that he who was undoubtedly most to blame should escape, and Wessner, who in the beginning was only his tool, be left to punishment.

But for Freckles, with Jack's fearful oath ringing in his ears, there was neither rest nor peace. He was almost ill when the day for the next study of the series arrived and he saw the Bird Woman and the angel com-

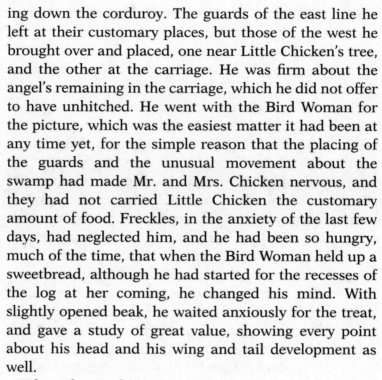

ing down the corduroy. The guards of the east line he
left at their customary places, but those of the west he
brought over and placed, one near Little Chicken's tree,
and the other at the carriage. He was firm about the
angel's remaining in the carriage, which he did not offer
to have unhitched. He went with the Bird Woman for
the picture, which was the easiest matter it had been at
any time yet, for the simple reason that the placing of
the guards and the unusual movement about the
swamp had made Mr. and Mrs. Chicken nervous, and
they had not carried Little Chicken the customary
amount of food. Freckles, in the anxiety of the last few
days, had neglected him, and he had been so hungry,
much of the time, that when the Bird Woman held up a
sweetbread, although he had started for the recesses of
the log at her coming, he changed his mind. With
slightly opened beak, he waited anxiously for the treat,
and gave a study of great value, showing every point
about his head and his wing and tail development as
well.

When the Bird Woman proposed to look for other
subjects about the line, Freckles went so far as to tell
her that Jack had made fearful threats against the angel. He implored her to take the angel home and keep
her under unceasing guard until Jack was located. He
wanted to tell her all about it, but he knew how dear the
angel was to her, and he dreaded to burden her with his
fears when they might prove groundless. He let her go,
and then blamed himself fiercely that he had done so.

Chapter XIV

WHEREIN FRECKLES NURSES A HEARTACHE AND BLACK JACK DROPS OUT

"McLean," said Mrs. Duncan, as the boss paused to greet her in passing the cabin, "do you know that Freckles hasna been in bed the last five nights, and all he's eaten in that many days ye could pack into a pint cup?"

"Why, what does the boy mean?" demanded McLean. "There's no necessity for his being on guard, with the watch I've set on the line. I had no idea he was staying down there."

"He's no' there," said Mrs. Duncan. "He goes some-where else. He leaves on his wheel juist after we're abed and rides in about cock-crow or a little earlier, and he's looking like death and nothing short of it."

"But, where does he go?" asked McLean, in astonish-ment.

"I'm no' given to bearing tales out of school," said
Sarah Duncan, "but in this case I'd tell ye if I could.
What the trouble is I dinna ken. If it is no' stopped, he's
in for dreadful sickness, and I thought ye could find out
and help him. He's in sair trouble; that's all I know."

McLean sat brooding as he stroked Nellie's neck.

At last he said, "I suspect I understand. At any rate, I
think I can find out. Thank you for telling me."

"Ye'll no' need telling, once ye clap your eyes on him,"
prophesied Mrs. Duncan. "His face is all a glist'ny, yellow and he's peaked as a starving caged bird."

McLean rode down to the Limberlost, and, stopping
in the shade, sat waiting for Freckles, whose hour for
passing the foot of the lease was near.

Along the north line came Freckles, fairly staggering.
When he turned east and reached Sleepy Snake Creek,
sliding through the swale like the long black snake for
which it was named, he sat down on the bridge and
closed his burning eyes, but they would not stay shut.
As if pulled by wires, the heavy lids flew open, and the
outraged nerves and muscles of his body danced,
twitched, and tingled.

He bent forward and idly watched the limpid little
stream flowing beneath his feet. Stretching back into
the swale, it came creeping between an impenetrable
wall of magnificent wild flowers, vines, and ferns. Milkweed, goldenrod, ironwort, fringed gentians, cardinal
flowers, and turtlehead stood on the very edge of the
creek, and every flower of them grew a double in the
water. Wild clematis crowned with snow the heads of
trees scattered here and there along the bank.

From afar the creek looked like murky, dirty water. Really it was clear and sparkling. The tinge of blackness was gained from its bed of muck showing through its transparent current. He could see small and wonderfully marked fish. What became of them when the creek spread into the swamp? For one thing, they would make mighty fine eating for the family of that self-satisfied old blue heron.

Freckles sat so still that presently the brim of his hat was covered with snake feeders, rasping their crisp wings and singing as they rested. Some of them settled on the club, and one on his shoulder. He was so quiet, and feathers, fur, and gauze were so accustomed to him, that all about the swale they went on with their daily life and forgot he was there.

The heron family were wading about the mouth of the creek. Freckles idly wondered whether the nerve-racking rasps they occasionally emitted indicated domestic felicity or a raging quarrel. He could not decide. A sheitpoke, with flaring crest, went stalking across a bare space near the creek's mouth. A stately brown bittern waded out into the clear-flowing water, lifting his feet high at every step, and setting them down gingerly, as if he dreaded wetting them, and, with slightly parted beak, stood eagerly watching about him for worms. Behind him were some mighty trees of the swamp above, and below the bank glowed a solid wall of goldenrod.

No wonder the ancients had chosen yellow as the color to represent victory, for the fierce, conquering hue of the sun was in it. They had done well, too, in choosing purple as the color of royalty. It was a dignified, compelling color, and in its warm tone there was a hint of blood.

It was the Limberlost's hour to proclaim her sovereignty and triumph. Everywhere she flaunted her yellow banner and trailed the purple of her mantle, which was paler in the thistle heads, took on strength in the first opening asters, and glowed and burned in the ironwort.

He gazed into her damp, mossy recesses where high-piled riven trees fell to decay under coats of living green, where dainty vines swayed and clambered, and here and there a yellow leaf, fluttering down, presaged the coming of winter. His love of the swamp laid hold of him and shook him with its force.

Compellingly beautiful was the Limberlost, but cruel withal. For back in there bleached the uncoffined bones of her victims, and she had missed cradling him, oh! so narrowly.

He shifted restlessly, and the movement sent the snake feeders skimming. The hum of life swelled and roared in his strained ears. Some small turtles, which had climbed on a log to sun, splashed clumsily into the water. Somewhere about the timber of the bridge a bloodthirsty little frog cried sharply, *"Keel'im! Keel'im!"*

Freckles muttered, "It's worse than that Black Jack swore to do to me, little fellow."

A muskrat waddled down the bank and swam for the swamp, its pointed nose riffling the water into a shining trail in its wake.

Then, just below the turtle log, a dripping silver-gray head, with shining eyes, was cautiously lifted, and

Freckles' hand slid around to his revolver. Higher and higher came the head, a long, heavy, fur-coated body rose, now half, now three-fourths out of the water. Freckles looked at his shaking hand and doubted, but he gathered his forces, the shot rang out, and the otter lay still. He hurried down and tried to lift it. He could scarcely muster strength to carry it to the bridge. The consciousness that he really could not go farther with it made Freckles realize the fact that he was well up to the limit of human endurance. He could bear it little, if any, longer. Every hour the dear face of the angel wavered before him, and behind it the awful distorted image of Black Jack, as he swore to the punishment he would mete out to her. He must go either to the lower camp to McLean, or else to town and find her father. Which should he do? He was almost a stranger, and the angel's father might not be so much impressed with what he said as he would if McLean went to him. Then he remembered that McLean had said he would come that morning. Freckles had never forgotten before. He hurried along the east trail as fast as his tottering legs would carry him.

He stopped when he came to the first guard, and telling him of his luck, asked him to go for the otter and carry it up to the cabin, as he was anxious to meet McLean.

Freckles passed the second guard without seeing him, and hurried up to the boss. He took off his hat, wiped his forehead, and stood silent under the eyes of McLean.

The boss was dumbfounded. Mrs. Duncan had led

him to expect that he would find Freckles in a bad way, but this was almost deathly. The fact was apparent that the boy scarcely knew what he was doing. His eyes had a glazed, farsighted look in them, which wrung the heart of the man that loved him. Without a thought of preliminaries, McLean leaned in the saddle and drew Freckles up to him.

"My poor lad!" he said. "My poor, dear lad; tell me, and we will try to right it!"

Freckles had twisted his fingers in Nellie's mane. At the kind words his face dropped on McLean's thigh and he shook with a nervous chill. McLean gathered him closer and waited.

When the guard came up with the otter, McLean without a word motioned him to lay it down and go back.

"Freckles," said McLean at last, "will you tell me, or must I set to work in the dark and try to find the trouble?"

"Oh, I want to tell you! I must tell you, sir," shuddered Freckles. "I cannot be bearing it the day out alone. I was coming to you when I remembered you would be here."

He lifted his face and gazed off across the swale, with his jaws set hard a minute, as if gathering his forces. Then he spoke. "It's the angel, sir," he said.

Instinctively McLean's grip on him tightened, and Freckles looked up into the boss's face in wonder.

"I tried hard the other day," said Freckles, "and I couldn't seem to make you see. It's only that there hasn't been an hour, waking or sleeping, since the day she parted the bushes and looked into me room, that

the face of her hasn't been before me in all the tinder-
ness, beauty, and mischief of it. She talked to me
friendly like. She trusted me entirely to take right care
of her. She helped me with things about me books. She
traited me like I was born a gentleman, and shared with
me like I was of her own blood. She walked the streets
of the town with me before her friends with all the pride
of a queen. She forgot herself and didn't mind the Bird
Woman, and run big risks to help me out that first day,
sir. This last time she walked into that gang of murderers, took their leader, and twisted him to the will of her.
She outdone him and raced the life almost out of her
trying to save me.

"Since I can remember, whatever the thing was that
happened to me in the beginning has been me curse.
I've been bitter, hard, and smarting under it hopelessly.
She came by and found me voice, and put hope of life
and success like other men into me in spite of it."

Freckles held up his maimed arm.

"Look at it, sir!" he said. "A thousand times I've
cursed it, hanging there helpless. She took it on the
street, before all the people, just as if she didn't see that
it was a thing to hide and shrink from. Again and again
I've had the feeling with her, if I didn't entirely forget it,
that she didn't see it was gone and I must pull her sleeve
and be pointing it out to her. Her touch on it was so
sacred-like, at times since I've caught meself looking at
the awful thing near like I was proud of it, sir. If I was
born your son she couldn't be treating me more as her
equal, and she can't help knowing you ain't truly me
father. Nobody can know the ugliness of the ignorance

of me better than I do, and all me lack of birth, home, relatives, and money, and what's it all to her?"

Freckles stepped back from McLean, squared his shoulders, and with a royal lift of his head looked straight into the boss's eyes.

"You saw her in the beautiful little room of hers, and you can't be forgetting how she begged and pleaded with you for me. She touched me body, and 'twas sanctified. She laid her lips on me brow, and 'twas sacrament. Nobody knows the height of her better than me. Nobody's studied my depths closer. There's no bridge for the great distance between us, sir, and clearest of all, I'm for realizing it. But she risked terrible things when she came to me among that gang of thieves. She wore herself past bearing to save me from such an easy thing as death! Now, here's me, a man, a big, strong man, and letting her live under that fearful oath, so worse than any death 'twould be for her, and lifting not a finger to save her. I cannot bear it, sir. It's killing me by inches! Black Jack's hand may not have been hurt so bad. Any hour he may be creeping up behind her! Any minute the awful revenge he swore to be taking may in some way fall on her, and I haven't even warned her father. I can't stay here doing nothing another hour. The five nights gone I've watched under her windows, but there's the whole of the day. She's her own horse and little cart, and's free to be driving about the town and country as she pleases. If any evil comes to her through Black Jack, it comes from her angel-like goodness to me. Somewhere he's hiding! Somewhere he is waiting his chance!

Somewhere he is reaching out for her! I tell you I cannot, I dare not be bearing it longer!"

"Freckles, be quiet!" said McLean, his eyes damp and his voice quivering with the pity of it all. "Believe me, I did not understand. I know the angel's father well. I will go to him at once. I have transacted business with him for the last three years. I will make him see! I am only just beginning to realize your agony, and the real danger there is for the angel. Believe me, I will see that she is fully protected every hour of the day and night until Jack is located and disposed of. And I promise you further, that if I fail to move her father or make him understand the danger, I will maintain a guard over her until Jack is caught. Now will you go bathe, drink some milk, go to bed, and sleep for hours, and then be my old brave, bright boy again?"

"Yes," said Freckles simply.

But McLean could see the flesh was twitching on the boy's bones.

"What was it the guard brought there?" McLean asked in an effort to distract Freckles' thoughts.

"Oh!" Freckles said, glancing where the boss pointed, "I forgot it! 'Tis an otter, and fine past believing, for this warm weather. I shot it at the creek this morning. 'Twas a good shot, considering. I expected to miss."

Freckles picked up the animal and started toward McLean with it, but Nellie pricked up her dainty little ears, danced out into the swale, and snorted with fright. Freckles dropped the otter and ran to her head.

"For pity's sake, get her on the trail, sir," he begged. "She's just about where the old king rattler crosses to go

into the swamp—the old buster Duncan and I have been telling you of. I haven't a doubt but it was the one Mother Duncan met. 'Twas down the trail there, just a little farther on, that I found her, and it's sure to be about yet."

McLean slid from Nellie's back, led her into the trail farther down the line, and tied her to a bush. Then he went to examine the otter. It was a rare, big specimen, with exquisitely fine, long, silky hair.

"What do you want to do with it, Freckles?" asked McLean, as he stroked the soft fur lingeringly. "Do you know that it is very valuable?"

"I was for almost praying so, sir," said Freckles. "As I saw it coming up the bank I thought this: Once somewhere in a book there was a picture of a young girl, and she was just a breath like the beautifulness of the angel. Her hands were in a muff as big as her body, and I thought it was so pretty. I think she was some queen, or the like. Do you suppose I could have this skin tanned and made into such a muff as that?—an enormous big one, sir?"

"Of course you can," said McLean. "That's a fine idea and it's easy enough. We must box and express the otter, cold storage, by the first train. You stand guard a minute and I'll tell Hall to carry it up to the cabin. I'll put Nellie to Duncan's rig, and we'll drive to town and call on the angel's father. Then we'll start the otter while it is fresh and I'll write your instructions later. It would be a mighty fine thing for you to give to the angel as a little reminder of the Limberlost before it is despoiled, and as a souvenir of her trip for you."

Freckles lifted a face with a glow of happy color creeping into it and eyes lighting with a former brightness. Throwing his arms about McLean, he cried, "Oh, how I love you! Oh, I wish I could make you know how I love you!"

McLean strained him to his breast.

"God bless you, Freckles," he said. "I do know! We're going to have some good old times out of this world together, and we can't begin too soon. Would you rather sleep first, or get a bite of lunch and have the drive with me and then rest? I don't know but sleep will come sooner and deeper to take the ride and have your mind set at ease before you lie down. Suppose you go."

"Suppose I do," said Freckles, with a glimmer of the old light in his eyes and newly found strength to shoulder the otter. Together they turned into the swale.

McLean noticed and spoke of the big black chickens.

"They've been hanging round out there for several days past," said Freckles. "I'll tell you what I think it means. I think the old rattler has killed something too big for him to swallow, and he's keeping guard and won't let the chickens have it. I'm just sure, from the way the birds have acted out there all summer, that it is the rattler's den. You watch them now. See the way they dip and then rise, frightened like!"

Suddenly McLean turned on him with blanching face.

"Freckles!" he cried.

"You think it's Jack!" shuddered Freckles.

He dropped the otter, caught up his club, and plunged into the swale. Reaching for his revolver,

McLean followed. The chickens circled higher at their coming, and the big snake lifted his head and rattled angrily. It sank in sinuous coils at the report of McLean's revolver, and together the boss and Freckles stood beside Black Jack. His fate was evident and most horrible.

"Come," said the boss at last. "We don't dare touch him. We will get a sheet from Mrs. Duncan and tuck over him, to keep these swarms of insects away, and set Hall on guard, while we go for the officers."

Freckles' lips closed resolutely. He deliberately thrust his club under Black Jack's body, and, raising him, rested it on his knee. He pulled a long silver pin from the front of the dead man's shirt and sent it spinning out into the swale. Then he gathered up a few crumpled bright flowers and dropped them into the pool far away.

"My soul is sick with the horror of this thing," said McLean, as he and Freckles drove toward town. "I can't understand how Jack dared risk creeping through the swale, even in desperation. No one knew its dangers better than he. And why did he choose the rankest, muckiest place to cross the swamp?"

"Don't you think, sir, it was because it was on a line with the Limberlost south of the corduroy? The grass was tallest there and he counted on those willows to screen him. Once he got among them, he would have been safe to walk by stooping. If he'd made it past that place, he'd been sure to get out."

"Well, I'm as sorry for Jack as I know how to be," said McLean, "but I can't help feeling relieved that our troubles are over, for now they are. With so dreadful a punishment for Jack, Wessner safe in jail, and warrants out for the others, we can count on their going away and staying. As for anyone else, I don't think they will care to attempt stealing my timber after the experience of these men. There is no one else about here with Jack's fine ability in woodcraft. He was an expert."

"Did you ever hear of anyone else that ever tried to locate any trees excepting him?" asked Freckles.

"No, I never did," said McLean. "I am sure there was no one besides him. You see, it was only with the arrival of our company that the other fellows scented good stuff in the Limberlost, and tried to work in. Jack knew the swamp better than anyone about here. When he found there were two companies trying to lease, he wanted to stand in with the one from which he could realize the most. Even then he had trees marked here that he was trying to dispose of. I think his sole intention in forcing me to discharge him from my gang was to come up here and try to steal timber. We had no idea, when we took the lease, what a gold mine it was."

"That's exactly what Wessner said that first day," said Freckles eagerly. "That 'twas a 'gold mine'! He said he didn't know where the marked trees were, but he knew a man that did, and if I would hold off and let them get the marked ones, there were a dozen they could take out in a few days."

"Freckles!" cried McLean. "You don't mean a dozen!"

"That's what he said, sir—a dozen. He said they couldn't tell how the grain of all of them would work up, of course, but they were all worth taking out, and five or six were real gold mines. This makes three they've tried, so there must be nine more marked, and several of them for being just fine."

"Well, I wish I knew which they were," said McLean, "so that I could get them out first."

"I have been thinking," said Freckles. "I believe if you will leave one of the guards on the line—say Hall—that I will begin on the swamp, at the north end, and lay it off in sections, and try to hunt out the marked trees. I suppose they are all marked something like that first maple on the line was. Wessner mentioned another good one not so far from that. He said it was best of all. I'd be having the swelled head if I could find that. Of course, I don't know a thing about the trees, but I could hunt for the marks. Jack was so good at it he could tell some of them by the bark, but all he wanted to take that we've got on to so far have just had a deep chip cut out, rather low down, and where the bushes were thick over it. I believe I could be finding some of them."

"Good head!" said McLean. "We will do that. You may begin as soon as you are rested. And about things you come across in the swamp, Freckles—the most trifling little thing that you think the Bird Woman would want, take your bicycle and go after her at any time. I'll leave two men on the line, so that you will have one on either side, and you can come and go as you please. Have you stopped to think of all we owe her, my boy?"

"Yes, and the angel—we owe her a lot, too," said Freckles. "I owe her me life and honor. It's lying awake nights I'll have to be trying to think how I'm ever to pay her up."

"Well, begin with the muff," suggested McLean. "That should be fine."

He bent down and ruffled the rich fur of the otter lying at his feet.

"I don't exactly see how it comes to be in such splendid fur in summer. Their coats are always finest in cold weather, but this could scarcely be improved. I'll wire Coopers to be watching for it. They must have it fresh. When it's tanned we won't spare any expense in making it up. It ought to be a royal thing, and somehow I think it will exactly suit the angel. I can't think of anything that would look nicer on her."

"Neither can I," agreed Freckles heartily. "When I get to the city there's one other thing, if I've the money after the muff is finished."

He told McLean of Mrs. Duncan's desire for a hat like the angel's. He hesitated a little in the telling, and kept sharp watch on McLean's face. When he saw the boss's eyes were full of comprehension and sympathy, he loved him anew, for, as ever, McLean was quick to understand. Instead of laughing, he said, "I guess you'll have to let me in on that, too. You mustn't be selfish, you know. I'll tell you what we'll do. Get it for Christmas. I'll be home then, and we can send a box. You get the hat. I'll add a dress and wrap. You get Duncan a hat and gloves. I'll send him a big overcoat, and we'll put in a lot of little stuff for the babies. Won't that be fun?"

Freckles fairly shivered with delight.

"That would be away too serious for fun," he said. "That would be heavenly. How long will it be?"

He fell to counting up the time, and McLean deliberately set himself to encourage Freckles and keep his
thoughts off the dark times of the last few days, for he
had been overwrought and needed quiet and rest.

Chapter XV

A week later everything at the Limberlost was precisely as it had been before the tragedy, except the case in Freckles' room now rested on the stump of the newly felled tree. Enough of the vines were left to cover it prettily, and every vestige of the havoc of a few days before was gone. The new guards were patrolling the trail. Freckles was roughly laying off the swamp in sections and searching for marked trees. In that time he had found one deeply chipped and the chip cunningly replaced and tacked in. It promised to be quite rare, so he was jubilant. He also found so many subjects for the Bird Woman that her coming was of almost daily occurrence, and the hours he spent with her and the angel were nothing less than golden.

223

The Limberlost was now arrayed like the Queen of Sheba in all her glory. The first frosts of autumn had bejeweled her crown in flashing topaz, ruby, and emerald. About her feet trailed the purple of her garments, and in her hand was her golden scepter. Everything was at full tide. It seemed as if nothing could grow lovelier, and it was all standing still a few weeks, waiting coming destruction.

The swamp was palpitant with life. Every pair of birds that had flocked to it in the spring was now multiplied by from two to ten. The young were tame from Freckles' tri-parenthood, and so plump and sleek that they were quite as beautiful as their elders, even if in many cases they lacked their brilliant plumage. It was the same story of increase everywhere. There were chubby little groundhogs scudding along the trail. There were cunning baby coons and opossums peeping from hollow logs and trees. Young muskrats followed their parents across the lagoons.

If you could come upon a family of foxes that had not yet disbanded, and see the young playing with a wild duck's carcass that their mother had brought, and note the pride and satisfaction in her eyes as she lay at one side guarding them, it would be a picture not to be forgotten. Freckles never tired of studying the devotion of a fox mother to her babies. To him, whose early life had been so embittered by continual proof of neglect and cruelty in human parents toward their children, the love of these furred and feathered folk of the Limberlost was even more of a miracle than to the Bird Woman and the angel.

The angel was wild about the baby rabbits and squirrels. Earlier in the season, when the young were still very small, it had so happened that at times Freckles could give into her hands one of these little ones. Then it was pure joy to stand back and watch her heaving breast, flushed cheek, and shining eyes. Hers were such lovely eyes. Freckles had discovered lately that they were not so dark as he had thought them at first, but that the length and thickness of lash by which they were shaded made them appear darker than they really were. They were forever changing. Now sparkling and darkling with wit, now damp with sympathy, now burning with the fire of courage, now taking on strength of color with ambition, now flashing indignantly at the abuse of any creature.

She had carried several of the squirrel and bunny babies home and had the conservatory littered with them. Her care of them was perfect. She was learning her natural history from nature, and was getting much healthful exercise. To her they were the most interesting of all, but the Bird Woman preferred the birds, with a close second in the butterflies.

Brown butterfly time had come. The outer edge of the swale was filled with milkweed, and other plants beloved of them, and the air was golden with the flashing satin wings of the monarch, viceroy, and argynnis. They outnumbered those of any other color three to one.

Among the birds it really seemed as if the little yellow fellows were in the preponderance. At least they were until the red-winged blackbirds and bobolinks, which had nested on the upland, suddenly saw in the swamp

the garden of the Lord and came swarming by hundreds to feast and adventure upon it these last few weeks before migration. Never was there a finer feast spread for the birds. The grasses were filled with seeds: so, too, were weeds of every variety. Fall berries were ripe. Wild grapes and black haws were ready. Bugs were creeping everywhere. The muck was yeasty with worms. Insects filled the air. Nature made glorious pause for holiday before her next change, and by none of the frequenters of the swamp was it more appreciated than by the big black chickens.

They seemed to feel the new reign of peace and fulness most of all. As for hunting, they didn't even have to hunt for themselves these days, for the bounty now being spread before Little Chicken every day was more than he could master, and he was glad to have his parents come down and feast with him.

He was a fine, big, overgrown fellow, and his wings, with quills of jetty black, gleaming with bronze, were so strong they almost lifted his body. He had three inches of tail, and his beak and claws were like steel. His muscles began to clamor for exercise. He raced the forty feet of his home back and forth many times every hour of the day. After a few days of that he began lifting and spreading his wings and flopping them until the down on his back was filled with elm fiber. Then he began jumping. The funny little hops, springs, and sidewise bounds he gave set Freckles and the angel, hidden in the swamp, watching him, into smothered chuckles of delight.

Sometimes he fell to coquetting with himself; and

that was the funniest thing of all, for he turned his head up, down, from side to side, and drew in his chin with prinky little jerks and tilts. He would stretch his neck, throw up his head, turn it to one side and smirk—actually smirk, the most complacent and self-satisfied smirk that anyone ever saw on the face of a bird. It was so comical that Freckles and the angel told the Bird Woman of it one day.

When she finished her work on Little Chicken, she left them the camera all ready for use, telling them they might hide back in the bushes and watch. If Little Chicken came out and truly smirked, and they could squeeze the bulb at just the proper moment to snap him, she would be more than delighted.

Freckles and the angel quietly curled down beside a big log, and with eager eyes and softest breathing they patiently waited. But Little Chicken had feasted before they told of his latest accomplishment. He was tired and sleepy so he went back into the log to bed and for an hour he never stirred.

They were becoming anxious, for the light would soon be gone and they had so wanted to try for the picture. At last Little Chicken lifted his head, opened his beak, and gaped widely. He dozed a minute or two more. The angel said that was his beauty sleep. Then he lazily gaped again and stood up, stretching and yawning. He ambled leisurely down toward the gateway and the angel said, "Now, we may have a chance, at last."

"I do hope so," shivered Freckles.

With one accord they rose to their knees and trained their eyes on the mouth of the log. The light was full

and strong. Little Chicken prospected again with no results. He dressed his plumage, polished his beak, and when he felt fine and in full toilet he began to flirt with himself. Freckles' eyes snapped and his breath sucked between his clenched teeth.

"He's going to do it!" whispered the angel. "That will come next. You'd best give me that bulb!"

"Yes," assented Freckles, but his eyes were fast on the log and he made no move to relinquish the bulb.

Little Chicken nodded daintily and ruffled his feathers. He gave his head sundry little sidewise jerks and rapidly shifted his point of vision. Once there was the fleeting little ghost of a smirk.

"Now!—No!" snapped the angel.

Freckles leaned toward the bird. Tense as a steel trap he waited. Unconsciously the hand of the angel clasped his. He scarcely knew it was there. Suddenly Little Chicken sprang straight up in the air and landed with a thud. The angel started slightly, but Freckles was immovable. Then, as if in approval of his last performance, the big, overgrown baby wheeled until he was more than three-quarters, almost full side, toward the camera, straightened on his legs, squared his shoulders, stretched his neck full height, drew in his chin, and smirked his most pronounced smirk, directly in the face of the lens.

Freckles' fingers closed on the bulb convulsively, and the angel's closed on his at the instant. Then the angel heaved a great sigh of relief and lifted her hands to push back the damp, clustering hair from her face.

"How soon do you s'pose it will be finished?" came Freckles' strident whisper.

For the first time the angel looked at him. He was on his knees, leaning far toward the log, his eyes set on the bird, the perspiration running in little streams down his red, mosquito-bitten face. His hat was awry, his bright hair rampant, his breast heaving with excitement, and he still gripped that bulb with every ounce of strength in his body.

"Do you think we were for getting it?" he asked.

The angel could only nod. Freckles heaved a great sigh of relief.

"Well, if that ain't the hardest work I ever did in me life!" he exclaimed. "It's no wonder the Bird Woman's for coming out of the swamp looking as if she's been through a fire, a flood, and a famine, if that's what she goes through day after day. But if you think we got it, why, it's worth all it took, and I'm glad as ever you are, sure!"

They put the holders in the case, carefully closed the camera, set it in also, and carried it out to the road.

Then Freckles cut loose. "Now, let's be telling the Bird Woman about it!" he shouted, wildly dancing and swinging his hat. "We got it! We got it! I bet a farm we got it!"

Hand in hand they ran for the north end of the swamp, yelling "We got it" like young Comanches, and never gave a thought to what they might do until a great blue-gray bird, with long neck and trailing legs, rose on flapping wings and sailed out over the Limberlost.

The angel went white to the lips and gripped Freckles

with both hands. He gulped with mortification and turned his back.

To carelessly frighten her subject away! It was the head crime in the Bird Woman's category. She extended her hands as she rose, baked, blistered, and dripping, and exclaimed, "Bless you, my children! Bless you!" And it truly sounded as if she meant it.

"Why, why—" stammered the bewildered angel.

Freckles hurried into the breach.

"You must be for blaming it every bit on me. I was thinking we got Little Chicken's picture real good. I was so drunk with the joy of it I lost all me senses and, 'Let's run tell the Bird Woman,' says I. Like a fool I was for running, and I sort of dragged the angel along."

"Oh, Freckles!" expostulated the angel. "Are you loony? Of course, it was all my fault! I've been with her hundreds of times. I knew perfectly well that I wasn't to let anything—*not anything*—scare her bird away! I was so crazy I forgot. The blame is all mine and she'll never forgive me."

"She will, too!" cried Freckles. "Wasn't you for telling me that very first day that when people scared her birds away she just killed them! It's all me foolishness, and I'll never forgive meself!"

The Bird Woman plunged into the swale at the mouth of Sleepy Snake Creek, and came wading out with a couple of cameras and dripping tripods.

"If you will permit me a word, my infants," she said, "I will explain to you that I have had three shots at that fellow."

The angel heaved a deep sigh of relief, and Freckles' face cleared a little.

"Two of them," continued the Bird Woman, "in the rushes—one facing, crest lowered; one light on back, crest flared; and the last on wing, when you came up. I had been simply praying for something to chase him up from that side, so that he would fly toward the camera, for he had waded around until in my position I couldn't do it myself. See? Behold in yourselves the answer to the prayers of the long-suffering!"

Freckles took a step toward her.

"Are you really meaning that?" he asked, wonderingly. "Only think, Angel, we did the right thing! She won't lose her picture through the carelessness of us, when she's waited and soaked nearly two hours! She's not angry with us!"

"Never was in a sweeter temper in my life," said the Bird Woman, busily cleaning and packing the cameras.

Freckles took off his hat and solemnly held out his hand. With equal solemnity the angel grasped it. The Bird Woman laughed alone, for to them the situation had been too serious to develop any of the elements of fun.

Then they loaded the carriage, and the Bird Woman and the angel started for their homes. It had been a hard time on all of them, and they were very tired, but they were happy. Freckles was so happy it seemed to him that life could hold no greater fullness of joy. As the Bird Woman was ready to drive away he laid his hand on the lines and looked up into her face.

"Do you suppose we got it?" he asked so eagerly that

she would have given much to be able to say yes with conviction.

"Why, my dear, I don't know," she said. "I've no way to judge. If you made the exposure just before you came to me, there was still a fine light there. If you waited until Little Chicken was far out in the entrance, you should have something good, even if you didn't catch just the fleeting expression for which you hoped. Of course, I can't say surely, but I think there is every reason to hope that you have it all right. I will develop the plate tonight, make you a proof from it early in the morning, and bring it when we come. It's only a question of a day or two now until the gang arrives. I want to work in all the studies I can before that time, for they are bound to disturb the birds. Mr. McLean will need you then, and I scarcely see how we are to do without you."

Moved by an impulse she never afterward regretted, she bent and laid her lips on Freckles' forehead, kissing him gently and thanking him for his many kindnesses to her in her loved work. Freckles started off walking on air, and he felt inclined to keep watching behind to see if the trail were not curling up and rolling down the line after him.

Chapter XVI

From afar Freckles saw them coming. The angel was standing, waving her hat. He sprang on his bicycle and raced, jolting and pounding, down the corduroy to meet them. The Bird Woman stopped the horse and the angel gave him the bit of print paper. Freckles leaned the wheel against a tree and took the proof with eager fingers. He had never before seen a study of any of his chickens. He stood staring. When he lifted his face to them it was transfigured with delight.

"You see!" he exclaimed, and fell to gazing again. "Oh, me Little Chicken!" he cried. "Oh, me elegant Little Chicken! I'd be giving all me money in the bank for you!"

Then he thought of the angel's muff and Mrs. Duncan's hat, and added, "or, at least, all but what I'm

233

needing bad for something else. Would you mind stopping at the cabin a minute and showing this to Mother
Duncan?" he asked.

"Give me that little book in your pocket," said the
Bird Woman.

She folded the outer edges of the proof so that it
would fit into the book, explaining as she did so its per-
ishable nature in that state. Freckles went hurrying on
ahead, and they drove up in time to see Mrs. Duncan
gazing as if awestruck, and to hear her bewildered,
"Weel, I be drawed on!"

Freckles and the angel helped the Bird Woman to establish herself for a long day at the mouth of Sleepy
Snake Creek. Then she sent them away and waited what
luck would bring to her.

"Now, what shall we do?" inquired the angel, who
was a bundle of nerves and energy.

"Would you like to go to me room awhile?" asked
Freckles.

"If you don't care to very much, I'd rather not," said
the angel. "I'll tell you. Let's go help Mrs. Duncan get
dinner and play with the baby. I love a nice, clean
baby."

They set out for the cabin. Every few minutes they
stopped to investigate something or to chatter over
some natural history wonder. The angel had quick eyes.
She seemed to see everything, but Freckles' were even
quicker for life itself had depended on their sharpness
ever since the beginning of his work at the swamp. They
saw it at the same time.

"Looks as if someone had been cutting a flagpole,"

said the angel, running the toe of her shoe around the small stump, evidently cut that season. "Freckles, what would anybody cut a tree as small as that for?"

"I don't know," said Freckles.

"Well, but I want to know!" said the angel. "Nobody came away in here and cut it just for fun. They've taken it away. Let's go back and see if we can see it anywhere around there."

She turned, retraced her footsteps, and began eagerly searching. Freckles did the same.

"There it is!" he exclaimed at last, "leaning just as naturally against the trunk of that big maple."

"Yes, and leaning there has killed a patch of bark," said the angel. "See how dried up it looks?"

Freckles stared at her.

"Angel!" he shouted, "I bet you it's a marked tree!"

"'Course it is!" cried the angel. "Nobody would cut that sapling and carry it away there and lean it up for nothing. I'll tell you! This is one of Jack's marked trees. He's climbed up there above anyone's head, peeled the bark, and cut into the grain enough to be sure. Then he's laid the bark back and fastened it with that pole to mark it. You see, there's a lot of other big maples close around it. Can you climb up to that place?"

"Yes," said Freckles, "if I take my wading boots off, I can."

"Then take them off," said the angel, "and do hurry! Can't you see that I am almost crazy to know if this tree is a marked one?"

They pushed the sapling over, and a piece of bark as big as the crown of Freckles' hat fell away.

"I believe it looks kind of nubby," encouraged the angel, backing away, with her face all screwed into a twist in an effort to intensify her vision.

Freckles reached the opening and then slid rapidly to the ground. He was almost breathless and his eyes were flashing.

"The bark's been cut clean with a knife, the sap scraped away, and a big chip taken out deep. The trunk is the twistiest thing you ever saw. It's full of eyes as a bird is of feathers!"

The angel was dancing and shaking his hand.

"Oh, Freckles," she cried, "I'm so delighted that you found it!"

"But I didn't," said the astonished Freckles. "That tree isn't my find, it's yours. I forgot it and was going on, and you wouldn't give up, and kept talking about it, and turned back. You found it!"

"You'd best be looking after your reputation for truth and veracity," said the angel. "You know you saw that sapling first!"

"Yes, after you took me back and set me looking for it," scoffed Freckles.

The clear, ringing echo of strongly swung axes came crashing through the Limberlost.

" 'Tis the gang!" shouted Freckles. "They're clearing a place to make the camp. Let's go help."

"Hadn't we better mark that tree again?" cautioned the angel. "It's away back in here. There's such a lot of them, and all so much alike. We'd feel good and green if we'd find it and then lose it."

Freckles lifted the sapling to replace it, but the angel motioned him away.

"Get out your hatchet," she said. "I predict this is the most valuable tree in the swamp. You found it. I'm going to play that you're my knight. Now, you nail my colors on it."

She reached up, and, pulling a blue bow from her hair, untied it and doubled it against the tree. Freckles turned his eyes from her and managed the fastening of it with shaking fingers. The angel had called him her knight! Dear Lord, how he loved her! She must not see his face, or surely her quick eyes would read what he was fighting to hide. He did not dare lay his lips on that ribbon then, but that night he would return to it. When they had gone a little distance they both looked back and the morning breeze set the bit of blue waving them a farewell.

They swung along together at a good pace.

"I am sorry about scaring the birds," said the angel, "but it's almost time for them to go anyway. I feel dreadfully over having the swamp ruined, but isn't it a delight to hear the good, honest ring of those axes, instead of straining your ears for stealthy sounds? Isn't it fine to go openly and freely, with nothing worse than a snake or a poison vine to fear?"

"Ah!" said Freckles, with a long breath, "it's better than you can dream, Angel. Nobody will ever be guessing some of the things I've been through trying to keep me promise to the boss, and to hold out until this day. That it's come with only one raw stump, and the log from that saved, and this new tree to report, isn't it

grand? Maybe Mr. McLean will be forgetting that stump when he sees this tree, Angel!"

"He can't forget it," said the angel. And in answer to Freckles' startled eyes she added, "Because he never had any reason to remember it. He couldn't have done a whit better himself. My father says so. You're all right, Freckles!"

She reached for his hand, and, like two children, they broke into a run as they came nearer the gang. They left the swamp by the west road and followed the trail until they found the men. To the angel it seemed complete chaos.

In the shadiest spot on the west side of the line, close to the swamp and very close to Freckles' room, they were cutting down bushes and clearing out space for a big tent for the men's sleeping quarters, another for a dining hall, and a board shack for the cook. The teamsters were unloading the materials, the horses were cropping leaves from the bushes; and each man was doing his part toward the construction of the new Limberlost quarters.

Freckles helped the angel climb on a wagonload of canvas parked in the shade. She removed her leggings, wiped her heated face, and glowed with happiness and interest.

The gang had been carefully sifted and McLean now felt that there was not a man remaining in it who was not trustworthy.

They had all heard of the angel's plucky ride for Freckles' relief, and several of them had been in the rescue party. Others, new since that time, had heard the tale rehearsed in its every aspect around the smudge fires at night. Almost all of them knew the angel by sight from her trips with the Bird Woman about their leases. They all knew her father, her position, and the luxuries of her home. Whatever course she had chosen with them they would scarcely have resented it, but the angel never had been known to choose a course. Her spirit of friendliness was inborn and inbred. She loved everybody and sympathized with everybody. Her generosity was only limited by what she could lay her hands on to give away.

She came down the trail, hand in hand with the red-haired, freckled timber guard whom she had worn herself past the limit of endurance to save only a few weeks before, racing in her eagerness to reach them, and laughing her "Good morning, gentlemen," right and left. When she was ensconced on the wagonload of tenting, she sat on a roll of canvas like a queen on her throne. There was not a man of the gang who would not have fought for her. She was a living exponent of universal brotherhood. There was no man among them who needed her exquisite face or dainty clothing to teach him that the deference due a gentlewoman should be paid her. That spirit of good-fellowship she radiated levied a special tribute of its own, and it became their delight to honor and please her.

As they raced toward the wagon—"Let me tell about the tree, please?" she begged Freckles.

"Why, sure!" said Freckles.

He would probably have said the same if she had proposed to cut off his head. When McLean rode up, he

found the angel sitting on the wagon, flushed and glowing, her hands already filled. One of the men, who was
cutting a scrub oak, had carried to her a handful of
crimson leaves. Another had picked a bunch of delicate
marsh-grass heads for her. Somebody else, in taking
out a bush, had found a daintily built and lined little
nest, fresh as when made.

She held up her treasures and greeted McLean,
"Good morning, Mr. Boss of the Limberlost!"

The gang shouted and McLean bowed profoundly before her.

"Everybody listen!" cried the angel, climbing a roll of
canvas. "I have something to say! Freckles has been
guarding here over a year now and he presents the
Limberlost to you, with every tree in it saved. And for
good measure he has just this morning located the rarest one of all: the one around in from the east line, that
Wessner spoke of that first day—nearest the one you
took out at first. All together! Everybody! Hurrah for
Freckles!"

With flushing cheeks and gleaming eyes, gaily waving
the grass above her head, she led them in three cheers.
Freckles slipped back into the swamp and held himself
tight, for fear he might burst wide open with pride and
with his great surging, throbbing love for her.

The angel subsided on the canvas and explained to
McLean about the maple. The boss was mightily
pleased. He took Freckles and set out to relocate and
examine the tree. The angel was interested in the making of the camp and preferred to remain with the men.
With her sharp eyes she was watching every detail of

construction. But when it came to the stretching of the dining-hall canvas she proceeded to take command. The men were driving the rope pins when the angel rose on the wagon and, leaning forward, spoke to Duncan, who was directing the work.

"I believe if you would swing that around a few feet farther you would find it better, Mr. Duncan," she said. "That way will let the hot sun in at noon, and the sides will cut off the best breeze."

"That's a fact," said Duncan, studying the condition.

So, by shifting the pins a little, they obtained comfort for which they blessed the angel every day. When they came to the sleeping tent, they consulted her about that. She explained the general direction of the night breeze and indicated the best position for the tent. Before anyone knew just how it happened, the angel was standing on the wagon, directing the location and construction of the cooking shack, the erection of the crane for the big boiling pots, and the building of the storeroom. She superintended the laying of the floor of the sleeping tent lengthwise, so that it would be easier to sweep, and suggested a new arrangement of the cots that would afford all the men an equal share of night breeze. She left the wagon, and, climbing up on the newly erected dining table, advised with the cook in placing his stove, table, and kitchen utensils.

When Freckles returned from the tree and joined in the work about the camp, he caught glimpses of her enthroned on a soapbox, cleaning beans. She called to him that they were invited to stay for dinner, and that they had accepted the invitation.

When the beans were steaming in the pot, the angel advised the cook to soak them overnight the next time, so that they would cook more quickly and not burst open. She was sure their cook at home did that way, and the chef of the gang thought it would be a good idea. The next Freckles saw of her she was paring potatoes. A little later she arranged the table.

She climbed on the table and swept it with a broom, instead of laying a cloth. She took the hatchet and hammered the worst dents out of the tin plates, and nearly skinned her fingers scouring the tinware with rushes. She set the plates an even distance apart, and laid the forks and spoons beside them. When the cook threw away half a dozen fruit cans, she gathered them up and melted off the tops, though she almost blistered her face and quite blistered her fingers doing it. Then she neatly covered these improvised vases with the manila paper from about the groceries, tying it on with wisps of marsh grass. These she filled with fringed gentians, blazing star, asters, goldenrod, and ferns, placing them the length of the dining table. In one of the end cans she placed her red leaves and in the other the fancy grass. Two men, watching her, went off and patted themselves and said that she was a born lady. She laughingly caught up a paper bag and fitted it jauntily to her head in imitation of a cook's cap. Then she ground the coffee, and beat a couple of eggs to put in, "because there is company," she gravely explained to the cook. She asked that delighted individual if he did not like it best that way, and he said he didn't know because he had never had a chance to taste it. The angel said that was her case exactly—she never had, either. She wasn't allowed anything stronger than milk. Then they laughed together.

She told the cook about camping with her father, and said that he fixed his coffee that way. When the steam began to rise from the big boiler, she stuffed the spout tightly with clean marsh grass, to keep the aroma in, placed the boiler where it would only simmer, and explained why. The influence of the angel's visit lingered with the cook through the rest of his life, and the men prayed for her frequent return.

She was having the time of her life when McLean came back, jubilant from his trip to the tree. How jubilant he only told the angel, for he had been obliged to lose faith in some trusted men of late and had learned discretion by what he suffered. He planned to begin clearing out a road to the tree that same afternoon, and to set two guards every night, for it promised to be a rare treasure, and he was eager to see it on the way to the mills.

"I am coming to see it felled," cried the angel. "I feel a sort of motherly interest in that tree."

McLean was highly amused. He would have staked his life on the honesty of either the angel or Freckles. Yet their versions of the finding of the tree differed widely.

"Tell me, Angel," the boss said jestingly. "I think I have a right to know. Who really did locate that tree?"

"Freckles," she answered, promptly and emphatically.

"But he says just as positively that it was you. I don't understand."

The angel's legal look flashed into her face. Her eyes grew tense with earnestness. She glanced about and, seeing no towel or basin, held out her hands for Sears to pour water over them. Then, using the skirts of her dress to dry them she climbed back on the wagon.

"I'll tell you, just word for word, how it happened," she said, "and then you shall decide, and Freckles and I will agree with you."

When she had finished her version, "Tell us, 'oh, most learned judge!'" she laughingly quoted, "which of us located that tree?"

"Blest if I know who located it!" exclaimed McLean. "But I have a pretty accurate idea as to who put the blue ribbon on it."

The boss smiled significantly at Freckles, who had just come up, for they had planned that they would instruct the company to reserve enough of the veneer from that very tree to make the most beautiful dressing table they could design for the angel's share of the discovery.

"What will you have for yours?" asked McLean of Freckles.

"If it's all the same to you, I'll be taking mine out in music lessons—begging your pardon—voice culture," said Freckles, with a grimace.

McLean laughed, for Freckles needed to see or hear but once to absorb learning as the thirsty earth sucks up water.

The angel gave McLean the head of the table. She took the foot, with Freckles on her right, and that lumber gang, washed, brushed, and straightened until they felt unfamiliar with themselves and each other, filled the sides. That imposed a slight constraint. Then, too, the men were afraid of the flowers, the polished tableware, and, above all, of the dainty grace of the angel. Nowhere do men so display lack of good breeding and culture as in dining. To sprawl on the table, scoop with their knives, chew loudly, gulp coffee, and duck their heads like snapping turtles for every bite, had not been noticed by them until the angel, sitting straight as an arrow, suddenly made them remember that they, too, were possessed of spines. Instinctively every man at the table straightened.

Chapter XVII

To reach the tree was a harder task than McLean had supposed. The gang could get nearest to it on the outside to the east, but after they reached the end of the east entrance there was still a mile of almost impenetrable thicket, trees big and little, and bushes of every variety and stage of growth. In several places the muck had to be filled in to give the horses and wagons something like a solid foundation over which to haul heavy loads. It was several days before they completed a road to the noble, big tree and were ready to fell it.

When the saw was well in, Freckles began watching down the road where it met the trail leading from Little Chicken's tree. He had gone to the tree ahead of the gang and taken down the blue ribbon. Carefully folded, it now lay over his heart. He was promising himself a

246

good deal of comfort with that ribbon when he should go to the city next month to begin his studies and dream the summer over again. It would help to make things tangible. When he was dressed like other men, and about his work, he knew where he meant to keep that precious bit of blue. It should be his good-luck token and he would wear it always to keep bright in memory the day on which the angel had called him her knight.

How he would study, and, oh, how he would sing! If he could fulfill McLean's expectations, and make the angel proud of him! If he could only be a real knight!

He could not understand why the angel had failed to come. She had wanted to see their tree felled. She would be too late if she did not arrive soon. He had told her it would be ready that morning and she had said she would surely be there. Why, of all mornings, was she late on this one?

McLean had ridden to town. If he had been there Freckles would have asked that they delay the felling, but he hardly liked to ask the gang. He really had no authority to do so, although he thought the men would wait. But some way he found such embarrassment in framing the request that he waited until the work was practically ended. The saw was out, and the men were sending ringing blows into the felling side of the tree when the boss rode up.

His first word was to inquire for the angel. When Freckles said she had not yet come, the boss at once gave orders to stop work on the tree until she arrived, for he felt that she had virtually located it and if she wanted to see it felled she should. As the men stepped back, a stiff morning breeze caught the top, which towered high above its fellows. There was an ominous grinding at the base, a shiver of the mighty trunk, and directly in line of its fall the bushes swung apart and the laughing face of the angel looked in on them.

A groan of horror burst from the dry throats of the men, and, reading the agony in their faces, she stopped short, glanced up, and understood.

"South!" shouted McLean. "Run south!"

The poor child was helpless. It was patent that she did not know which way south was. There was another slow shiver of the big tree. The rest of the gang stood as if rooted, but Freckles sprang past the trunk and went leaping in great bounds. He caught up the angel and dashed through the thicket for safety. The swaying trunk was half over when, just for an instant, a nearby tree stayed its fall. They saw Freckles' foot catch and with the angel he plunged headlong.

A terrible cry broke from the men and McLean covered his face. Instantly Freckles was up, with the angel in his arms, plunging on again. The outer limbs were on them when they saw Freckles hurl the angel, face down, in the muck, as far from him as he could send her. Springing after, in an attempt to cover her body with his own, he whirled to see if they were still in danger, and with outstretched arms braced himself for the shock. The branches shut them from sight, and the awful crash rocked the earth.

McLean and Duncan ran with axes and saws. The rest of the gang followed, and they worked like madmen. It

seemed an age before they caught a glimpse of the angel's blue dress and it renewed their vigor. Duncan fell
on his knees beside her and tore the muck from under-
neath her with his hands. In a few seconds he dragged
her out choking and stunned, but surely not fatally
hurt.

Freckles lay a little farther under the tree, a big limb
pinning him down. His eyes were wide open. He was
perfectly conscious. Duncan began mining beneath
him, but Freckles stopped him.

"You can't be moving me," he said. "You must cut off
the limb and lift it. I know."

Two men ran for the big saw. A number of them laid
hold of the limb and bore up. In a little time it was off
and Freckles lay free.

The men bent over him to lift him, but he motioned
them away.

"Don't be touching me until I rest a bit," he pleaded.

Then he twisted his head until he saw the angel, who
was digging muck from her eyes and wiping it off her
face on the skirt of her dress.

"Try to get up," he begged.

McLean laid hold of the angel and helped her to her
feet.

"Do you think any bones are broken?" gasped
Freckles.

The angel shook her head and wiped muck.

"You see if you can find any, sir," Freckles commanded.

The angel yielded herself to McLean's touch, and he
assured Freckles that she was not seriously injured.

Freckles settled back with a smile of ineffable tenderness on his face.

"Thank the Lord!" he hoarsely whispered.

The angel broke from McLean.

"Now, Freckles, you!" she cried. "It's your turn. Please get up!"

A pitiful spasm swept Freckles' face. The sight of it washed every vestige of color from the angel's. She took hold of his hand.

"Freckles, get up!"

It was half command, half entreaty.

"Easy, Angel, easy! Let me rest a bit first!" implored Freckles.

She knelt beside him. He reached his arm about her and drew her up closely. He looked at McLean in an agony of entreaty that brought the boss to his knees on the other side.

"Oh, Freckles!" McLean cried. "Not that! Surely we can do something! We must! Let me see!"

He tried to unfasten Freckles' neckband, but his fingers shook so clumsily that the angel pushed them away and herself laid Freckles' chest bare. With just one hasty glance, she gathered the clothing together and slipped her arm under his head. Freckles lifted eyes of agony to hers.

"You see?" he said.

The angel nodded dumbly.

Freckles turned to McLean.

"Thank you for everything," he panted. "Where are the boys?"

"They are all here," said the boss, "except a couple

that have gone for doctors, Mrs. Duncan, and the Bird Woman."

"It's no use trying to do anything," said Freckles. "You won't forget the muff and the Christmas box. The muff especial?"

There was a movement above them so pronounced that it attracted Freckles' attention, even in that extreme hour. He looked up and a pleased smile flickered into his drawn face.

"Why, if it ain't me Little Chicken!" he cried hoarsely. "He must be making his very first trip from the log. Now Duncan can have his big watering trough."

"It was Little Chicken that made me late," faltered the angel. "I was so anxious to get here early I forgot to bring his breakfast from the carriage. He must have been very hungry, for when I passed the log he started after me. He was so wobbly, and so slow getting from tree to tree and through the bushes, I just had to wait for him, for I couldn't drive him back."

"Of course you couldn't! Me bird has too amazing good sense to go back when he could be following you," exulted Freckles, just as if he did not realize that the delay was the price of his life. Then he lay silently thinking, but presently he asked slowly, "And so 'twas me Little Chicken that was making you late, Angel?"

"Yes," said the angel.

A spasm of fierce pain shook Freckles and a look of uncertainty crossed his face.

"All summer I've been thanking God for the falling of the feather and all the delights it's brought me," he muttered, "but this looks like—"

He stopped short and raised questioning eyes to McLean.

"I can't help being Irish, but I can help being superstitious," he said. "I mustn't be laying it to the Almighty, nor to me bird, must I?"

"No, dear lad," said McLean, stroking the brilliant hair. "The choice lay with you. You could have stood like a rooted dolt, like all the rest of us. It was through your great love and your high courage that you made the sacrifice."

"Don't you be so naming it, sir!" cried Freckles. "It's just the reverse. If I could be giving me body the hundred times over to save hers from this, I'd be doing it and take joy with every pain.

He turned with a smile of adoring tenderness to the angel. She was ghastly white, and her eyes were dull and glazed. She scarcely seemed to hear or understand what was coming, but she bravely tried to answer that smile.

"Is my forehead covered with dirt?" he asked.

She shook her head.

"You did once," he gasped.

Instantly she laid her lips on his forehead, then on each cheek, and then in a long kiss on his lips.

Then McLean bent over him.

"Freckles," he said brokenly, "you will never know how I love you. You won't go without saying good-bye to me?"

That word stung the angel to quick comprehension. She started as if rousing from sleep.

"Good-bye?" she cried sharply, her eyes widening and

the color rushing into her white face. "Good-bye! Why, what do you mean? Who's saying good-bye? Where could Freckles go, when he is hurt like this, but to the hospital? You needn't say good-bye for that. Of course, we will all go with him! You call up the men. We must start right away."

"It's no use, Angel," said Freckles. "I'm thinking every bone in me breast is smashed. You'll have to be letting me go!"

"I will not," said the angel flatly. "It's no use wasting precious time talking about it. You are alive. You are breathing. And no matter how badly your bones are broken, what are great surgeons for but to fix you up and make you well again? You promise me that you'll just grit your teeth and hang on when we hurt you, for we must start with you as quickly as it can be done. I don't know what has been the matter with me. Here's good time wasted already."

"Oh, Angel!" moaned Freckles, "I can't! You don't know how bad it is. I'll die the minute you are for trying to lift me!"

"Of course you will, if you make up your mind to do it," said the angel. "But if you are determined you won't, and you set yourself to breathing deep and strong, and hang on to me tight, I can get you out. Really you have to do it, Freckles, no matter how it hurts you, for you did this for me, and now I must save you, so you might as well promise."

She bent over him, trying to smile encouragement with her fear-stiffened lips.

"You will promise, Freckles?"

Big drops of cold sweat ran together along Freckles'
temples.

"Angel, darlin' Angel," he pleaded, taking her hand in
his. "You ain't understanding, and I can't for the life of
me be telling you, but, indeed, it's best to be letting me
go. This is just my chance. Please say good-bye and let
me slip off quick!"

He appealed to McLean. "Dear Boss, you know! You
be telling her that, for me, living is far worse pain than
dying. Tell her you know death is the best thing that
could ever be happening to me!"

"Merciful heaven!" burst in the angel. "I can't bear
this delay!"

She caught Freckles' hand to her breast, and, bending
over him, looked deep into his stricken eyes.

" 'Angel, I give you my word of honor that I will keep
right on breathing.' That's what you are going to promise me," she said. "Do you say it?"

Freckles hesitated.

"Freckles!" imploringly commanded the angel, *"you
do say it!"*

"Yes," gasped Freckles.

The angel sprang to her feet.

"Then that's all right," she said, with a tinge of her
old-time briskness. "You just keep sawing away like a
steam engine, and I will do all the rest."

The eager men gathered about her.

"It's going to be a tough pull to get Freckles out," she
said, "but it's our only chance, so listen closely and
don't for the lives of you fail me in doing quickly what I
tell you. There's no time to spend falling down over

each other. We must have some system. You four there get on those wagon horses and ride to the sleeping tent. Get the stoutest cot, a couple of comforts, and a pillow. Ride back with them some way to save time. If you meet any other men of the gang, send them on here to help carry the cot. We won't risk the jolt of driving with him. The rest of you clear a path out to the road. And, Mr. McLean, you take Nellie and ride to town. Tell my father how Freckles is hurt and that he risked it to save me. Tell him I'm going to take Freckles to Chicago on the noon train and I want him to hold it if we are a little late. If he can't, then have a special ready at the station and another on the Pittsburgh at Fort Wayne, so we can go straight through. You needn't mind leaving us. The Bird Woman will be here soon. We will rest a little."

She dropped back into the muck beside Freckles and began stroking his hair and hand. He lay with his face of agony turned to hers, and fought to smother the groans that would tell her what he was suffering.

When they stood ready to lift him, the angel bent over him in a passion of tenderness.

"Dear old Limberlost guard, we're going to lift you now," she said. "I suspect you will faint from the pain of it, but we will be just as easy as ever we can, and don't you dare forget your promise!"

A whimsical half-smile touched Freckles' quivering lips.

"Angel, can a man be remembering a promise when he ain't knowing?" he asked.

"You can," said the angel stoutly, "because a promise means so much more to you than it does to most men."

A look of strength flashed into Freckles' face at her words.

"I am ready," he said.

With the first touch his eyes closed, a mighty groan was wrenched from him, and he lay senseless. The angel gave Duncan one panic-stricken look. Then she set her lips and gathered her forces again.

"I guess that's a good thing," she said. "Maybe he won't feel how we are hurting him. Oh, boys, are you being quick and gentle?"

She stepped to the side of the cot and bathed Freckles' face. Taking his hand in hers she gave the word to start. She told the men to ask every able-bodied man they met to join them so that they could change carriers often and make good time.

The Bird Woman insisted upon taking the angel into the carriage and following the cot, but the angel refused to leave Freckles, and suggested that the Bird Woman drive ahead, pack them some clothing, and be at the station ready to accompany them to Chicago. All the way the angel walked beside the cot, shading Freckles' face with a branch, and holding his hand. At every pause to change carriers she moistened his face and lips and counted each breath with heartbreaking anxiety.

She scarcely knew when her father joined them, and, taking the branch from her, slipped an arm about her waist and almost carried her along. To the city streets and the swarm of curious, staring faces she paid no more attention than she had to the trees of the Limberlost. When the train pulled in and the gang placed Freckles aboard, big Duncan made a place for the angel beside the cot.

With the best physician to be found, and with the Bird Woman and McLean in attendance, the four-hour run to Chicago began. The angel constantly watched over Freckles, bathed his face, stroked his hand, and softly fanned him. Not for an instant would she yield her place, or allow anyone else to do anything for him. The Bird Woman and McLean regarded her in amazement. There seemed to be no end to her resources and courage. The only time she spoke was to ask McLean if he was sure the special would be ready on the Pittsburgh line. He replied that it was made up and waiting.

At five o'clock, Freckles lay stretched on the operating table of Lake View Hospital, while three of the greatest surgeons in Chicago bent over him. At their command, McLean picked up the unwilling angel and carried her out to the nurses to be bathed, have her bruises attended to, and be put to bed.

In a place where it is difficult to surprise people, they were astonished women as they removed the angel's dainty stained and torn clothing, peeled off hose muck-baked to her limbs, soaked the dried loam from her silken hair, and washed the beautiful scratched, bruised, dirt-covered body. The angel fell fast asleep long before they had finished, and lay deeply unconscious while the fight for Freckles' life was being waged.

Three days later she was the same angel as of old, except that Freckles was constantly in her thoughts. The anxiety and responsibility that she felt for his condition had bred in her a touch of womanliness and au-

thority that was new. That morning she was up early and hovering near Freckles' door. She had been allowed to remain with him constantly, for the nurses and surgeons had learned, with his returning consciousness, that for her alone would the active, highly-strung, pain-racked sufferer be quiet and obey orders. When she was dropping from loss of sleep, the threat that she would fall ill had to be used to send her to bed. Then, by telling Freckles that the angel was asleep and they would waken her the moment he moved, they were able to control him for a short time.

The surgeon was with Freckles. The angel had been told that the word he brought that morning would be final, so she curled up in a windowseat, dropped the curtains behind her, and, in dire anxiety, waited for the opening of that closed door.

Just as it opened, McLean came hurrying down the hall and up to the surgeon, but with one glance at his face he stepped back in dismay. And the angel, who had risen, sank to the seat again, too dazed to come forward. The men faced each other. The angel, with parted lips and frightened eyes, bent forward in tense anxiety.

"I—I thought he was doing nicely?" faltered McLean.

"He bore the operation well," replied the surgeon, "and his wounds are not necessarily fatal. I told you that yesterday, but I did not tell you that something else would probably kill him, and it will. He need not die from the accident, but he will not live the day out."

"But why? What is it?" asked McLean, hurriedly. "We all dearly love the boy. We have millions among us to do anything that money can accomplish. Why must he die, if those broken bones do not kill him?"

"That is what I am going to give you the opportunity of telling me," replied the surgeon. "He need not die from the accident, yet he is dying as fast as his splendid physical condition will permit, and it is because he so evidently prefers death to life. If he were full of hope and ambition to live, my work would be easy. If all of you love him as you prove you do, and there is unlimited means to give him anything he wants, why should he desire death?"

"Is he dying?" demanded McLean.

"He is," said the surgeon. "He will not live this day out, unless some strong reaction sets in at once. He is so low that, preferring death to life, nature cannot overcome his inertia. If he is to live he must be made to desire life. Now he undoubtedly wishes for death, and that it come quickly."

"Then he must die," said McLean.

His broad shoulders shook convulsively. His strong hands opened and closed mechanically.

"Does that mean that you know what he desires and cannot, or will not, supply it?"

McLean groaned in misery.

"It means," he said desperately, "that I know what he wants, but it is as far removed from my power to give it to him as it would be to give him a star. The thing for which he will die he can never have."

"Then you must prepare for the end very shortly," said the surgeon, turning abruptly away.

McLean caught his arm roughly.

"You look here!" he cried in desperation. "You say that as if I could do something if I would. I tell you the boy is dear to me past expression. I would do anything —spend any sum. You have noticed and repeatedly commented on the young girl with me. It is that child that he wants! He worships her to adoration and knowing he can never be anything to her, he prefers death to life. In God's name, what can I do about it?"

"Barring that missing hand, I never handled a finer man," said the surgeon, "and she seems perfectly devoted to him. Why cannot he have her?"

"Why?" echoed McLean. "Why? Well, for a good many reasons. I told you he was my son. You probably knew that he was not. A little over a year ago I had never seen him. He joined one of my lumber gangs from the road. He is a stray, left at one of your homes for the friendless here in Chicago. When he grew up the superintendent bound him out to a brutal man. He ran away and landed in one of my lumber camps. He has no name or knowledge of legal birth. The angel—we have talked of her. You see what she is, physically and mentally. She has ancestors reaching back to Plymouth Rock, and across the sea for generations back of that. She is an idolized, petted only child, and there is great wealth. Life holds everything for her, nothing for him. He sees it more plainly than anyone else could. There is nothing for the boy but death, if it is the angel that is required to save him."

The angel stood between them.

"Well, I just guess not!" she cried. "If Freckles wants me, all he has to do is to say so and he can have me!"

The amazed men stepped back, staring at her.

"That he will never say," said McLean at last, "and you don't understand, Angel. I don't know how you came here. I wouldn't have had you hear that for the world, but since you have, dear girl, you must be told that it isn't your friendship or your kindness Freckles wants. It is your love."

The angel looked straight into the great surgeon's eyes with her clear, steady orbs of blue, and then into McLean's with unwavering frankness.

"Well, I do love him," she said simply.

McLean's arms dropped helplessly.

"You don't understand," he reiterated patiently. "It isn't the love of a friend, or a comrade, or a sister, that Freckles wants from you. It is the love of a sweetheart. And if to save the life he has offered for you, you are thinking of being generous and impulsive enough to sacrifice your future—in the absence of your father it will become my plain duty, as the protector in whose hands he has placed you, to prevent such rashness. The very words you speak, and the manner in which you say them, proves that you are a mere child and have not dreamed what love is."

Then the angel grew splendid. A rosy flush swept the pallor of fear from her face. Her big eyes widened and dilated with intense lights. She seemed to leap to the height and the dignity of superb womanhood before their wondering gaze.

"I have never had to dream of love," she said proudly. "I have never known anything else, in all my life, but to love everyone and to have everyone love me. And there

has never been anyone so dear as Freckles. If you will
remember, we have been through a good deal together.
I do love Freckles, just as I say I do. I don't know anything about the love of sweethearts, but I love him with
all the love in my heart and I think that will satisfy
him."

"Surely it ought!" muttered the surgeon.

McLean reached to take hold of the angel, but she
saw the movement and swiftly stepped back.

"As for my father," she continued, "he at once told me
what he learned from you about Freckles. I've known all
you know for several weeks. That knowledge didn't
change your love for him a particle. I think the Bird
Woman loved him more. Why should you two have all
the fine perceptions there are? Can't I see how brave,
trustworthy, and splendid he is? Can't I see how his soul
vibrates with his music, his love of beautiful things, and
the pangs of loneliness and heart-hunger? Must you two
love him with all the love there is, and I give him none?
My father is never unreasonable. He won't expect me
not to love Freckles, or not to tell him so, if the telling
will save him."

She darted past McLean into Freckles' room, closed
the door, and turned the key.

Chapter XVIII

Freckles lay raised on a flat pillow, his body immovable in a plaster cast, his maimed arm, as always, hidden. His greedy eyes fastened at once on the angel's face. She crossed to him with light step and bent over him with infinite tenderness. Her heart ached at the change in his appearance. He seemed so weak, so heart-hungry, so utterly hopeless, and so alone. She could see that the night had been one long terror.

For the first time she tried putting herself in Freckles' place. What would it mean to have no parents, no home, no name? No name! That was the worst of all. That was to be lost, indeed—utterly and hopelessly lost. The angel lifted her hands to her dazed head and reeled, as she tried to face that proposition. She dropped on

263

her knees by the bed, slipped her arm under the pillow, and, leaning over Freckles, set her lips on his forehead. He smiled faintly, but his wistful face looked worse for it. It cut the angel to the heart.

"Dear Freckles," she said, "there is a story in your eyes this morning, tell me?"

Freckles drew a long, wavering breath.

"Angel," he begged, "be generous! Be thinking of me a little. I'm so homesick and worn out, dear Angel, be giving me back me promise. Let me go?"

"Why, Freckles!" faltered the angel. "You don't know what you are asking. 'Let you go!' I cannot! I love you better than anyone, Freckles. I think you are the very finest person I ever knew. I have our lives all planned. I want you to go to be educated and learn all there is to know about singing, just as soon as you are well enough. By the time you have completed your education I shall have finished college, and then I want," she choked on it a second, "I want you to be my real knight, Freckles, and come to me and tell me that you like me— a little. I have been counting on you for my sweetheart from the very first, Freckles. I can't give you up, unless you don't like me. But you do like me—just a little— don't you, Freckles?"

Freckles lay whiter than the coverlet, his staring eyes on the ceiling and his breath wheezing between dry lips.

The angel awaited his answer a second, and when none came she dropped her crimsoning face beside him on the pillow and whispered in his ear, "Freckles, I—I'm trying to make love to you. Oh, can't you help me just a little bit? It's awful hard all alone! I don't know how, when I really mean it, but Freckles, I love you. I must have you, and now I guess—I guess maybe I'd better kiss you next."

She lifted her shamed face and bravely laid her feverish, quivering lips on his. Her breath, like clover bloom, was in his nostrils and her hair touched his face. Then she looked into his eyes with reproach.

"Freckles," she panted, "Freckles! I didn't think it was in you to be mean!"

"Mean, Angel! Mean to you?" gasped Freckles.

"Yes," said the angel. "Downright mean. When one kisses you, if you had any mercy at all you'd kiss back, just a little bit. Now, I'm going to try it again and I want you to help me a little. You aren't too sick to help me just a little, Freckles?" she implored.

Freckles' sinewy fist knotted into the coverlet. His chin pointed ceilingward and his head rocked on the pillow.

"Oh, Jesus!" burst from him in agony. "You ain't the only one that was crucified!"

The angel caught Freckles' hand and carried it to her breast.

"Freckles!" she wailed in terror, "Freckles! Is it a mistake? Is it that you don't want me?"

Freckles' head rolled on in wordless suffering.

"Wait a bit, Angel?" he panted at last. "Be giving me a little time!"

The angel rose with controlled features. She bathed his face, straightened his hair, and held water to his lips. It seemed an age before he reached for her. In-

stantly she knelt again, carried his hand to her breast, and leaned her cheek upon it.

"Tell me, Freckles," she whispered softly.

"If I can," said Freckles, in biting agony. "It's just this. Angels are from above. Outcasts are from below. You've a sound body and you're beautifulest of all. You have everything that loving, careful raising and money can give you. I have so much less than nothing that I don't suppose I had any right to be born. It's a sure thing— nobody wanted me afterward, so, of course, they didn't before. Some of them should have been telling you long ago."

"If that's all you have to tell, Freckles, I've known that quite a while," said the angel stoutly. "Mr. McLean told my father and he told me. That only makes me love you more, to pay for all you've missed."

"Then I'm wondering at you," said Freckles, in a voice of awe. "Can't you see that if you were willing and your father would come and offer you to me, I couldn't be touching the soles of your feet, in love—me, whose people brawled over me, cut off me hand, and throwed me away to freeze and to die! Me, who has no name just as much because I've no *right* to any as because I don't know it. When I was little, I planned to find me father and mother when I grew up. Now I know me mother deserted me, and me father was maybe a thief and surely a liar. The pity of me suffering and the watching over me has gone to your head, dear Angel, and it's me must be thinking for you. If you could be forgetting me lost hand, where I was raised, and that I had no name to give you, and if you would be taking me as I am, some day people such as mine must be might come upon you. I used to pray every night and morning and many times the day to see me mother. Now I only pray to die quickly and never risk the sight of her. 'Tain't no ways possible, Angel! It's a wildness of your dear head. Oh, do, for mercy sake, kiss me once more and be letting me go!"

"Not for a minute!" cried the angel. "Not for a minute, if those are all the reasons you have. It's you that have the wildness in your head, but I can understand just how it happened. Being shut up in that home most of your life, and seeing children every day whose parents did neglect and desert them, makes you sure yours did the same. And yet there's a lot of other things that could have happened so much more easily than that. There are thousands of young couples who come to this country and start a family with none of their relatives here. Chicago is a big, wicked city, and grown people could be wiped out in a lot of ways, and who would there ever be to find to whom their little children belonged? The minute my father told me how you felt, I began to study this thing over and I've made up my mind you are dead wrong. I meant to ask my father or the Bird Woman to talk to you before you went away to school, but the way things are right now I guess I'll just do it myself. It's all so plain to me. Oh, if I could only make you see!"

She buried her face in the pillow and presently lifted it, transfigured.

"Now I have it!" she cried. "Oh, dear heart! I can make it so plain! Freckles, can you imagine you see the old Limberlost trail? Well, when we followed it, you

know there were places where ugly, prickly thistles
overgrew the path and you went ahead with your club
and bent them back to keep them from stinging
through my clothing. Other places there were great
shining pools where lovely, snow-white lilies grew, and
you waded in and gathered them for me. Oh, dear
heart, don't you see? It's this! Everywhere the wind carried that thistledown, other thistles sprang up and grew
prickles; and wherever those lily seeds sank to the mire,
the pure white of other lilies bloomed. But, Freckles,
there was never a place anywhere about the Limberlost,
or in the whole world, where the thistledown floated
and sprang up and blossomed into white lilies! Thistles
grow from thistles, and lilies grow other lilies. Dear
Freckles, think hard! You must see it! You are lily,
straight through! You never, never could have drifted
from the thistle patch.

"Where did you get the courage to go into the
Limberlost and face its terrors? You inherited it from
the blood of a brave father, dear heart. Where did you
get the pluck to hold for over a year a job that few men
would have taken at all? You got it from a plucky
mother, you bravest of boys. You waded single-handed
into a man almost twice your size, and fought like a
demon just at the suggestion that you could be decep-
tive and dishonest. Could your mother or your father
have been untruthful? Here you are, so hungry and
starved out that you are dying for love. Where did you
get all that capacity for loving. You didn't inherit it from
hardened, heartless people, who would disfigure you
and purposely leave you to die, that's one sure thing.

You once told me of saving your big bullfrog from a rattlesnake. You knew you risked a horrible death when you did it. Yet you will spend miserable years torturing yourself with the idea that your own mother might have cut off that hand. Shame on you, Freckles! Your mother would have done this—"

The angel deliberately turned back the cover, slipped up the sleeve, and laid her lips on the scars.

"Freckles! Wake up!" she cried, almost shaking him. "Come to your senses! Be a thinking, reasoning man! You have brooded too much, and been all your life too much alone. It's all as plain as plain can be to me. You just must see it! Like breeds like in this world! You must be some sort of a reproduction of your parents, and I am not afraid to vouch for them, not for a minute!

"And then, too, if more proof is needed, here it is: Mr. McLean says that you have never once failed in tact and courtesy. He says that you are the most perfect gentleman he ever knew, and he has traveled the world over. How does it happen, Freckles? Nobody at that home taught you that. Hundreds of men couldn't be taught it even in a school of etiquette; so it must be instinctive with you. If it is, why, that means that it is born in you, and a direct inheritance from a race of men that have been gentlemen for ages, and couldn't be anything else.

"Then there's your singing. I don't believe there ever was a mortal with a sweeter voice than yours, and while that doesn't prove anything, there is a point that does. Just the little training you had from that choirmaster won't account for the wonderful accent and ease with

which you sing. Somewhere in your close blood is a
marvelously trained vocalist; we every one of us believe
that, Freckles.

"Why does my father refer to you constantly as being
of fine perceptions and honor? Because you are,
Freckles. Why does the Bird Woman leave her precious
work and stay here to help look after you? I never heard
of her losing any time over anyone else. It's because she
loves you. And why does Mr. McLean turn all of his
valuable business over to hired men and watch over you
personally? And why is he hunting excuses every day to
spend money on you? My father says McLean is full
Scottish—close with a dollar. He is a hardheaded business man, Freckles, and he is doing it because he finds
you worthy of it. Worthy of all we can all do and more
than we know how to do, dear heart! Freckles, are you
listening to me? Oh! won't you see it? Won't you believe
it?"

"Oh, Angel!" chattered the bewildered Freckles, "are
you truly meaning it? Could it be?"

"Of course it could," flashed the angel, "because it just
is!"

"But you can't prove it," wailed Freckles. "It ain't giving me a name, or me honor!"

"Freckles," said the angel sternly, "you are unreasonable! Why, I *did* prove every word I said! Everything
proves it! You look here! If you knew for sure that I
could give you your name and your honor, and prove to
you that your mother did love you, why, then, would
you just go to breathing like perpetual motion and hang
on for dear life and get well?"

A great light leaped into Freckles' eyes.

"If I knew that, Angel," he said solemnly, "you couldn't be killing me if you felled the biggest tree in the Limberlost smash on me!"

"Then you go right to work," said the angel, "and before night I'll prove one thing to you: I can show you easily enough how much your mother loved you. That will be the first step and then the rest will all come. If my father and Mr. McLean are so anxious to spend some money, I'll give them a chance. I don't see why we haven't comprehended how you felt and been at work weeks ago. We've been awfully selfish. We've all been so comfortable, we never stopped to think what other people were suffering before our eyes. None of us has understood. I'll hire the finest detective in Chicago and we'll go to work together. This isn't anything compared with things people do find out. We'll go at it, beak and claw, and we'll show you a thing or two."

Freckles caught her sleeve.

"Me mother, Angel! Me mother!" he marveled hoarsely. "Did you say you could be finding out today if me mother loved me? How? Oh, Angel! All the rest don't matter, *if only me mother didn't do it!*"

"Then you rest easy," said the angel, with great confidence. "Your mother didn't do it! Mothers of sons like you don't do such things as that. I'll go to work at once and prove it to you. The first thing to do is to go to that home where you were and get the little clothes you wore the night you were left there. I know that they are required to save those things carefully. We can find out

almost all there is to know about your mother from them. Did you ever see them, Freckles?"

"Yes," said Freckles.

The angel literally pounced on him.

"Freckles! Were they white?" she cried.

"Maybe they were once. They're all yellow with laying, and brown with bloodstains now," said Freckles, the old note of bitterness creeping in. "You can't be telling anything at all by them, Angel!"

"Well, but I just can!" said the angel, positively. "I can see from the quality what kind of goods your mother could afford to buy. I can see from the cut whether she had good taste. I can see from the care she took in making them how much she loved and wanted you."

"But how? Angel, tell me how!" implored Freckles, with trembling eagerness.

"Why, easily enough," said the angel. "I thought you'd understand. People that can afford anything at all, always get white for little new babies—linen and lace, and the very finest things to be had. There's a young woman living near us who cut up her wedding clothes to have fine things for her baby. Mothers that love and want their babies don't buy little rough, ready-made things, and they don't run up what they make on an old sewing machine. They make fine seams and tucks, and put on lace and trimming by hand. They sit and stitch, and stitch—little, even stitches, every one just as careful. Their eyes shine and their faces glow. When they have to quit to do something else they look sorry, and fold up their work so carefully. There isn't much worth knowing about your mother that those little clothes won't tell. I can see her putting the little stitches into them and smiling with shining eyes over your coming. Freckles, I bet you a dollar those little clothes of yours are just alive with the dearest, tiny handmade stitches."

A new light dawned in Freckles' eyes. A tinge of warm color swept into his face. Renewed strength was noticeable in his grip on her hands.

"Oh, Angel! Will you go now? Will you be hurrying?" he cried.

"Right away," said the angel. "I won't stop for a thing, and I'll hurry with all my might."

She smoothed his pillow, straightened the cover, gave him one steady look in the eyes, and went quietly from the room.

Outside the door, McLean and the surgeon anxiously awaited her. McLean caught her shoulders.

"Angel, what have you done?" he demanded desperately.

The angel smiled defiance into his eyes.

"What have I done?" she repeated. "I've tried to save Freckles."

McLean groaned.

"What will your father say?" he cried.

"It strikes me," said the angel, "that what Freckles said would be to the point."

"Freckles!" burst out McLean. "What could he say?"

"He seemed to be able to say several things," said the angel sweetly. "I fancy the one that concerns you most at present was that if my father would offer me to him he would not have me."

"And no one knows why better than I do," thundered

McLean. "Every day he must astonish me with some new fineness."

He gripped the surgeon until he almost lifted him from the floor.

"Save him!" he commanded. "Save him!" he implored. "He is too fine to be sacrificed."

"His salvation lies here," said the surgeon, stroking the angel's sunshiny hair, "and I can read in the face of her that she knows how she is going to work it out. Don't trouble for the boy. She will save him."

The angel sped laughingly down the hall, and into the street, just as she was.

"I have come," she said to the matron of the home, "to ask if you will allow me to examine, or, better still, to take with me, the little clothes that a boy you called Freckles, discharged last fall, wore the night you took him in."

The woman eyed her in greater astonishment than the case called for.

"Well, I'd be glad to let you see them," she said at last, "but the fact is we haven't them. I do hope we haven't made some mistake. I was thoroughly convinced, and so was the superintendent. We let his people take those things away yesterday. Who are you and what do you want with them?"

The angel stood staring at the matron, dazed and speechless.

"There couldn't have been a mistake," continued the matron, seeing the angel's pitiful distress. "Freckles was here when I took charge, ten years ago. These people had it all proven plain as day that he belonged to them.

They had him traced to where he ran away down in Illinois last fall, and there they completely lost track of him. I'm sorry you seem so terribly disappointed, but it was all right. The man was his uncle, and as like the boy as he could possibly be. He was almost killed to go back without him. If you know where Freckles is they'd give big money to find out."

The angel laid a hand along each jaw to steady her chattering teeth.

"Who are they?" she stammered. "Where are they going back to?"

"They are Irish folks, Miss," said the matron. "They have been in Chicago and over the country for the last three months, hunting him everywhere. They have given up and are starting home today. They—"

"Did they leave an address? Where could I find them?" interrupted the angel.

"They left a card, and I notice the morning paper has the man's picture and is full of them. They've advertised a great deal in the city papers. It's a wonder you haven't seen something."

"Trains don't run right. We never get Chicago papers," snapped the angel. "Please give me that card quickly. They may get away from me. I simply have to catch them!"

The matron hurried to the secretary and came back with a card.

"Their addresses are on there," she said. "Both here in Chicago and at their home. They made them full and plain, and I was to cable at once if I got the least clue of him at any time. If they've left the city, you can stop

them in New York. You're sure to catch them before
they sail—if you hurry."

The matron caught up a paper and thrust it into the
angel's hand as she rushed for the street.

The angel glanced at the card. The Chicago address
was Suite Eleven, Auditorium. She laid her hand on her
driver's sleeve and looked into his eyes.

"There is a fast-driving limit?" she asked.

"Yes, Miss."

"Will you crowd it all you can without danger of arrest? I will pay well. I must catch some people!"

Then she smiled at him. The hospital, an orphans'
home, and the Auditorium seemed a queer combination
to that driver, but the angel was always and everywhere
the angel, and her ways were strictly her own.

"I will get you there just as quickly as any man could
with a team," he said promptly.

Slamming the door, he sprang to the box and gave
the horses a cut that rolled the angel from the seat.

She clung to the card and paper, and, as best she
could in the lurching, swaying cab, read the addresses
over.

"O'More, Suite Eleven, Auditorium."

" 'O'More,' " she repeated. "Seems to fit Freckles to a
dot. Wonder if that could be his name? 'Suite Eleven'
means that you are pretty well fixed. Suites in the Auditorium come high."

Then she turned the card and read on its reverse,
Lord Maxwell O'More, M. P., Killvany Place, County
Clare, Ireland.

The angel sat well on the edge of the seat, bracing her

feet against the one opposite, as the cab pitched and swung around corners and past vehicles. She mechanically fingered the pasteboard and stared straight ahead. Then she drew a deep breath and read the card again.

"A Lord-man!" she groaned despairingly. "A Lord-man! Bet my hoecake's scorched! Here I've gone and pledged my word to Freckles I'd find him some decent relatives, that he could be proud of, and now there isn't a chance out of a dozen but he'll have to be ashamed of them after all. It's too mean!"

The tears of vexation rolled down the tired, nerve-racked angel's cheeks.

"This isn't going to do," she said, resolutely wiping her eyes with the palm of her hand and gulping down the nervous spasm in her throat. "I must read this paper before I meet Lord O'More."

She blinked back the tears and, spreading the paper on her knee, read: "After three months' fruitless search, Lord O'More gives up the quest for his lost nephew and leaves Chicago today for his home in Ireland."

She read on, and absorbed every word of it. The likeness settled it. It was Freckles over again, only older and elegantly dressed. There was not a chance to doubt.

"Well, I must catch you if I can," muttered the angel. "But when I do, if you are a gentleman in name only, you shan't have Freckles; that's flat. You're not his father and he is twenty. Anyway, if the law will give him to you for one year, you can't spoil him, because nobody could, and," she added, brightening, "he'll probably do you a lot of good. Freckles and I both have to study years yet, and you ought to be something that will

save him. I guess it will come out all right. At least, I
don't believe you can take him away if I say no."

"Thank you; and wait, no matter how long," she said
to her driver.

Catching up the paper, she hurried to the desk and
laid down Lord O'More's card.

"Has my uncle started yet?" she asked, sweetly.

The surprised clerk stepped back on a bellboy, and
covertly kicked him for being in the way.

"His Lordship is in his room," he said, with a low
bow.

"All right," said the angel, picking up the card. "I
thought he might have started. I'll see him."

The clerk shoved the bellboy toward the angel.

"Show Her Ladyship to the elevator and Lord
O'More's suite," he said, bowing double.

"Aw, thanks," said the angel, with a slight nod, as she
turned away.

"I'm not sure," she muttered to herself as the elevator
shot upward, "whether it's the Irish or the English that
say 'Aw, thanks,' but it's probable he isn't either. And,
anyway, I just had to do something to counteract that
'All right.' How stupid of me!"

At the bellboy's tap, the door swung open and the
liveried servant thrust a card tray before the angel. The
opening of the door created a current that swayed a
curtain aside, and in an adjoining room, lounging in a
great chair, with a paper in his hand, sat the man who
was beyond question of Freckles' blood and race.

With perfect control the angel dropped Lord O'More's

card in the tray, whipped past his servant, and stood before his lordship.

"Good morning," she said with tense politeness.

Lord O'More said nothing. He carelessly glanced her over with amused curiosity, until her color began to deepen and her blood to run hotly.

"Well, my dear," he said at last, "how can I serve you?"

Instantly the angel bristled. She had been so shielded in the midst of almost entire freedom, owing to the circumstances of her life, that the words and the look appeared to her as almost insulting. She lifted her head with a proud gesture.

"I am not your 'dear,'" she said, with slow distinctness. "There isn't a thing in the world you can do for me. I came here to see if I could do something—a very great something—for you. But if I don't like you, I won't do it!"

Then Lord O'More did stare. Suddenly he broke into a ringing laugh. Without a change of attitude or expression, the angel stood looking steadily at him.

There was a silken rustle and a beautiful woman with cheeks of cherry bloom, hair of jet, and eyes of pure Irish blue, moved to Lord O'More's side, and, catching his arm, shook him impatiently.

"Terence! Have you lost your senses?" she cried. "Didn't you understand what the child said? Look at her face! See what she has!"

Lord O'More batted his eyes and sat up. He did look at the angel's face intently, and suddenly found it so

good that it was hard to follow the next injunction. He came to his feet instantly.

"I beg your pardon," he said. "The fact is I am leaving Chicago sorely disappointed. It makes me bitter and reckless. I thought it was some more of those queer, useless people that have thrust themselves on me constantly, and I was careless. Forgive me, and tell me why you came."

"I will if I like you," said the angel stoutly, "and if I don't, I won't!"

"But I began all wrong and now I don't know how to make you like me," said his lordship, with sincere penitence in his tone.

The angel found herself yielding to his voice. He spoke in a soft, mellow, smoothly flowing, Irish tone, and though his speech was perfectly correct it was so rounded, and accented, and the sentences so turned, that it was Freckles over again. Still, it was a matter of the very greatest importance and she must be sure. So she looked into the beautiful woman's face.

"Are you his wife?" she asked.

"Yes," said the woman. "I am his wife."

"Well," said the angel judicially, "the Bird Woman says no one in the whole world knows all a man's bignesses and all his littlenesses as his wife does. What you think of him ought to do for me. Do you like him?"

The question was so earnestly asked that it met with equal earnestness. The dark head moved caressingly against Lord O'More's sleeve.

"Better than anyone in the whole world," said Lady O'More promptly.

The angel mused a second, and then her legal tinge
came to the fore again.

"Yes, but have you anyone you could like better, if he
wasn't all right?" she persisted.

"I have three of his sons, two little daughters, a father,
mother, and several brothers and sisters," came the
quick reply.

"And you like him best?" persisted the angel, with
finality.

"I love him so much that I would give up every one of
them with dry eyes, if by so doing I could save him,"
said Lord O'More's wife.

"Oh!" cried the angel. "Oh, my!"

She lifted her clear eyes to Lord O'More's and shook
her head.

"She never, never could do that!" she said. "But it's a
mighty big thing to your credit that she *thinks* she
could. I guess I'll tell you why I came."

She laid down the paper and touched the portrait.

"When you were just a boy, did people call you
Freckles?" she asked.

"Dozens of good fellows all over Ireland and the Con-
tinent are doing it today," answered Lord O'More.

The angel's face lighted with her most beautiful
smile.

"I was sure of it," she said, winningly. "That's what we
call him, and he is so like you I doubt if any one of those
three boys of yours is more so. But it's been twenty
years. Seems to me you've been a long time coming!"

Lord O'More caught the angel's wrists and his wife
slipped her arms about her.

"Steady, my girl!" said the man's voice hoarsely. "Don't make me think you've brought word of the boy at this last hour, unless you know surely."

"It's all right," said the angel. "We have him and there's no chance of a mistake. If I hadn't gone to that home for his little clothes, and heard of you and been hunting you, and had met you on the street, or anywhere, I should have stopped you and asked you who you were, just because you are so like him. It's all right. I can tell you where Freckles is. But whether you deserve to know—that's another matter!"

Lord O'More did not hear her. He dropped back in his chair, and, covering his face, burst into those terrible sobs that shake and rend a strong man. Lady O'More hovered over him, weeping.

"Umph! Looks pretty fair for Freckles," muttered the angel. "Lots of things can be explained. Now perhaps they can explain this."

They did explain so fully that in a few minutes the angel was on her feet hurrying Lord and Lady O'More to reach the hospital.

"You said Freckles' old nurse knew his mother's picture instantly," said the angel. "I want that picture and the bundle of little clothes."

Lady O'More gave them into her hands.

The likeness was a large miniature, painted on ivory, with a frame of beaten gold, and the face that looked out of it was of extreme beauty and surpassing sweetness. Surrounded by masses of dark hair was a delicately cut face with big eyes. In the upper part of it there was no trace of Freckles, but the lips curving in a smile were his very own. The angel gazed as if she could never leave off. Then with a quivering breath she laid the portrait aside and reached both arms for Lord O'More's neck.

"That will save Freckles' life and ensure his happiness," she said, positively. "Thank you, oh, thank you for coming!"

She kissed and hugged him, and then the wife who had come with him. She opened the bundle of yellow and brown linen and gave just a glance at the texture and work. Then she gathered the little clothes and the picture to her heart and led the way to the cab.

Ushering Lord and Lady O'More into the reception room, she said to McLean, "Please go call up my father and ask him to come on the first train."

She swung the door after him.

"These are Freckles' people," she said to the Bird Woman. "You can find out about each other. I'm going to him."

And she was gone.

Chapter XIX ——————————————————

WHEREIN FRECKLES FINDS HIS BIRTHRIGHT AND
THE ANGEL LOSES HER HEART

The nurse left the room quietly as the angel entered,
still carrying the bundle and picture. When they
were alone, the angel turned to Freckles and saw that
the crisis was, indeed, at hand.

That she had good word to give him was his salvation, for despite the heavy plaster jacket that held his
body immovable, his head was lifted clear of the pillow.
Both arms reached for her. His lips and cheeks flamed
scarlet. His eyes flashed with excitement.

"Angel," he panted. "Oh, Angel! Did you get them? Are
they white? Are the little stitches there? *Oh, Angel! did
me mother love me?*"

The words seemed to leap from his burning lips. The
angel dropped the bundle on the bed and laid the pic-

ture face down across his knees. She gently pushed his head to the pillow and caught his arms in a firm grasp.

"Yes, dear heart," she said with fullest assurance. "No little clothes were ever whiter. I never in all my life saw such dainty, fine little stitches. And as for loving you, no boy's mother ever loved him more!"

A great trembling seized Freckles.

"Sure? Are you sure?" he urged, with clicking teeth.

"I know," said the angel firmly. "And, Freckles, while you rest and be glad, I want to tell you a little story. When you feel stronger we will look at the clothes together. They are here. They are all right. But when I was at the home getting them, I heard of some people who were hunting a lost boy. I went to see them, and what they told me was all so exactly like what might have happened to you that I must tell you. Then you'll see that things could be very different from what you have always tortured yourself with thinking. Are you strong enough to listen? May I tell you?"

"Maybe 'twasn't me mother! Maybe someone else made those little stitches!"

"Now, goosie, don't you begin that," said the angel, "because I know that it was!"

"Know!" cried Freckles, his head springing from the pillow. "Know! How can you know?"

The angel gently soothed him back.

"Why, because nobody else would ever sit and do it the way it was done. That's how I know," she said emphatically. "Now you listen while I tell you about this lost boy and his people, who have hunted for months and can't find him."

Freckles lay quiet under her touch, but he did not hear a word that she was saying until his roving eyes rested on her face. He immediately noticed a remarkable thing. For the first time she was talking to him and doing everything but meet his eyes. That was not like the angel at all. It was the delight of hearing her speak that she always looked one squarely in the face and with perfect frankness. There were no side glances and down-drooping eyes when the angel talked. She was business straight through. Now she was engrossed with his hand, the coverlet, the ceiling, anything to avoid meeting his eyes. Instantly Freckles' wandering thoughts fastened on her words.

"—and he was a sour, grumpy, old man," she was saying. "He always had been spoiled, because he was an only son, and had a title, and a big estate. He would have just his way, no matter about his sweet little wife, or his boys, or anyone. So when his eldest son fell in love with a beautiful girl with a title, the very girl of all the world his father wanted him to, and added a big adjoining estate to his, why that pleased him mightily.

"Then he went and ordered his other son to marry a poky kind of a girl, who nobody liked, to get another big estate on the other side, and that was different. That was all the world different, because the eldest son had been in love all his life with the girl he married, and, oh, Freckles, it's no wonder, for I saw her! She's a royal beauty, and she has the sweetest way.

"But that poor younger son, he had been in love with the village vicar's daughter all his life. That's no wonder either, for she was more beautiful yet. She could sing

like the angels, but she hadn't a cent. She loved him to
death, too, if he was bony and freckled and red-haired—
I don't mean that! They didn't say what color his hair
was, but his father's must have been the reddest ever,
for when he found out about them, and it wasn't anything so terrible, *he just caved!*

"The old man went to see the girl—the pretty one
with no money, of course—and he hurt her feelings until she ran away. She went over to London and began
studying music. Soon she grew to be a lovely singer and
then she joined a company and came to this country.

"When the younger son found that she had left London he ran off and followed her. When she got here all
alone, and afraid, and saw him coming to her, why, she
was so glad she up and married him, just like anybody
else would have done. He didn't want her to travel with
the troupe, so when they got to Chicago they thought
that would be a good place, and they stopped, and he
hunted work. It was slow business, because he had
never been taught to do a useful thing, and he didn't
even know how to hunt work, least of all to do it when
he found it. So pretty soon things were going wrong.
But if he couldn't find work, she could always sing, so
she sang at night and made little things in the daytime.
He didn't like her to sing in public, and he wouldn't let
her when he could help himself. But winter came, it
was very cold, and firewood was expensive. Rents went
up and they had to move farther out to cheaper and
cheaper places. And you were coming—I mean, the boy
that is lost was coming—and they were almost distracted.

"Then the man wrote and told his father all about it. And his father sent the letter back unopened and wrote him to never write again. When the baby came, there was mighty little left to pawn for food and a doctor, and nothing at all for a nurse. So an old neighbor woman went in and took care of the young mother and the little baby, just because she was so sorry for them. By that time they were away out in the suburbs on the top floor of a little wooden house, among a lot of big factories, and it kept getting colder, with less to eat. Then the man got desperate and he went out to just find something to eat. And the woman was desperate, too. She got up, left the old woman to take care of her baby, and went into the city to sing for some money. The woman got so cold she put the baby in bed and went home. Then a boiler blew up in a big factory beside the little house and set it on fire. A piece of iron was pitched across the little house and broke through the roof. It came down smash, and cut just one little hand off the poor baby. He screamed and screamed and the fire kept coming closer and closer.

"The old woman ran out with the rest of the people and saw what had happened. She knew there wasn't going to be time to wait for firemen or anything, and she ran into the building. She could hear the poor little baby screaming and she couldn't stand that. So she worked her way up to him. There he was, all hurt and bleeding. Then she was scared almost to death over thinking what his mother would do to her for going off and leaving him, so she ran to a home for little friendless babies, which was near, and banged on the door.

Then she hid across the street until the baby was taken in, and then she ran back to see if her own house was burning. The big factory and the little house and a lot of others were all gone. The people there told her that the beautiful lady came back and ran into the house to find her baby. She had just gone in when her husband came, and he went in after her, and the house went down over both of them."

Freckles lay rigid, with his eyes on the angel's face, and she talked rapidly to the ceiling.

"Then the old woman was just sick about that poor little baby. She was afraid to tell them at the home, because she knew she never should have left him, but she wrote a letter and sent it to where the beautiful woman, when she was ill, had said her husband's people lived. She told all about the little baby that she could remember. When he was born, how he was named for the man's elder brother, that his hand had been cut off in the fire, and where she had put him to be doctored and taken care of. She told them that the baby's mother and father were both burned, and she begged and implored them to come and get him.

"You think it would have melted a heart of ice, but that old man hadn't any heart to melt, for he got that letter and read it. He hid it away among his papers and never told a soul. A few months ago he died. When his elder son went to settle up his business, he found that letter almost the first thing. He dropped everything and came, with his wife, to hunt that baby, because he had always loved his brother dearly and wanted him back. He had hunted for him all he dared all these years, and

when he got here you were gone—I mean the baby was gone, and I had to tell you, Freckles, for you see, it might have happened to you like that just as easy as to that other lost boy."

Freckles reached up and turned the angel's face until he compelled her eyes to meet his.

"Angel," he asked softly, "why don't you look at me when you are telling about that lost boy?"

"I—I didn't know I wasn't," faltered the angel.

"It seems to me," said Freckles, his breath beginning to come in sharp wheezes, "that you got us pretty well mixed, and it ain't like you to be mixing things till one can't be knowing. If they were telling you so much, did they say which hand was for being off that lost boy?"

The angel's eyes escaped again.

"It—it was the same as yours," she ventured, barely breathing in her fear.

Still Freckles lay rigid and whiter than the coverlet.

"Would that boy be as old as me?" he asked.

"Yes," said the angel faintly.

"Angel," said Freckles at last, catching her wrist, "are you trying to tell me that there is somebody hunting a boy that you're thinking might be me? Are you believin' you've found me relations?"

Then the angel's eyes came home. The time had come. She pinioned Freckles' arms to his sides and bent above him.

"How strong are you, dear heart?" she breathed. "How brave are you? Can you bear it? Dare I tell you that?"

"No!" gasped Freckles. "Not if you're sure! I can't bear it! I'll die if you do!"

The day had been one unremitting strain for the angel. Nerve tension was drawn to the finest thread. It snapped suddenly.

"Die?" she flamed. "Die, if I tell you that! You said this morning that you would die if you *didn't* know your name, and if your people were honorable. Now I've gone and found you a name that stands for ages of honor, a mother who loved you enough to go into the fire and die for you, and the nicest kind of relatives, and you turn round and say you'll die over that! *You just try dying and you'll get a good slap!*"

The angel stood glaring at him. One second Freckles lay paralyzed and dumb with astonishment. The next the Irish in his soul rose above everything. A roar of laughter burst from him. The terrified angel caught him in her arms and tried to stifle the sound. She implored and commanded. The tears rolled from Freckles' eyes and he wheezed on. When he was too worn out to utter another sound, his eyes laughed silently.

After a long time, when he was quiet and rested, the angel began talking to him softly, and this time her great eyes, damp with tenderness and mellow with happiness, seemed as if they could not leave his face.

"Dear Freckles," she was saying, "across your knees there is the face of the mother that went into the fire for you, and I know the name—old and full of honor—to which you were born. Dear heart, which will you have first?"

Freckles was very tired, and the big drops of perspiration ran together on his temples, but the watching angel caught the words his lips formed, "Me mother!"

She lifted the lovely pictured face and set it in the nook of his arm. Freckles caught her hand and drew her down beside him and together they gazed at the picture while the tears slid over their cheeks.

"Me mother! Oh, me mother! Can you ever be forgiving me? Oh, me beautiful little mother!" chanted Freckles over and over in exalted wonder, until he was so completely exhausted that his lips refused to form the question in his weary eyes.

"Wait!" cried the angel with inborn refinement, for she could no more answer that question than he could ask. "Wait, I will write it!"

She hurried to the table, caught up the nurse's pencil and, on the back of a prescription tablet scrawled it, "Terence Maxwell O'More, Dunderry House, County Clare, Ireland."

Before she had finished came Freckles' voice, "Angel, are you hurrying?"

"Yes," said the angel. "I am. But there is a good deal of it. I have to put in your house and country, so that you will feel located."

"Me house?" marveled Freckles.

"Of course," said the angel. "Your uncle says your grandmother left your father her dower house and estate, because she knew his father would cut him off. You get that and all your share of your grandfather's property besides. It is all set off for you and waiting. Lord O'More told me so. I suspect you are richer than McLean, Freckles."

She closed his fingers over the slip and straightened his hair.

"Now you are all right, dear Limberlost guard," she said. "You go to sleep and don't think of a thing but just pure joy, joy, joy! I'll keep your people until you wake up. You are too tired to see anyone else just now."

Freckles caught her skirt as she turned from him.

"I'll go to sleep in five minutes," he said, "if you will be doing just one thing more for me. Send for your father! Oh, Angel, send for him quick! How will I ever be waiting until he gets here?"

One instant the angel stood looking down on him. The next a crimson wave darkly stained her lovely face. Her chin began a spasmodic quivering and the tears sprang into her eyes. Her hands caught at her chest as if she were stifling. Freckles' grasp on her tightened until he drew her up to and then down beside him. He slipped his arm about her and drew her face close to his pillow.

"Don't, Angel. For the love of mercy don't be doing that," he implored. "I can't be bearing it. Tell me. You must tell me."

The angel shook her head.

"That ain't fair, Angel," said Freckles. "You made me tell you when it was like tearing the heart raw from me breast. And you was for making everything heaven— just heaven and nothing else for me. If I'm so much more now than I was an hour ago, maybe I can be thinking of some way to fix things. You will be telling me?" he coaxed softly, moving his cheek against her hair.

The angel's head moved in negation. Freckles did a moment of intent thinking.

"Maybe I can be guessing," he whispered. "Will you be giving me three chances?"

There was just the faintest possible assent.

"You didn't want me to be knowing me name," guessed Freckles.

The angel's head sprang from the pillow and her tear-stained face flamed with outraged indignation.

"Why, I did too!" she burst out angrily.

"One gone," said Freckles calmly. "You didn't want me to have relatives, a home, and money."

"I did!" screamed the angel. "Didn't I go myself, all alone, into the city, and find them when I was afraid as death? I did too!"

"Two gone," said Freckles. "You didn't want the beautifulest girl in the world to be telling me—"

Down went the angel's face and a heavy sob shook her. Freckles' clasp tightened about her shoulders, and his face, in its conflicting emotions, was a study. He was so stunned and bewildered over the miracle that had been performed in bringing to light his name and relatives that he had no strength left for elaborate mental processes. Despite all it meant to him to know at last his name, and that he was of honorable birth—knowledge without which life was an eternal disgrace and burden —the one thing that was hammering in Freckles' heart and beating in his brain past any attempted expression was the fact that, while nameless and possibly born in shame, the angel had told him that she loved him. He could find no word with which to begin to voice the rapture of his heart over that. But if she regretted it—if it had been a thing done out of her pity for his condition, or her feeling of responsibility, if it killed him after all, there was only one thing left to do. Not for McLean, not for the Bird Woman, not for the Duncans would Freckles have done it, but for the angel—if it would make her happy—he would do anything.

"Angel," whispered Freckles, with his lips against her hair, "you haven't learned your history book very well, or else you've forgotten."

"Forgotten what?" sobbed the angel.

"Forgotten about the real knight, Ladybird," breathed Freckles softly. "Don't you know that, if anything happened that made his lady sorry, a real knight just simply couldn't be remembering it? Angel, darling little Swamp Angel, you be listening to me. There was one night on the trail, one solemn, grand, white night, that there wasn't ever any other like before or since, when the dear boss put his arm about me and told me that he loved me. But if you care, Angel, if you don't want it that way, why, I ain't remembering that anybody else ever did— not in me whole life."

The angel lifted her head and looked into the depths of Freckles' honest gray eyes, and they met hers unwaveringly. But the pain in them was pitiful.

"Do you mean," she demanded, "that you don't remember that a brazen forward girl told you, when you hadn't asked her, that she"—the angel choked on it a second, but she gave a gulp and brought it out bravely— "that she loved you?"

"No!" thundered Freckles. "No! I don't remember anything of the kind!"

But all the songbirds of his soul burst into melody
over that one little clause: "When you hadn't asked her."

"But you will," said the angel. "You may live to be an
old, old man and then you will."

"I will not!" cried Freckles. "How can you think it,
Angel?"

"You won't even *look* as if you remember!"

"I will not!" persisted Freckles. "I'll be swearing to it if
you want me to. If you wasn't too tired to think this
thing out straight, you'd be seeing that I couldn't—that I
just simply couldn't! I'd rather give it all up now and go
out into eternity alone, without ever seeing a soul of me
same blood, or me home, or hearing another man call
me by the name I was born to, than to remember anything that would be hurting you, Angel. I should think
you'd be understanding that it ain't no ways possible for
me to do it."

The angel's tearstained face flashed into dazzling
beauty. A half-hysterical little laugh broke from her
heart and bubbled over her lips.

"Oh, Freckles, forgive me!" she cried. "I've been
through so much that I'm scarcely myself, or I wouldn't
be here bothering you when you should be sleeping. Of
course you couldn't! I knew it all the time! I was just
scared! I was forgetting that you were you! You're too
good a knight to remember a thing like that. Of course
you are! And when you don't remember, why, then it's
the same as if it never happened, I was almost killed

because I'd gone and spoiled everything, but now it will be all right. Now you can go on and do things like other men, and I can have some flowers, and letters, and my sweetheart coming, and when you are *sure*, why, then *you* can tell *me* things, can't you? Oh, Freckles, I'm so glad! Oh, I'm so happy! It's dear of you to not remember, Freckles, perfectly dear! It's no wonder I love you so. The wonder would be if I did not. Oh, I should like to know how I'm ever going to make you understand how much I love you!"

Pillow and all, she caught him to her breast one long second and then she was gone.

Freckles lay dazed with astonishment. At last his batting eyes rolled about the room, searching for something approaching the human to which he could appeal, and, falling on his mother's portrait, he set it up before him.

"For the love of life! Me little mother," he panted, "did you hear that? Did you hear it! Tell me, am I living, or am I dead and all heaven come true this minute? Did you hear it?"

He shook the frame in his impatience at getting no answer.

"You are only a pictured face," he said at last, "and of course you can't talk. But the soul of you must be somewhere, and surely in this hour you are near enough to be hearing. Tell me, did you hear that? I can't ever be telling a living soul. But darling little mother, that gave your life for mine, I can always be talking of it to you! Every day we'll talk it over and try to understand the

miracle of it. Tell me, are all women like that? Were you like me Swamp Angel? If you were, then I'm understanding why me father followed you across the ocean and went into the fire after you."

Chapter XX ――――――――――――――――――

*WHEREIN FRECKLES RETURNS TO THE
LIMBERLOST, AND LORD O'MORE SAILS FOR
IRELAND WITHOUT HIM*

Freckles' voice trailed off, his eyes dropped shut, and his head rolled back from sheer exhaustion. Later in the day he insisted on seeing Lord and Lady O'More, but he fainted before the look of his own face on that of another man and gave all of his friends a terrible fright.

The next morning, the angel's father, with a heart filled with misgivings, undertook the interview on which Freckles insisted. His fears were without cause. Freckles was the soul of honor and simplicity.

"Have they been telling you what's come to me?" he asked without even waiting for a greeting.

"Yes," said the angel's father.

"Do you think you have the very worst of it clear to your understanding?"

Under Freckles' earnest eyes he answered soberly, "I think I have, Mr. O'More."

That was the first time Freckles heard his name from the lips of another man. One second he lay overcome, the next, great tears filled his eyes, and he reached out his hand. Then the angel's father understood, and he clasped that hand and held it in a strong, firm grasp.

"Terence, my boy," he said, "let me do the talking. I came in here with the understanding that you wanted to ask me for my only child. I should like, at the proper time, to regard her marriage, if she has found the man she desires to marry, not as losing all I have, but as gaining a man I can depend on to love as a son and to take charge of my affairs for her when I retire from business. Bend all of your energies toward rapid recovery, and from this hour understand that my daughter and my home are yours."

"You're not forgetting this?"

Freckles lifted his right arm.

"Terence, I'm sorrier than I have words to express about that," he said. "It's a damnable pity! But if it's up to me to choose whether I give all I have left in this world to a man with a hand off his body, or to one of these gambling, tippling, immoral spendthrifts of to-day, with both hands and feet off their souls, and a rotten spot in the core, I choose you. And it seems that my daughter does the same. Put what is left you of that right arm to the best uses you can in this world, and never again mention or feel that it is defective as long as you live. Good day, sir!"

"One minute more," said Freckles. "Yesterday the angel was telling me that there was money coming to me from two sources. She said that me grandmother had left me father all of her fortune and her house, because she knew that his father would be cutting him off, and that me uncle had also set aside for me what would be me father's interest in his father's estate.

"Whatever the sum is that me grandmother left me father, because she loved him and wanted him to be having it, that I'll be taking. 'Twas hers from her father, and she had the right to be giving it as she chose. Anything from the man that knowingly left me father and me mother to go cold and hungry, and into the fire in misery, when just a little would have made life so beautiful to them, and saved me this crippled body—money that he willed from me when he knew I was living, of his blood and on charity among strangers, I don't touch, not if I freeze, starve, and burn too! If there ain't enough besides that, and I can't be earning enough to fix things for the angel—"

"We are not discussing money!" burst in the angel's father. "We don't want any blood money! We have all we need without it. If you don't feel right and easy about it, don't you touch a cent of any of it."

"It's right I should have what me grandmother intended for me father, and I want it," said Freckles, "but I'd die before I'd touch a cent of me grandfather's money!"

"Now," said the angel, "we are all going home. We have done all we can for Freckles. His people are here. He needs to know them. They are very anxious to get acquainted with him. We'll turn him over to them and go home. When he is well, why, then he will be perfectly free to go to Ireland or come to the Limberlost, just as he chooses. We will go right away."

McLean bore it for a week and then he could stand it no longer. He was heart-hungry for Freckles. Communing with himself in the long, soundful nights of the swamp, he had learned to his astonishment that for the last year his heart had been circling the Limberlost with Freckles. He began to wish that he had not left him. Perhaps the boy—his boy by first right, after all—was being neglected. If the boss had been a nervous old woman, he could scarcely have imagined more things that might be going wrong.

He started for Chicago, loaded with a big box of goldenrod, asters, fringed gentians, and crimson leaves, which the angel had carefully gathered from Freckles' room, and a little, long slender package. He traveled with biting, stinging jealousy in his heart. He would not admit it even to himself, but he was unable to remain longer away from Freckles and leave him to the care of Lord O'More.

In a few minutes' talk, while McLean awaited admission to Freckles' room, his lordship had genially chatted of Freckles' rapid recovery, of his delight that he was unspotted by his early surroundings, and his desire to visit the Limberlost with Freckles before they sailed. He expressed the hope that he could prevail on the angel's father to place her in his wife's care and have her education finished in Paris. He said they were anxious to do all they could to help bind Freckles' arrangements with the angel, as both he and Lady O'More regarded her as the most promising girl they knew, and one that could be fully fitted to fill the high position in which Freckles would place her.

Every word he uttered was pungent with bitterness to McLean. The swamp had lost its flavor without Freckles. And yet, as Lord O'More talked, McLean fervently wished that he was in the heart of it. As he entered Freckles' room he almost lost his breath. Everything was changed.

Freckles lay by a window where he could follow Lake Michigan's blue until the horizon dipped into it. He could see great soft clouds, white-capped waves, shimmering sails, and big, puffing steamers trailing billowing banners of lavender and gray across the sky. Gulls and curlews wheeled over the water and dipped their wings in the foam. The room was filled with every luxury that taste and money could introduce there.

All the tan and sunburn had been washed from Freckles' face in sweats of agony. It was a smooth, even white, its brown rift showing but faintly. What the nurses and Lady O'More had done to Freckles' hair McLean could not guess, but it was the most beautiful that he had ever seen. Fine as floss, bright in color, waving and crisp, it fell about the white face.

They had gotten his arms into and his chest covered with a finely embroidered, pale-blue silk shirt, with a soft, white tie at the throat. Among the many changes that had taken place during his absence, the fact that Freckles was most attractive and barely escaped being handsome remained almost unnoticed by the boss, so

great was his astonishment at seeing both cuffs turned
back and the right arm in view. Freckles was using the
maimed arm that heretofore he had always hidden.

"Oh, Lord, sir, but I'm glad to see you!" burst out
Freckles, almost rolling from the bed as he reached for
him. "Tell me quick, is the angel well and happy? Can
me Little Chicken spread six feet of wing and sail to his
mother? How's me new father, the Bird Woman, Duncans, and Nellie—darling little high-stepping Nellie? Me
Aunt Alice is going to pick the hat just as soon as I'm
mended enough to be going with her. How are all the
gang? Have they found any more good trees? I've been
thinking a lot, sir. I believe I can find others near that
last one. Me Aunt Alice thinks maybe I can and Uncle
Terence says it's likely. Golly, but they're nice, elegant
people. I tell you I'm proud to be the same blood with
them! Come closer, quick! I was going to do this yesterday, and somehow I just felt that you'd surely be coming today, and I waited. I'm picking the angel's ring
stone. The ring she ordered me is done and they sent it
to keep me company. See? It's an emerald—just me
color, Lord O'More says."

Freckles flourished his hand.

"Ain't that a beauty? Never took so much comfort
with anything in me life. Every color of the old swamp
is in it. I asked Angel to have a little shamrock leaf cut
on it, so every time I saw it I'd be thinking of the love,
truth, and valor of that song she was teaching me. Ain't
that a beautiful song? Some of these days I'm going to
make it ring. I'm a little afraid to be doing it with me

voice yet, but me heart's just tuning away on it every blessed hour. Will you be looking at these now?"

Freckles tilted about a tray of unset stones from Peacock's that would have ransomed several valuable kings. He held them out to McLean, stirring them about with his right arm.

"I tell you I'm glad to see you, sir," he said. "I tried to tell me uncle what I wanted, but this ain't for him to be mixed up in, anyway, and I don't think I made it clear to him. I couldn't seem to say the words I wanted. I can be telling you, sir."

McLean's heart began to thump like a lover's.

"Go on, Freckles," he said assuringly.

"It's this," said Freckles. "I told him that I would pay only three hundred dollars for the angel's stone. I'm thinking that with what he has laid up for me, and the bigness of things that the angel did for me, that seems like a stingy little sum to him. I know he thinks I ought to be giving a lot more, but I feel as if I just had to be buying that stone with money I earned meself. And that is all that I have saved of me wages. I don't mind paying for the muff, or the dressing table, or Mrs. Duncan's things, from that other money, and later the angel can have every last cent of me grandmother's, if she'll take it; but just now—oh, sir, can't you see that I have to be buying this stone with what I have in the bank? I'm feeling that I couldn't do any other way, and don't you think the angel would rather have the best stone I can buy with the money I earned meself than a finer one paid for with other money?"

"In other words, Freckles," said the boss, in a thick

voice, "you don't want to buy the angel's ring with money. You want to give for it your first awful fear of the swamp. You want to pay for it with the loneliness and heart-hunger you have suffered there, with last winter's freezing on the line and this summer's burning in the sun. You want it to stand to her for every hour in which you risked your life to honorably fulfill your contract. You want the price of that stone to be the fears that have chilled your heart—the sweat and blood of your body."

Freckles' eyes were floating in tears and his face quivering with feeling.

"Dear Mr. McLean," he said, reaching up with a caress over the boss's black hair and along his cheek. "Dear Boss, that's why I've wanted you so. I knew you would know. Now you will be looking at these? I don't want emeralds, because that's what she gave me."

He pushed the green stones back into a little heap of rejected ones. Then he singled out all the pearls.

"Ain't they pretty things?" he said. "I'll be getting her a lot of those later. They are like lily faces, turtlehead flowers, or dewdrops in the shade or moonlight, but they haven't the life in them that I want in the stone I give to the angel right now."

Freckles heaped the pearls with the emeralds. He studied the diamonds a long time.

"These things are so fascinating like they almost tempt one, though they ain't quite the proper thing," he said. "I've always dearly loved to be watching yours, sir. I must get her some of these big ones, too, some day. They're like the Limberlost in January, when it's all ice-coated, and the sun gets over in the west and shines through and makes all you can see of the whole world look like fire and ice; but fire and ice ain't like the angel."

The diamonds joined the emeralds and pearls. There was left a little red heap, and Freckles' fingers touched it with a new tenderness. His eyes were flashing.

"I'm thinking here's me Angel's stone," he exulted. "The Limberlost, and me with it, grew in mine. But it's going to bloom, and her with it, in this! There's the red of the wild poppies, the cardinal flowers, and the little bunch of crushed foxfire that we found where she put it to save me. There's the light of the campfire, and the sun setting over Sleepy Snake Creek. There's the red of the blood we were willing to give for each other. It's like her lips, and like the drops that dried on her beautiful arm that first day, and I'm thinking it must be like the brave, tender, clean red heart of her."

Freckles lifted the ruby to his lips and handed it to McLean.

"I'll be signing up me checks and you have it set," he said. "I want you to draw me money and pay for it with those very same dollars, sir."

Again the heart of McLean took hope.

"Freckles, may I ask you something?" he said.

"Why, sure," said Freckles. "There's nothing you would be asking that it wouldn't be giving me joy to be telling you."

McLean's eyes traveled to Freckles' right arm with which he was pushing the jewels about.

"Oh, that!" cried Freckles with a merry laugh. "You're

wanting to know where all the bitterness is gone? Well, sir, 'twas carried from me soul, heart, and body on the lips of an angel. Seems that hurt was necessary in the beginning to make today come true. The wound had always been raw, but the angel was healing it. If she doesn't care, I don't. Me dear new father doesn't, nor me aunt and uncle, and you never did. Why should I be fretting all me life about what can't be helped. The real truth is that, since what happened to it last week, I'm so everlastingly proud of it I catch meself sticking it out on display a bit."

Freckles looked the boss in the eyes and burst into a laugh.

"Well, thank heaven!" said McLean.

"Now it's me turn," said Freckles. "I don't know as I ought to be asking you, and yet I can't see a reason good enough to keep me from it. It's a thing I've had on me mind every hour since I've had time to straighten things out a little. May I be asking you a question?"

McLean reached over and took Freckles' hand. His voice was shaken with feeling as he replied, "Freckles, you almost hurt me. Will you never learn how much you are to me? How happy you make me in coming to me with anything, no matter what!"

"Then it's this," said Freckles, gripping the hand of McLean strongly. "If this accident, and all that's come to me since, had never happened, where was it you had planned to send me to school? What was it you meant to do with me?"

"Why, Freckles," answered McLean, "I'm hardly prepared to state definitely. My ideas were rather hazy. I thought we would make a beginning and see which way things went. I figured on taking you to Grand Rapids first and putting you in the care of my mother. I had an idea it would be best to get a private tutor to coach you for a year or two, until you were fit to enter Ann Arbor or the Chicago University in good shape. Then I thought we'd finish in this country at Yale or Harvard, and end with Oxford, to get a good, all-round flavor."

"Is that all?" asked Freckles.

"No. That's leaving the music out," said McLean. "I intended to have your voice tested by some master, and if you really were endowed for a career as a great musician, and had inclinations that way, I wished to have you drop some of the college work and make music your chief study. Finally, I wanted us to take a trip over Europe and clear around the circle together."

"And then what?" queried Freckles, breathlessly.

"Why, then," said McLean, "you know that my heart is hopelessly in the woods. I will never quit the timber business while there is timber to handle and breath in my body. I thought if you didn't make a profession of music, and had any inclination my way, we would stretch the partnership one more, and take you into the firm, placing your work with me. Those plans may sound jumbled in the telling, but they have grown steadily on me, Freckles, as you have grown dear to me."

Freckles lifted anxious and eager eyes to McLean.

"You told me once on the trail, and again when we thought that I was dying, that you loved me. Do these

things that have come to me make any difference in any
way with your feeling toward me?"

"None," said McLean. "How could they, Freckles?
Nothing could make me love you more, and you will
never do anything that will make me love you less."

"Glory be to God!" burst out Freckles. "Glory to the
Almighty! Hurry and be telling your mother I'm coming! Just as soon as I can get on me feet I'll be taking
that ring to me Angel, and then I'll go to Grand Rapids
and be making me start just as you planned, only that I
can be paying me own way. When I'm educated enough,
we'll all—the angel and her father, the Bird Woman,
you, and me—all of us will go together and see me
house and me relations and be taking that trip. When
we get back, we'll add O'More to the lumber company,
and golly, sir, but we'll make things hum! Good land,
sir! Don't do that! Why, Mr. McLean, dear boss, dear
father, don't be doing that! What is it?"

"Nothing, nothing!" boomed McLean's deep bass,
"nothing at all!"

He abruptly turned away and hurried to the window.

"This is a mighty fine view," he said. "Lake's beautiful
this morning. No wonder Chicago people are so proud
of their city's location on its shore. But, Freckles, what
is Lord O'More going to say to this?"

"I don't know," said Freckles. "I am going to be cut
deep if he cares, for he's been more than good to me,
and Lady Alice is next to me Angel. He's made me feel
me blood and race me own possession. She's talked to
me by the hour of me father and mother and me grandmother. She's made them all that real I can lay claim to

them and feel that they are mine. I'm very sorry to be hurting them, if it will, but it can't be changed. Nobody ever gets the width of the ocean between me and the angel. From here to the Limberlost is all I can be bearing peaceable. I want the education, and then I want to work and live here in the country where I was born and where the ashes of me father and mother rest.

"I'll be glad to see Ireland, and glad especial to see those little people that are my kin, but I ain't ever staying *long*. All me heart is the angel's and the Limberlost is calling every minute. You're thinking, sir, that when I look out of that window I see the beautiful water, ain't you? I'm not.

"I see soft, slow clouds oozing across the blue, me big black chickens hanging up there, and a great feather softly sliding down. I see mighty trees, swinging vines, bright flowers, and always masses of the wild roses, with the wild rose face of me Ladybird looking through. I see the swale rocking, smell the sweetness of the blooming things, and the damp, mucky odor of the swamp. And I hear me birds sing, me squirrels bark, the rattlers hiss, and the step of Wessner or Black Jack coming. And whether it's the things that I loved or the things that I feared, it's all a part of the day.

"Me heart's all me Swamp Angel's and me love is all hers, and I have her and the swamp so confused in me mind I never can be separating them. When I look at her, I see blue sky, the sun rifting through the leaves and pink and red flowers; and when I look at the Limberlost I see a pink face with blue eyes, gold hair, and red lips, and, it's the truth, sir, they're mixed till they're one to me!

"I'm afraid it will be hurting some, but I have the feeling that I can be making my dear people understand, so that they will be willing to let me come back home. Send Lady O'More to put these flowers God made in the place of these glasshouse elegancies, and please be cutting the string of this little package the angel's sent me."

As Freckles held up the package, the lights of the Limberlost flashed in the emerald on his finger. On the cover was printed: "To the Limberlost Guard!" Under it was a big, crisp, iridescent black feather.